THE
PRISONER
OF
BRENDA BROWN

To Judy & Paul
My amazing friends
all best wishes

Love
Geoff x

Geoff Green

Chapter 1

Brenda Brown pushed the carton of cold soup toward her basement prisoner. Melvyn Greenstone was asleep, snoring and dribbling, his beard now into its third week. Already he could double for Papillon, the convict held in solitary confinement on Devil's Island.

She'd decided on the nickname Pap, for short, a name no one would recognise, three letters that struck a chord. And when Greenstone enquired about his new title, Brenda said he could look it up…if he ever got out.

Pap hated soup, particularly broccoli, but she could tell he was getting rather partial to it. That's the way it goes when you're hungry, you'll eat anything. She'd taken his belt at the start and he was having trouble keeping his trousers up. Must have been pigging it out for years, 'cos he was losing pounds faster than melting butter.

Upstairs, away from the gloom of the single basement light bulb controlled by a dimmer switch, the sun was shining through a bay window. She looked at the first green leaves coating The Avenue with a new spring day. Cars were moving out of drives and kids were joshing along in close knit groups, eating and texting or doing other stuff on their iPhones. She was a keen texter herself. Composing her messages one-handed, despite the new nail extensions, was legendary. Pap was a recent addition to her contacts, but exclusive. Only one person got news of her prisoner, someone who needed to be kept in the loop. And if Brenda should ever lose her mobile, Melvyn Greenstone would be untraceable on it.

Normal day then: feed prisoner, go to work, think about the move to Australia and not too frequently, wonder how Pap's incarceration would end. No hurry, she'd had several ideas about that.

The basement, originally used by Brenda's recently departed husband for his string of hobbies, consisted of one large area, thirty feet by twenty, divided by two supporting walls directly in line with the room layout above. So three sections; the furthest from the staircase, leading from the kitchen above, was now Pap's prison. It had a narrow ventilation shaft, a toilet, and a tiny corner washbasin with a single cold tap. The centre of the floor had a drain, a small gulley that took waste water when the cement floor was washed, which Brenda's husband had taken some pride in doing with a jet hose, after his hobby weekends.

She'd added a few essentials, including a single wooden bed with a thin mattress but no sheets. She wouldn't be doing Pap's washing. It wasn't cold down there, so one thick army type blanket was enough. To keep relatively clean, she supplied Pap with a hand towel that Arthur had been using for over a decade. It resembled coarse grade sandpaper with a matching flannel, less used but with a similar history. The handle of a toothbrush had been shortened and sanded smooth, keeping it small and less like a weapon. Plus a bit of luxury, a bar of soap and some toothpaste in one of those soft plastic squishy tubes. No razors. Not that he was likely to cut his own throat, but he might be tempted to cut hers, if he got the chance.

Chapter 2

Brenda's husband Arthur had been dead for over a year. He had been a good deal older than her and statistics show that women, as a general rule, live longer than men. She still missed him. Well, not so much missed, more remembered. He was never still. Passionate interests came and went like tube trains on the Metropolitan Line. They always involved dust and dirt. Odd, since he was so keen on making sure his workroom shone after each session, always hosing it down before he took a long hot shower. She used to think his strict rule of cleanliness was in preparation for a night of passion. But no, it was a sign that his day was over, in every possible way. It reminded Brenda of her mother, who'd told her that the tunes from the ice cream van signalled they'd run out of ice cream...A similarly disappointing memory.

But thankfully, as far as women were concerned, Arthur was a safe pair of hands, courteous without an agenda. Not like Pap. She didn't think Arthur ever made the connection between a woman's latent desire for sex and a nodding fascination for his latest project. All it needed was a smile and a look of expectant interest and she'd get both barrels; on the best way of using a tenon saw, or how to drill a piece of timber without it spinning, something which Arthur failed to mention he had yet to master. In fact Arthur had failed to mention many of his shortcomings.

All his hobbies were disasters. Like a man born with two left feet who couldn't dance, Arthur's hands were similarly inept at creating something useful. Give him a piece of wood and a chisel and you'd just end up with less wood and a pile of sawdust.

So what was the attraction in the first place? After a run of bad choices on Brenda's part, he was a breath of fresh air. So easy to be with, undemanding, generous with his time, eager to do the right thing, apologising when he failed to *manage things* in the bedroom—something he never did when he fell short with one of his projects. But they did have some passionate times at first. He was a late starter so Brenda, not that experienced herself, tried to encourage him. She didn't think Arthur ever enjoyed sex. He never said so and she never asked. It would have been unladylike and might have crushed Arthur's confidence.

Chapter 3

At first, Melvyn had no idea why Brenda was keeping him locked up. Couldn't think of a single reason how it could possibly benefit her. Who the hell did she think she was anyway? He vaguely remembered meeting her somewhere, at a party or something like that, but she wasn't someone he'd had a relationship with or even been out with. Why would a virtual stranger go to so much trouble? She'd not mentioned money or any other trade-off. It was a mystery.

For Melvyn, the unfolding of the mystery was to be protracted and painful. Things were starting to come to light and he was really pissed off. He wondered who'd spilt the beans, how she'd managed to dig up so much dirt. She'd read out a list of what she called 'his victims', as if he was a serial killer. There were a lot of women on that list, lots of memories too, though he could hardly remember the early stuff. In fact, one or two names escaped him completely.

No need to worry about his job, not yet, but it was getting close to *report back with results* time. He was always travelling, always completing his projects on schedule and didn't need to check in unless there was a problem. Free agent, more or less.

He heard the clatter of the basement door as Brenda opened it, then locked it behind her, before pattering down the stairs in her slippers. She was humming something, not loud, just meaningless enough to irritate the hell out of him. Pap inhaled her strong perfume before she'd got halfway down the wooden steps. Tight dress, full figure, auburn hair, unnaturally long eyelashes and kind of sexy in a matron-due-for-a-good-night-out sort of way.

'Don't ask what the food is. I want it to be a surprise. You need one after being down here for three weeks. Even after what you've done...' Her voice trailed off. Brenda wasn't smiling. 'Step to the back wall and I'll put it through the bars.'

Pap shuffled back, hitching his trousers up as he watched her slip the cardboard carton onto the floor his side of the bars. 'Bloody broccoli!'

'Couldn't be bothered making your usual treat after the last batch ran out. You'll be pleased to know the broccoli stalks are nice and cold, just like the soup,' she said, gleefully. 'And by the way, Pap, it's not nice to swear in front of a lady. Do it again and I'll punish you. I won't tolerate it!'

When she'd gone, Pap gobbled the soggy vegetable as if it was his favourite food. He hadn't eaten since yesterday. This couldn't go on, a plan was shaping up, and when he got out, Brenda was gonna be one sorry bitch.

He'd gotten used to the cardboard food containers. Brenda, quite wisely, decided that nothing resembling a weapon—shard of china, glass, tin or metal of any sort—should be allowed into Pap's cell. She'd seen things on telly, desperate men stabbing their captor with something unexpected, like a paperclip or sharpened matchstick. Plus Pap was doing involuntary 'cold turkey', drying out from alcohol and fags. He must be getting healthier by the day. He wasn't the type to do push-ups, or run back and forth across the ten foot space to keep his muscles toned. He was more the park-as-close-as-you-can-to-wherever-you-wanted-to-be kind of a guy. But still testosterone driven and quite capable of getting nasty, of that she was certain.

Pap felt he'd been wrongly accused. He couldn't help himself, he loved women with a genuine affection, heartfelt, no harm intended.

But he did have a problem; falling head over heels within moments, an emotion so overwhelming that he had to share it, fairly urgently as it turned out. The trouble was, he fell out of love just as quickly.

How had he felt so smitten in the first place? He didn't have an answer to this paradox. The falling out came so suddenly he could never find the courage to tell them. He just had to leave. Unfortunately it left some severely upset and angry women, a few with reasons as to why they'd like to castrate Melvyn Greenstone.

But there were others who'd been only too pleased to see Pap leave. They'd not complained when he'd suddenly disappeared. Pap didn't reason why, but if he had, he would have realized that women can also fall in and out of love easily. Lovers who only wanted, and expected, a short intense relationship fuelled by a bit of high living. And should Pap give them a call, they might still consider a one-night stand in a luxury hotel with all the trimmings.

Chapter 4

'How was your weekend, Brenda, anything exciting?' asked her young boss, Raymond, as she walked into the office. 'Raymondo', the staff called him when he wasn't around, was okay. Fancied himself a bit—a young entrepreneur, regular estate agent type: confident, sticky-up gelled hair, Mini Cooper, shiny suit, good teeth—but one of her better employers.

'Not too exciting. Still miss Arthur... All work at the moment,' she replied, switching on the kettle before hanging up her coat.

'We're going to miss you. Pleased to hear the house sale's gone through without a hitch,' he said, handing her the day's schedule.

The buyers would have blown a gasket, had they ever found out about Pap spending time there. But she'd worked it out like a military exercise. Knew who the buyers were going to be, they'd been interested for a long time. Last year they even stuck a note through her door: *...if you ever think of selling, please consider us first...* And she'd found out they weren't in a hurry to move in, just wanted to make sure it was theirs. Despite that, they'd spent some time bargaining, trying to reduce the price, making all sorts of excuses as to why Brenda should knock thousands off. Arthur's DIY had, apparently, reduced the value of the house. She'd had to admit that some of his work was not quite up to scratch and had to pay local builders to sort it out. On a couple of occasions, Arthur had forgotten to apply for building regulations, a minor fact that only came to light when a local surveyor filed a report for the new buyers. So they ended up buying at a knockdown price, reducing Brenda's expected sales figure by twenty grand.

Then a stroke of good luck. Following the exchange of paperwork and payment, the buyers had to go away for two months. So even less hurry to move out, just enough time for her plan with Pap to run its course and deliver some justice in this sad world. Plenty of time to finish what she'd started.

She poured four coffees, all black, no sugars, the latest corporate health initiative. Raymondo had already banned electronic cigarettes. They looked too much like the old habit, and anyway vaping irritated his sinuses.

Brenda sat down with her coffee and texted Raihana: *All going to plan, you wouldn't recognise him. See you Thursday x*

'Any second thoughts?' asked Raymondo, looking at himself in the glass reflection and straightening his tie. His company, Butts, had been passed on from his father. Raymondo had missed the irony of the company name. All his staff were smokers, confined to a quick one outside the office, keeping their half smoked butts for later and never daring to leave the evidence in the yard for Raymondo to grumble about.

'I've enjoyed it here,' said Brenda. 'I'll miss you all. But Australia and that climate is too hard to resist,' she continued, sipping her coffee distractedly, aware of what she still had to do before leaving.

When her new friend Raihana was looking to buy a place to stay, she'd chosen Butts because, apart from being in the area she'd needed to be, the name intrigued her. It was a common family name in Pakistan and she'd wondered, being new to the UK, if there was some kind of connection with an Asian family. Maybe the owner was from her home city, Lahore. There was no such link, but it did mean she'd met Brenda. And Brenda and Raihana would turn from friends to partners in crime, in no time at all.

Chapter 5

The smell was awful. She gagged as she went down the stairs. Pap had used the floor as a toilet. He was grinning.

'Sorry about this, Brenda. The loo was blocked, and what with all that broccoli soup... I called, but I guess you wouldn't have let me out anyway. You'll have to do something. Hand me some mops and cleaning stuff and I'll try and sort it out.'

'You think I'm going to give you a weapon? A mop is a big stick, Pap. Can't risk it, sorry.'

'If you leave it much longer it'll stink the whole house out. This smell will go through anything in time.'

'Don't worry, Pap. I've thought of everything. Especially stunts from you.' *But not quite this*, she decided.

'Take your clothes off and stand in the corner, away from the bed.'

'No way. You can't make me do that.'

'But you always enjoyed taking your clothes off, Pap. Don't you remember? You've spent a lifetime doing it.'

'No.'

'You can leave your underpants on.'

'What the hell for? I refuse.'

'You'll be sorry,' she said, taking the stairs two at a time, back to the main house.

Pap was worried now. But reason told him that she couldn't physically force him to undress. Then he heard clattering, scraping, an odd banging on the cellar wall as Brenda struggled down the staircase with Arthur's yellow Karcher jet spray.

Pap looked on in horror.

'It's make your mind up time, sunshine. You want a dry bed don't you? And if you don't want your clothes to get wet, take them off now and stand in the corner.' She plugged the Karcher into the single socket and tested it on the basement floor. The hose nearly leapt out of her hand with the force of water jetting out of the narrow slit, cutting neat strips of cleanliness across the basement floor.

Pap turned pale and quickly took off his clothes, keeping his underpants on, holding them up with one hand while protecting his vital parts with the other. He'd put his clothes on the bed.

It hit him like a water cannon, knocking him back against the wall. So powerful, it brought blotches of red out on his skin. His pants were slipping as the jet strummed down his legs. He turned to the wall. Brenda was in playful mood, cutting across his backside sideways leaving strips of scarlet against his pale skin. He shouted out. The spray was stingingly cold.

The pressure was ferocious. He gasped for breath and signalled frantically for her to stop. She switched the Karcher off. Pap's head dropped forward, exhausted. He wondered if this contravened his human rights.

Brenda switched to shampoo mode. Pap took on the sad image of a melting snowman. Then she rinsed, on high power.

Brenda brought the hose down from Pap's body, bounced the jet into the toilet and hosed the disgusting floor in clean frothy swathes straight into the gully.

'Now flush that loo. I want it working before I leave.'

Pap, head still bowed, underpants low and stuck to his skin, looked like Ghandi in a monsoon. Ghandi flushed the loo. It worked first time, like it had never been blocked.

'One last word, Pap, I'll outsmart you every time. If you pretend to be ill, or have a coughing fit or any of that stuff we've seen on telly—ploys to overpower the guard—forget it. And if you're really ill, I'll let you die anyway. So don't bother.'

Chapter 6

Brenda needed Pap to know he was in deeper trouble than he'd ever imagined. She knew too much. Most of it discovered, first by texting and Facebook, followed by her own brand of sleuthing, including some very personal interviews with those who would be thrilled to hear the recent good news; Melvyn Greenstone, aka Pap, was in solitary...

Pap was lying on his bed, with nothing to do but think. He was racking his brain, trying to recall anything that would have led Brenda to such a bizarre plan. She was risking an awful lot, so there must be something he'd missed.

Could she have a connection to someone he'd upset in the past, another woman, more than one maybe! Most of them had been willing participants in his amorous pursuits, but not all... There was nothing obvious. Anyway, the past was over. Why did women insist on dragging it up to beat you over the head with when they wanted attention, or use it as leverage to make you feel guilty?

Brenda padded down the steps and delivered his soup of the day. He didn't have to guess what was on the menu.

'Stand back, Pap.' He took four steps backward and stood erect against the wall, as if he'd been on a successful dog training course. He closed his eyes and sighed; he didn't even want to look at her. He was angry enough to throttle Brenda, but he wasn't going to show it. Not yet. He wasn't a killer type really, never hurt anyone physically, never hit a woman in his life—but there's always a first time. He'd always shown the utmost respect. Therein lay the problem, he was a slave to women, a slave to love.

Brenda walked to the back of the basement and dragged an old Bentwood chair to within six feet of the cell. She sat down and stared at Pap, his eyes still closed, the cold soup looking like— well, looking like cold soup, on his cell floor.

'You need to know why you're here, Pap. Crimes against women. And now it's payback time.'

He cleared his throat as if to speak, then decided against it. All Pap's efforts to stop a particular event in his past trying to assert itself, had failed.

'Do you remember groping me, at one of those company seminars—and while my Arthur was there too?'

Pap had a hard enough time trying to remember all the women in his life, never mind the blokes.

To Brenda, it looked as if he was searching his memory. She felt insulted: the bastard.

'Vaguely. I was drunk, didn't mean nothin'. It was the booze. Didn't fancy you or anything like that.' He smiled, as if he'd struck the right note with his explanation.

'You're the only person I can think of who would believe that statement to be a compliment,' sniffed Brenda.

Pap said nothing.

'Well, you'll be interested to know I've put a file together. Pretty incriminating: lots of evidence, lots of witnesses waiting to come forward. It might make you evaluate your future. Not exactly your plan 'A', you can be sure of that.'

Pap's turn to sniff. 'You can't take the law into your own hands. Who are these so-called witnesses anyway? As far as I know I haven't committed any crime, haven't even got a parking ticket.'

Brenda ignored Pap's response. He was obviously in denial—about his whole bloody life by the sounds of it. 'I know a leopard can't change its spots but we can give the leopard a lesson or two on how to behave. You should be in a proper jail. But I thought something might be learned from a little gentle isolation, a spell of meditation maybe. Ever heard of meditation, Pap? I doubt it because that would involve thinking, being quiet and reflective. This could be a big opportunity for you to practise.'

Chapter 7

Over the recent past, Pap had gone global with his amours.

It was Thursday and Raihana was due for an update.

Brenda was sitting in Coffee 4 Us, across from the bus station. The new owners had recently put up a trendy sign: *small batch coffee*. Same old coffee it ever was, as far as she could tell, but they'd changed the decor and the cup size and boasted fresh croissants with more fillings than you could imagine. And almost next door, the pizza people must have got hold of the same marketing magician because they'd taken down the *Any Pizza for £12* sign, and replaced it with, *Handcrafted Sourdough Pizza*. Surprisingly for her, both establishments had attracted a new clientele; younger punters from the offices and businesses around the station. *It's all about marketing now*, she thought. Didn't matter if it was the same old stuff, repackaged and robustly advertised with a promise that their products could change lives. They'd actually printed, *life-changing coffee*, on the cups at Coffee 4 Us. This was a philosophy Pap could really connect with: change the advertising without changing the product. Deception.

Brenda watched her friend cross the street. As she approached the coffee shop Raihana stopped for a moment and closed her eyes briefly before tapping on the window. She pressed her palm to the glass and smiled, followed by a look that Brenda sensed was not quite joy.

The place wasn't crowded. Half the morning business had left for work. Raihana ordered two cortados, small batch, of course. They'd been intrigued by the name, sounded like a Spanish bullfighter and it had become their Thursday tipple, a coffee without too much froth. They sat in the little conservatory, now signposted, *The Little Conservatory*.

'How you doing? How's the patient?' said Raihana, scanning the tables, aware that she shouldn't mention *prisoner*.

'Coming along nicely, even getting to like broccoli.'

Raihana laughed. She remembered eating at Pap's swish hotel, when she'd met him in Lahore. He was served it in the restaurant once. He'd had a few drinks and told the manager that broccoli should be taken off the menu and certainly never billed as *vegetable of the day*.

Brenda leaned closer to her friend and whispered, 'I asked him to take his clothes off.'

Raihana looked horrified. Had Brenda succumbed to Pap's advances?

Brenda told her about the blocked toilet and the Karcher. Raihana's laugh was embarrassing; unstoppable giggling with a bit of snorting and hooting. People turned to watch. It was infectious. In moments, the place was alive with smiles and laughter. They hadn't a clue.

Raihana wiped her eyes, smearing makeup across her high cheekbones, before fiddling nervously with her cup of coffee. She'd overdone the giggling, didn't feel chirpy at all, not right now. Brenda would notice.

Brenda had sensed something wrong when her friend had tapped on the window, something about that quickly fading smile.

'I think I'm pregnant, Brenda.'

Chapter 8

Pap was disappointed that his shit plan had turned out to be such a shit plan. He almost smiled at his witty reflection. No matter. Once he'd got over the shock of the Karcher and his reddened skin had calmed down, he felt like he'd been on a pamper day—full body massage plus various painful procedures to tone him up—an indulgence that usually cost a couple of hundred quid.

Time for the next plan; maybe break the toilet, or pull the sink away from the wall and let the place flood. The bloody Karcher would be useless then. And madam wouldn't want her house ruined with rising damp. These lime-plastered basement walls would suck water up like a sponge and cost a fortune to put right.

Plan B had occurred to him before. But during the first two weeks of his incarceration, he was in sheer terror following Brenda's threats to torture him, described in the most graphic detail. Then he began to realise that her threats were empty words, physical violence was not what she'd planned and he was feeling more optimistic about getting out alive. Now was the time to take a chance. He felt up to it.

Much to his surprise, being on the broccoli and water diet, being forced to give up booze and fags, no longer seemed too much of a punishment. He had more energy, a clearer head and a strong plan to get out of this hole, perhaps leave the UK for good...And with a bit of luck, he'd manage to give Brenda a bloody nose before he left.

'Cooee, my little broccoli addict, I'm home,' shouted Brenda as she opened the basement door. She clacked down the stairs in her heels and stood, hands on hips, in the centre of the basement. 'I have some bad news for you. I'm moving abroad shortly and there's no set plan to let you out. You'll miss the company, and my soup. Not sure what the new owners will do when they find they have a sitting tenant.'

Brenda hooted, and Pap remained stony-faced.

'Obviously you have plans of your own. I would have, in your position. I'd probably tear the basin off the wall and flood the place, or wreck the toilet. No doubt you've thought of that. But given I won't be here to help clear up, you may need to rethink.'

Pap tried not to show disappointment. Plan C then.

'You'll have to let me out. They'll call the police. You'll be arrested, Brenda. I'd hate to see you banged up… And what about my human rights?' he added, weakly.

Brenda laughed exaggeratedly. 'You really have no idea, Pap. When I leave, the shit really *is* going to hit the fan.'

Pap frowned but could see something positive in Brenda leaving and the new folk finding him, a bedraggled prisoner ready to be released after his terrifying ordeal in the basement. But whatever she was going to do, he wished she'd do it now and get it over with.

But *when* he would be out was hard to guess, so planning ways to escape was worth the effort. Soldiers of war considered breaking out, even as liberating armies were poised to release them. Escape from captivity is hot-wired into the male genes: think of those prisoners in *The Great Escape* and *Bridge Over the River Kwai.*

There'd be no point going down the sympathy route, it would have to be something that left her no choice, a fit, or some medical emergency. Not quite up to faking a plausible fit but he could manage a half decent coma. What would make it believable? He could try the-diabetic-without-his-insulin card ploy. His knowledge of the subject of diabetes was sketchy, to say the least, but he knew it was some sort of medical emergency. Diabetics died without insulin, he'd heard about that. He could fake a coma pretty convincingly. Hadn't he played a corpse in the school murder play? A part his teacher said would suit his acting talent to a 'T', adding sarcastically: *You're at the top of your game, straight out of Central Casting, Greenstone.* Well now was his chance to shine. Worth a go...She'd threatened to let him die before but he was now beginning to think she wasn't that cruel.

Chapter 9

Brenda considered the latest developments. She wasn't quite sure how Raihana's pregnancy was going to impact on the end game. All sorts of complications could arise, but if all went well, it shouldn't detract from Brenda's plan.

Brenda had removed two mobiles from Pap's pockets when she'd imprisoned him; one for daily use; office, business, pals etc. and the other, a dinky little thing, a fully loaded pay-as-you-go with an interesting collection of women's names. This list of female contacts did not include his wife Gloria, who he'd kept on his reliable-normal-husband phone along with his pals and business contacts. Brenda had charged both phones up and been having fun. She'd found out that when Pap was away on business, he and Gloria favoured texting.

The start of Brenda texting Gloria began the day after Pap had left the marital home, his first day in Brenda's care: *Hi, arrived safely, good flight, will text in a couple of days, when I've settled in.* Brenda had nearly blown it from the get go. She was about to add: *love you, Pap*—or stick a kiss on the end. That's what most couples do when they're away. And wouldn't Gloria have flipped at the name Pap on the end of his text? She could imagine Gloria thinking: *what the hell!*

Fortunately, she'd checked his text messages. He never sent kisses or love to his wife. Nor she to him! *Cheers* at the end of a text, was the best Gloria could hope for. After scrutinising the grammatical style of their messaging, she found it was easy to keep the reassuring texts going.

Pap (now Brenda) and Gloria texted each other several times, usually brief messages. Gloria had received several phone calls that worried her, the callers having put down the phone as soon as they'd heard her voice.

Chapter 10

Pap was trying to recall the day he'd been tricked into the basement. He'd finished at the office and was feeling relaxed about his impending trip. The memory was hazy, he was drunk. A woman had sidled up to him in The Crown and asked if he remembered her. He hadn't. She offered to buy him a drink. His flight to Morocco wasn't until later the following day so... He'd already downed a fair bit, but when this attractive woman turned up and offered to buy him another, he should have been suspicious. Traditionally, it was the man's role to sidle up and buy drinks. This was something new, the event had bypassed his bullshit detector which, to be honest, often failed when a combination of blondes (or brunettes or redheads) and booze appeared in the same scene. Not that he wasn't attractive, women told him he was, but that compliment was more likely after they'd been drinking a while... 'That's why God created alcohol', a dumped girlfriend had told him; blokes you thought unappealing at first, always looked better after a glass or two.

The woman who'd bought the fatal round was with him in the cell at first, stroking his aching head, calming him, staying silent.

She'd listened to his ramblings—'Where am I? Who are you? Is this your house?'—and a host of other slurred questions, before leaving him flat out on the single hard divan. Then she'd leapt up too fast for Pap's pickled brain to register, before slamming the door of the cell as she left. Pap never saw her again. Bitch.

But he did see Brenda, that very same day. His foggy recall gathered he'd met Brenda briefly, way back, remembered her being married or shacked up with some dull bloke.

'Get yourself a drink,' she said, 'cardboard cup next to your bed, cold tap in the corner.'

Pap knew this had to be a joke. He was supposed to be away on business. Not totally, some would be leisure time, but his wife would text him soon, if he didn't contact her...

'What's this about? Are you having a laugh or what? I'll raise merry hell if you don't let me out.'

'One scream out of you, sunshine and we *will* kill you. That's how angry we are.'

We? This mad woman was obviously in a gang.

'If you want to stay alive, with your bones and health intact, do as you're told. Before your peanut brain starts to work out the possibilities of ever getting out, I'll tell you about this little paradise you'll be staying in. My husband Arthur, who died last year, had the place soundproofed. Arthur liked opera you see, liked it full blast while he whittled away at pieces of wood or took things to pieces. Things that never quite managed to acquire their intended purpose in life,' she said, smiling at the memory of her husband.

'Do you like opera, Pap? Not that you'll get any here. I want you to have peace and quiet, some thinking time. You need to reflect on your past, realise what a bastard you've been.'

Pap preferred a bit of rock and roll, even heavy metal in small doses, but never opera. If it ever came on the radio he'd switch it off.

'The quartet from Verdi's *Rigoletto* was his favourite,' said Brenda. At the height of a deep intake of breath, she remembered Pavarotti and Joan Sutherland singing that very piece. 'So full blast it should have lifted the roof. But do you know what, Pap?'

No, he didn't know what. Pap had an aversion to anything Italian, even hated pasta, ever since he'd got clobbered in Tuscany for trying to chat up some bird. She wasn't alone or as lonely, as he'd first thought. Her guy came out with a bottle of wine halfway through Pap's monologue. He hadn't expected Italians to be so touchy.

'If I was upstairs or in the garden I really couldn't hear anything. Even the fresh air vent is taken care of, Arthur put some sort of duct isolator in there, so don't think of trying to shout up there either. No point, no one's going to hear you, and anyway, the outlet is tucked away behind the shed, lots of bushes between here and the closest neighbours.'

The cell became peculiarly silent. Just Pap breathing, a throaty pant like a dog just finishing its run. It had been some while since somebody threatened him with the possibility of death, but it wasn't totally outside his experience.

Chapter 11

Brenda had slipped easily into her role as gaoler. Pap had been tried, by consensus, and sentenced by the small jury. She, the judge, had worked out his punishment which would be just and fair with all the loose ends tied up and Pap learning the biggest lesson of his sordid existence. And if she played it right, it would eventually go viral.

Raihana's engagement ring looked capacious, cheap, with a chunky fake diamond. She slid it across the table to Brenda, during an emergency visit to Coffee 4 Us.

'I never wore it,' she said, '...my parents. It's not like here in the UK. Mum and Dad still think arranged marriages are best; usually someone from the same community or having the same ethnicity. Things are changing in Pakistan, in some places, semi-arranged marriages are acceptable, where the couple have a final say. But they still tend to keep things within the community. Then there's the other end of the scale; honour killings, a thousand in Pakistan last year, even some where I live, in Lahore.

'You see, Brenda, in Pakistan women and girls embody family honour, a woman's identity, and her family's sense of social respect is measured by her acceptance of family demands, like marrying the man they choose for her.'

'Mum doesn't have any idea about life in the West and they both have a strict Muslim view toward sex and marriage. If this

situation arose in Lahore,' she said dropping her gaze, 'I would be
hidden until the birth of the baby. It would probably be adopted, to
save the family from shame. Horrible things can happen. I heard of
a woman being stoned to death by her family for getting pregnant
outside marriage. Another was locked in a cell, like Pap, until the
birth. And he's a white European! I've got no chance, they'd kill
me! It's tough, Brenda. Not sure how I can cope...'

Brenda put the ring in her pocket, patted Raihana's hand and,
unsure how to respond to Raihana's fears, asked how she felt,
pregnancy-wise.

'A bit of morning sickness, nothing awful.'

'Any news from home? I guess your friends have been
keeping you up to speed.'

'I heard that Mum's been crying a lot since I left Lahore to
find Melvyn Greenstone. And Dad has spread the word, tells
everyone he no longer has a daughter,' she said, touching the
finger where the ring should have been. 'Can't blame him for that,
he's from a different world. As far as Dad is concerned my life is
over. I'll never have a respectable marriage.'

Brenda squeezed Raihana's hand, realising that this was the
worst possible scenario for her friend. Pregnancy outside marriage,
particularly with such a cheating bastard, would ruin Raihana's
future, regardless of anything Brenda could do. Her desire to act as
the lone avenger hadn't considered such an outcome. But there
were other women to think about. Not all of them would be happy
with the revelations but then justice leaves its inevitable legacy, not
always perfect, even for the victims.

Pap was supine on the floor trying to look pale and pathetic. He'd
heard Brenda coming down the stairs. She gasped when she saw
him, lying still as a rock.

Pap had turned his eyes upward for effect, showing only the
whites. He wondered if he'd ever be able to see properly again.
Perhaps he'd go cross-eyed and stay that way. His mother had

predicted this when he'd come home from school showing off his cross-eyed stunt, which had spread through the boys' class like a virus.

Brenda clapped her hands as hard as she could. The eyes that he thought would never move again, flickered and rolled back in their sockets. Pap coughed: he'd blown it.

'What's up now, Pap?'

'Dial 999. I think I've been in a coma.'

'All of your life probably. No change there, sunshine. And no doctor.'

'It's serious. I nearly died last time.'

Brenda laughed. 'What last time? What is it, Pap?'

'Diabetes.'

'Dickabetes more likely. Surprised it hasn't dropped off with all that extramarital activity.'

'Give me something sweet soon, or I'll die. That would ruin your plan, Brenda,' he said, still trying to look as ill as he could on the basement floor, thoughts of Brenda ever calling a doctor fading fast.

'What type?' She'd already worked out that if he'd really had insulin dependent diabetes, he'd have been in a coma within a day of his captivity. The guy should have done his research.

Pap was racking his brain trying to remember what his doctor had said when he went for a routine check-up. He'd been screened for...ah yes....

'Type two.'

'Snap. Same as me, everything is gonna be fine, Pap, I have insulin in the fridge and a bloody great needle in a sterile pack. I'll go get it.'

Pap started to get up, his plan unravelling. He was breaking out in a sweat and had gone genuinely pale. He was terrified of needles.

'I'm having a hyper attack, just give me some chocolate, I'll be fine.'

'The word is hypo, Pap and it's not an attack. If it's anything like my condition you're overdue on your insulin. We'll soon have you sorted,' she said, taking the stairs two at a time, arriving back almost at once with a phial of insulin and a hypodermic.

That man was definitely not diabetic, Brenda would stake her life on it. If he was, he'd have gone hypo the day she locked him up. He was an eater of anything going. She could believe that a doctor's check-up would put him in the borderline pre-diabetic group, if it hadn't been done already. But she was going to play him along. When she mentioned needles he almost passed out, which suited her nicely. Despite her intention, she needed to be careful; obviously didn't want to get in the cell with him.

He hadn't thought this through. Brenda looked suspicious, perhaps he'd have been better off blaming the coma on something more obscure. But he didn't have enough medical knowledge to explain his case.

He stood, gripping the bars, urging Brenda to give him a piece of chocolate first. 'It usually works,' he lied.

She stuck the needle into the phial and drew out a measured amount of insulin.   Pointing the hypodermic toward the ceiling, she pressed the plunger and a spurt of insulin shot into the air, four feet from Pap. He'd watched it spray, reminding him of lethal injections in docudramas, the ones given to prisoners on Death Row.

'You know what to do, Pap. Roll up your sleeve and stick your arm through the bars. Don't try and grab my hand else I might inject the lot into you. Then boy, oh boy, you really will be in trouble. You might even die in that cell after all.'

Pap was trembling with fear. 'Why are you shaking, Pap? You'll be fine once you've had the insulin...'

'Just give me some chocolate, Brenda. Please. It'll stop me shaking. Promise.'

'Be a man for once in your life.'

He attempted to be a man, rolled up his sleeve, and tried to convince himself it would be over in seconds. Brenda stood one hand on hip, the other waving the syringe threateningly.

He never reached the bars of the cell. A build-up of terror rushed through his veins and tried to exit somewhere through the top of his skull; everything went black and Pap went down like a sack of potatoes. Not faking at all.

She plugged in the Karcher, turned the pressure down and gave Pap a quick blast across the back of his head. He sat bolt upright, still shaking.

The diabetic ploy had gone completely pear-shaped. Brenda couldn't stop laughing and that made it so much worse. Failure was one thing, but failure in front of the *she devil* was doubly worse.

He shook for most of the night. Not from the cold, but from the thought of Brenda actually sticking a needle in him.

Chapter 12

Pap wasn't going to call any of the shots. No way! The insulin incident hadn't ended well. No matter. Now Brenda had an even bigger plan to spook her captive. It was time for him to get another wake-up call. Call being the operative word.

'Listen up, Pap. It's time for a little entertainment.'

Pap grunted without getting up off the bed. He noticed her hands were empty, no Karcher or anything, so he relaxed a bit.

Brenda sat in the old chair, away from Pap's cell and took his mobiles out of her pocket. She laid them on the chair, before flexing her wrists and cracking her knuckles, like a virtuoso about to play a Rachmaninov concerto. Text time!

Pap twitched. He recognised his mobiles.

The welcome screen lit up her smile from below as she turned on one of the phones. Selecting contacts, she held back, pausing for effect, deciding who was going to get the first text to be sent, with her prisoner as a spectator.

Pap was now alert, sitting up, leaning forward, colour draining from his face.

'Thought you might like a bit of company, so I'm going to sit here and we'll catch up with a few people. Don't mind me using your mobiles, do you? I've charged them up. Pretty good reception here, for a cellar…Wow, lots of contacts, Pap, you're a popular guy. Nice wife by the look of things; seen your little messages to each other. Not a lot of affection there, Pap. Gone off the boil has it, this marriage? Well, nothing lasts forever. Three years is a long time for someone like you to stick with a woman.'

The prisoner said nothing.

''Spect you're wondering how I knew it was three years. So sweet of you to put anniversaries with your contact details. It's all there, Pap, all your little reminders.'

Sweat appeared on Pap's forehead, he felt clammy. 'You've gone far enough, Brenda, tell me what you want. I've learnt my lesson so let's get it over with, you need to get back to a normal life.'

'I already have a normal life, Pap. You being down here is nothing, hardly know you're around most of the time.

'Ready, Pap? No secrets from my end: I've already swapped a few texts, kept people in the loop, nothing meaningful: *I'm on the plane, I'm at the hotel, I'm off for a meeting...* Don't worry, I'll be reading the important stuff out loud as I text. Which phone, who shall we call first? There's so many to choose from, but let's start with number one, wifey.' She was tempted to crack her knuckles again, for effect; something quite disturbing about the cracking of joints, like fingers breaking.

She tapped the keypad. '*Hi Gloria.* That's how you start, isn't it, Pap, none of this mushy, dearest Gloria or darling stuff?' Pap closed his eyes and gripped the bars of his cell, knuckles ivory white.

Brenda read aloud to Pap as she composed the text. '*I guess you've been wondering why I haven't texted you over the last few days. It's been complicated. I tried to ring but couldn't get through. Didn't really want you to get this news by text. Not fair. You've been good to me.*'

Pap's knuckles turned whiter.

'*Right out of the blue, I swear it, I bumped into an old flame and, long story short, realised we'd had something special. I know we did too but I have to be honest, I can't carry on with our marriage any longer, I'd be living a lie. File for divorce, Gloria. I wouldn't blame you. I'll make sure you get a good settlement. Cheers, Pap.*

She emphasised *Pap* to make him think she'd made a mistake but actually signed off with Melvyn…'There you go,' she said, making a big show of pressing the send button.

Pap turned away from Brenda. He held back a Jack Nicholson grin, an evil smirk, because Gloria would know it wasn't from him! 'Who the hell's Pap?' she'd say. He felt confident that Brenda's plan was about to unravel and Gloria would pull out all the stops to find him.

Chapter 13

Brenda hadn't pressed 'send', only 'save draft'. She'd check it again before she'd let it go; one slip could ruin everything. The whole point was that Melvyn would be pissing his pants at the thought of texts going out all over the place.

Despite the shock of Brenda having his mobiles, Pap was feeling somewhat optimistic about getting out. Gloria wouldn't be a problem; he'd tell her the truth about the text from Pap. In fact the whole world would know that he'd been kept prisoner, had his mobiles stolen, mentally tortured, kept without proper food and, more or less, water-boarded while in captivity. Yeah that works, the Karcher was as close to water-boarding as you could get.

But what would Gloria do first? She'd wonder how Pap, whoever he was, had got hold of his phone, the one she would have known about at least. She'd look through his address book, maybe phone a few of his friends, check with his boss and colleagues and if all else failed she'd call the police.

Maybe she'd pick up the land line thinking something might be askew with her cell phone reception, and then try his mobile again. It would go straight to voicemail. She'd try texting, *Who is Pap*? Of course, nothing would come back that day or the next, unless Brenda decided on adding a bit more to her sham texts. Gloria would be worried, notice his messages weren't genuine. She was a cute cookie was Gloria, she'd get right on it as soon as she saw Brenda's big mistake: texting *Pap*, on the end of the message to her.

Chapter 14

A brief flash caught Pap's eye as he gazed out at the empty basement. He'd woken from a disturbed night, most nights were these days. But he hadn't heard Brenda come downstairs and leave the ring on the basement floor, just feet from his cell. His breath caught. He recognised it. Cheap, with a chunky diamond, not quite in the three-for-the-price-of-two bracket but worth buying a few at the time, he remembered. They'd looked so good, expensive. Let's face it, some women needed a certain reassurance before they got to the bed stage.

How the hell did Brenda get hold of it, whose was it? Three possibilities, but with Brenda holding the reins and his mobiles...

Brenda came down the stairs with his soup. 'Spotted the ring then?' she said. 'I've brought you another present. Stand back and I'll push it through.'

She squeezed a paper bag through the bars, didn't want to risk polythene, he may decide to suffocate himself.

'What's this?'

'Don't you just love presents, Pap? It's getting a bit smelly down here. Those clothes you're wearing need chucking now. I've bought you something new to wear.'

Pap opened the bag and took out a disposable boiler suit, bought from Amazon and delivered to Brenda the next day, compliments of her Prime Membership. It was made of a thin papery material, orange, same colour worn by the Guantanamo Bay inmates, high-vis.

'It'll suit you, Pap, matches your eyes, saves on laundry. Not that I'll be doing any. When that one wears out, I have a stock, they come in packs of five. You'll smell better.'

Pap swallowed hard. Didn't mind the boiler suit as much as the information Brenda had a stock, indicating she meant to keep him there for some time yet.

He was racking his brain as to who might have given Brenda the ring. Some of his conquests lived abroad. No one in the UK with a ring, as far as he could remember, that would have been too risky.

'When you've got your new gear on, Pap, just push your old clothes through the bars. I'll be wearing rubber gloves, don't want to catch anything, do I? Stand back and I'll put your soup in. Big day, Pap, diamond ring returned, as new, fresh clothes. I'm getting soft, spoiling you now.'

When Brenda left, he took off his clothes and donned the boiler suit. He felt instantly cleaner. There was plenty of room in it.

He had an idea. Holding one arm of his filthy shirt he flicked the other through the bars like a lasso. After several tries he managed to catch the ring on the folded cuff and draw it toward his cell. He pocketed it, bundled up his old clothes, and stuffed them through the bars.

Using the star-shaped head of the cold water tap, he prised the ring apart. It snapped easily, roughly where the gem setting met the ring band, leaving a small hook-like end. He flattened the circular structure on the edge of the sink and held the result up to the light. He wasn't an expert but this looked remarkably like a lock pick: the ones he'd seen on telly where, with a bit of patience, you wiggled them around in the lock, heard the innards drop systematically into the right place and… you're free.

Chapter 15

Thank God she hadn't sent the draft. But Pap wouldn't know that. She'd said 'Pap' out loud when she'd finished the text to Gloria. His brain would now be working overtime thinking Brenda had made a mistake. But once she'd considered it, sending that very text might have the effect she wanted. But not yet, there were other things to put into place first. Had to be coordinated and timed to perfection. The important thing was that Pap thought she'd sent it.

Had Arthur constructed the barred door to Pap's cell, Pap would have been out and running down The Avenue the day of his incarceration. But she'd paid two illegal immigrants a hefty sum to make and fit it, spot-welded to Forth Bridge standards with a decent lock. They'd delivered the cell door disguised as a single mattress—padding, cell door, more padding, mattress cover, polythene—in a hired van with the legend: *Big White Van Man: no job too small*. In broad daylight in the middle of a school and working day, it was not seen as suspicious. Just as well, or the guys delivering it would have been back on a bus, plane or boat, to wherever they came from.

Pap would not be escaping anytime soon.

Brenda texted more numbers on Pap's mobile. She needed anecdotes for her 'Pap file' and got responses. Many were surprised that he'd contacted them. 'A woman scorned', didn't come close to some of the replies she was getting.

Her list was growing. Probably enough. Might get a few quotes from others later, something extra to read to Pap during his long boring days in the cellar.

All communications were by text, so none of the recipients would doubt their origin. As far as they were concerned, it would be their old lover Melvyn Greenstone trying to woo them back into his life. Some of the responses were hilarious. 'Fuck off' was overused in Brenda's mind, but there were still some willing to meet up and carry on where they'd left off. Surprise, surprise.

Chapter 16

Gloria picked up the phone, which was ringing as she walked in from the garden.

'Hi, Gloria, Simon here, we're trying to contact Melvyn. He's not picking up. We have a problem.'

She walked over to the window and looked across the terrace to the immaculate lawn. She flopped into the most comfortable chair, her back still aching from the ride-on mower, a fiftieth birthday present from Melvyn. 'You like gardening,' he'd said, as he took her outside to show her the pink ribboned machine.

Hope you enjoy the ride, had been carefully printed on the card around the flowery design. Inside it added: *Didn't get you a card with fifty on it as I know you hate being reminded of your age. Cheers, Melvyn.* Bumping around a landscaped acre on a machine that had never been introduced to a shock absorber, was a bit more than the fine gardening she'd had in mind.

Simon, Melvyn's boss, started the company from scratch. Hands-on guy most of the time, but once he'd given instructions, his super salesman Melvyn Greenstone was left alone. His brief: travel abroad and buy cheap goods to sell at a profit in the UK. And if he saw an opportunity to invest in naive but struggling small companies—often found by trawling the Internet, making a few phone calls and targeting his quarry—he could formulate rescue plans and offer to buy them too. Simon gave him a budget for these dubious transactions. Melvyn was used to being off the radar but always managed to finish the deals on time, which was all Simon needed.

'Sorry, Simon. We've been texting each other but I haven't tried to call him yet. We tend to stick to texting while he's away, unless there's a real problem. Anything I can do? Have you tried texting him yourself?'

Simon only did phoning, bosses need to give strong verbal messages. Texting was a leisure activity, as far as he was concerned. 'Please keep trying,' he replied. 'Nothing else you can help with, Gloria, but thanks for the offer. Tell him it's urgent, we need him back before Saturday.'

In all the years she'd known Simon, Gloria could count his calls to the house on one hand. It was rare, because when the boss rang Melvyn's mobile, he'd always pick up, no matter where he was or what he was doing...

She tried ringing Melvyn's phone first. Voicemail. She left a message, *'Call Simon. Urgent.'* Then texted: *Simon called. He has a problem. Contact him asap. I think he wants you back by Saturday.*

Brenda thought this might happen, but all was going to plan. She might have to consider bringing Pap's release date forward a bit. She read the text to Pap...

'You'll have to let me go now, Brenda. The shit's gonna hit the fan for you. They'll know I'm missing now. My boss knows people, tough people, he'll need me back, I'm his key man.'

'You haven't got it yet, have you? I'm the gaoler you're the prisoner. I can leave, you can't. But don't worry, Pap, I intend to let you go...when I'm ready.'

Pap sank back on his bed, thinking about Gloria. He was really getting to like her, almost to the point of being faithful. But he knew his terrible affliction, genetic for sure; alcohol and women had led him to make less than satisfactory choices in life.

'Don't worry about Simon. He'll soon find someone else, Pap.'

'I'm his top man, Brenda. It won't be that simple. Simon won't give up that easily.'

'This might help move the situation on,' she said, starting to text. 'Here's my latest, or should I say your latest, to Gloria, Pap.'

'Gloria. Sorry to ask you to do this, but Simon needs to know right away. I'm not coming back. I'm quitting the company. I've got other plans, been thinking about leaving for ages. Tell him my letter of resignation is on its way. Sorry.'

Brenda had already Googled Pap's company. She'd checked out what they did, taken a look at the staff his boss Simon employed and found out that Pap's rather grand title was, *Procurement Consultant.* Pap looked good on the company web page: extensive CV, nice pic of him smiling in his expensive suit and tie, plus some shots of him in far-off lands strutting his stuff. No hobbies, she noted, well not proper ones, only golf and sailing. She could add some interesting snippets to that section.

Chapter 17

Brenda's footsteps sounded ominous, heavier, as if she was angry about something. She took her time looking around the basement floor. Placing the ring right there was only meant to wind Pap up, make him think a bit more on what misery he might have caused during his little escapades.

'Give it back, Pap, or I'll get the Karcher out.'

'Give what back?' he said.

'The ring!'

'What ring?'

'The cheap diamond ring, Pap, the one you gave Raihana. It was here,' she said, pointing to a spot a few feet from Pap's cell.

Bugger: the Pakistani chick. 'What was it doing on the floor anyway?' he said, knowing it was something to do with his captor's subtle system of mental torture. 'Don't know if you noticed, Brenda, but, even if there had been a ring, my arms aren't four foot long. I haven't anything to reach out with. Check my cell... You must have picked it up with that bundle of clothes.'

Brenda hadn't thought of that. She hadn't missed the ring at first, until she'd spoken to Raihana who'd asked what she'd done with it. She'd put Pap's dirty clothes in a plastic bag and hidden them in the rubbish bin, due for collection...this morning! She dashed upstairs and made her way out to the back garden just in time to hear the dustcart pull away from the house and out of The Avenue.

There was one thing she certainly wouldn't be doing, she'd not even turn the key in Pap's cell door let alone search for the ring, far too dangerous. Then she reasoned, what could he do with it anyway? He wouldn't wear it! Even though it looked big enough to fit his stubby fingers. And he wasn't likely to do anything dramatic with it, like sock her in the face with the fake diamond. She'd never get that close.

Chapter 18

Shah-Alam Market, Shalmi Market to the locals, one of more than two dozen street markets in Lahore, was the one Melvyn had liked best. He'd seen most of the others but the goods looked better quality and the people friendlier. It was his business to get the best deals on products or buy the companies that would turn over a decent profit in the UK.

The place was a mixture of shops and stalls; some commercial structures were so flimsy he could well believe they'd been put up by a playful child and not meant to last more than a night.

He'd had forewarning about how easily he could be taken for a ride here. The locals stared a lot and he was advised to respond to this curiosity with a smile. Too much of a smile, however, could indicate overfriendliness, which could get you into a whole lot of trouble. Melvyn had already discussed etiquette with his boss before he left. They'd checked Wikipedia for tips, watched YouTube videos of market life in Lahore: looked up how to say, in Urdu; 'Do you speak English?', 'Good morning', 'How much?' 'Thank you' and 'I couldn't give this deal to anyone else.' Melvyn was useless at languages and often resorted to speaking louder or using hand signals, a strategy he felt tended to work pretty well most of the time. The people he'd met usually had a smattering of English anyway, picked up from tourists, the Internet, or television.

A big part of making these successful deals was to check out the local trading practices: rules of the game that made a region unique in the way its economy functioned. Always worth the effort, particularly when he found out that police were often involved in corruption and various scams when working in concert with 'creative' businessmen.

Some of Pakistan's major exports were handicrafts, leather and textiles, an area Melvyn loved to deal in: products bought cheaply and sold for a huge profit in the UK.

*

Melvyn coughed as trucks, cars and motorbikes filled the air with diesel fumes. He lit a cigarette which seemed to help. By the time the tuk tuk dropped him off at the Shah-Alami Gate, he'd already worked out exactly where he was headed: the Khans' place. With boss Simon he'd done some research, made calls and stuck pins in a map of Lahore indicating exactly where they should be focusing their efforts.

*

The man who approached Raihana was obviously British. Her parents spoke of them, not unkindly, but rather as if they did not fit in, not in Lahore anyway. Her father—a strict Muslim from northern Pakistan, a *Pashtun*, with links across the border to Afghanistan—forbade her contact with males, any males, unless it was for business and only on condition that he was around to supervise the transactions.

Lahore welcomed new trade, but old customs and culture prevailed. Melvyn was surprised to learn there was no caste hierarchy here, but a well-respected class system: high, middle and low income groups. Women were still expected to spend most of their lives looking after the house, the children, and the needs of their men and were compelled, in all matters, to follow the advice of their parents.

However, women could vote, be well educated and, in some circumstances, were allowed to enter business and follow chosen career paths. Things were changing even more rapidly for the next generation. Raihana had, along with so many other younger Pakistanis, been exposed to Western ways through social media. She'd been excited by the apparent freedom, broadcast easily across the Internet; parents who allowed their children to mix with other races and cultures and even allowed them to marry a foreigner. She and her friends had European contacts on their mobile contact lists; on Facebook and on laptops, for those who could afford them, and hidden away from authoritarian parents. Some were eager to escape their roots and meet foreigners with money.

In Lahore's terms, Raihana was relatively well off, making a decent profit through her clever marketing, selling local, handmade quality goods. Tourists paid good prices and some of Lahore's middle class frequented her stall too.

*

The European smiled and walked toward her. He looked friendly, well dressed, even wealthy, she imagined. But then many of the foreigners who came here looked rich. Top of the range hotels were fifteen hundred pounds a week, one hundred and forty eight thousand rupees, a fortune.

'What's your name?' Melvyn asked, turning over various objects and asking about prices. He was lightly tanned and dressed to impress, in a smart linen suit with a crisp open-neck shirt. His hair was neatly cut in a style a bit too young for him, a little quiff poking up at an odd angle.

'Raihana...Miss Khan,' she added, to keep it formal. 'Can I help you with anything?' she asked, the use of her name, striking her as overly intimate for a new customer. Unsure of his intentions she distracted herself by rearranging the display and not looking up.

Melvyn smiled. 'I want to buy the lot, everything on the stall. Name your price,' he said, confident of a decent profit. 'Here's my business card.'

There was a long silence. She was blushing. Embarrassed, whether by his directness or the shock of possibly selling her whole stock in a moment, was hard to tell. She looked at his card: *Ethical Global Logistics. Melvyn Greenstone: Procurement Consultant.* There was an international number to call, an email address, a website and *follow me* on Facebook and Twitter logos. The company looked respectable.

'Ray...sorry, what was it again?'

'Raihana,' she reminded him.

'Raihana,' he repeated. 'What do you think?' he asked, realising that buying the lot must have been something of a surprise.

'I'll need to discuss this with my parents,' she replied, trying to look business-like.

'Is it not your stall?'

'Of course, but here in Lahore, it is customary to consult parents on big decisions.'

Providing the price was right, Melvyn couldn't understand why selling the whole stall in one go should need any consideration at all. But he'd taken a shine to Raihana and was in no particular hurry to close the deal. This was relatively small beer, but he knew from his enquiries that she had other stalls, and an introduction to her parents might lead to more contacts. He was going to spend time in a pretty decent hotel. And who knows, Raihana might like a bit of company.

'Shall I come back tomorrow? I'd be happy to meet your parents too, if that's the best way to do things here. If you need to call me in the meantime, I'll write my personal mobile number on the back of the card.'

Raihana tucked Melvyn's card into her pocket and couldn't wait to rush home and tell her father the good news. She knew he'd view the deal with suspicion and wonder if there was a catch. But she also felt that Melvyn was a man to be trusted. He hadn't even asked about discounts, deals for bulk buy; unheard of in Lahore.

Raihana's parents had turned up early in what Melvyn considered pyjamas; *Shalwar Kameez*, long loose tops and baggy trousers. Mr. and Mrs. Khan were standing either side of Raihana's stall when Melvyn arrived. He sensed they were suspicious of his motives, probably because he was European, and a stranger. They looked serious. Melvyn became even more aware that his offer to buy the lot must have seemed ludicrous, particularly as he hadn't tried to fix a price. The products were of such good quality that he was thinking of offering Raihana a contract to supply goods exclusively to him. He would arrange shipping back to the UK.

'We understand you want to buy my daughter's products. Everything on the stall, you said?' asked Mr. Khan.

Melvyn nodded and smiled. 'That's right. I have instructions to buy the best products for sale in my country.' He thought a little flattery wouldn't go amiss.

'You are a business man from the West, I expect you'll want a good price... But our profit is small,' said Mr. Khan. Raihana nodded but didn't speak.

Melvyn was aware that many Eastern markets thrived on barter and bargain but he didn't have the patience for it. He knew what he wanted to pay and hoped the Khans would feel overwhelmed by his generosity. 'What is your price?' said Melvyn, restraining himself from taking a wad of notes and counting out whatever was asked for. He just knew it would be a bargain.

Mr. Khan spoke in Urdu to Raihana and gently nudged his daughter forward. She presented Melvyn with a stock list, each item priced, a discount for bulk purchase and a final figure; cheaper than even Melvyn would have guessed.

'That looks fair,' said Melvyn. He went behind the drape at the back of the stall, accessed his money belt and counted the cash out in the preferred currency, the dollar.

Raihana and her parents looked at each other. Mr. Khan whispered to Raihana before turning to face Melvyn. 'Aren't you going to bargain with us?' he said, looking as if he'd been gravely insulted.

'I think you are very fair and you've worked hard for this,' said Melvyn, directly to Raihana. Very fair to Melvyn but not fair to the people of Lahore. In England this would have been considered an out and out rip off.

'I'll send a man to help you pack everything up. He'll do most of the work and it will be shipped to the UK.' Eventually the parents smiled, shook hands, and embraced Melvyn, who'd almost had an attack of conscience. Then they offered him coffee.

Raihana felt a huge excitement build. Her products were going to be sold—in England!

'Can I buy you all dinner?' offered Melvyn, 'wherever you choose.' The family were smitten, but it wouldn't last.

*

There were a few reasons why Raihana ended up sleeping with Melvyn. Apart from the fact he treated her well, he was mildly attractive, in a cuddly bear sort of way and was liked, as much as a foreigner could be, by her overbearing parents. Pakistani women had a harder time than Westerners, a great percentage were underprivileged, undereducated and more exposed to physical abuse than their Western counterparts. So Melvyn was on the list of men that she did like. She'd heard that, on the whole, a European businessman was a pretty good deal for a liberated Asian woman. These men were richer and seemed happier too. She was almost certain that doing good business with him would be bound to meet with parental approval. They'd been impressed when Raihana showed them the Ethical Global Logistics website on her laptop, complete with Melvyn's extensive CV and the trading history of his company.

Although old-school, Raihana's parents were quite picky about the local men she'd been attracted to so far. And Raihana had not been overwhelmed by any of them, so covert sex with cuddly, wealthy, Melvyn, who'd promised her more riches than she'd ever dreamed of, seemed a risk worth taking. Especially when he talked about a serious relationship, travel and possibly marriage. He made her feel like the most important person in the world, something that never happened with the men she'd met in Lahore. When he'd confirmed his intention by slipping a diamond ring on her finger, Raihana was swept off her feet. There was a lot of space between the ring and her finger; she'd blushed and slipped it off as soon as she was on her own. Her parents would have killed her.

Chapter 19

Pap's attempt at picking his cell lock was not going well. He had to twist his wrist and arm to access the lock from inside the cell, his weak muscles straining with the contortions. Everything hurt. He fully appreciated the antics of Houdini who, until now, he'd considered nothing more than a cheap trickster. Picking locks was no mean feat. But there was an optimistic side; the ring was holding up, hadn't lost its shape and still had the little hooked end he'd started with. Time was on his side and he was getting the hang of angles and twists that might yet see him up, out and away.

Footsteps. Quickly, ring in pocket.

'Haven't heard from Gloria or Simon since you chucked your job in, Pap, wonder what on earth's going on. Think they've thrown the towel in? Given up on you?' Brenda asked Pap to stand back while she slipped his carton of soup through the bars.

'The only thing they'll get up to, Brenda, is to start a search going. And when the cops find out you've imprisoned me and stuck your fingerprints all over my mobiles, they'll know how sick you are. All those false messages. Impersonating me!'

'You seem to be forgetting something, Pap. No one's gonna have sympathy for a cheating liar who's just got his comeuppance. And if they do ever find you, it might be too late...' She let the words hang in the musty basement air.

Pap swallowed hard, uncertain of how he was going to end up.

Escape was on his mind, or release at some point, but every now and again, Brenda said something that sent a shiver down his spine.

The perfume followed her up the stairs and left Pap in a bad mood.

*

Mr. and Mrs. Khan had been discussing Raihana's association with Melvyn. Mrs. Khan viewed it in a more positive light. 'The business arrangement is a good deal, Khan, the world is changing, we have to make allowances otherwise we will be left behind,' said Mother. She always called her husband Khan and he always addressed her as Mother. It suited the old hierarchy of male-female relationships and class, and Khan was a powerful name, respected, feared even: an old Pashtun tribal surname. He liked being called Khan.

'I will not have my daughter flaunting herself in front of a foreigner,' he said, wagging his finger, a habit that Mother hated. Sometimes she felt like grasping that damn finger and snapping it!

'She's not flaunting, Khan, she's doing business. When the deal is done Mr. Greenstone will be gone and we will be so much richer. Surely that's worth a little discomfort on your part?'

Khan grunted. He could see the point but he was not happy, especially as his daughter had insisted on attending some meetings with Melvyn alone. She needed their trust and didn't want Melvyn to think she wasn't worldly, or sophisticated. It seemed ridiculous, in this day and age, that parents should accompany a grownup daughter to every damn business meeting she'd set up. Raihana had been courteous enough to let her parents in at the start of the enterprise. They must see that he was a genuine guy, serious about business. That should be enough.

'Certainly not,' said Khan, brow knitting, eyes darkening as Raihana explained her reasons for meeting Melvyn on her own.

Mother gripped Khan's arms and directed her gaze directly into his troubled face. 'Do you love your daughter, Khan?'

'Of course, what's that got to do with it?'

'Then you have to trust her,' she said, gripping Khan tighter. 'Has she ever given you any reason to doubt her love for us, has she ever done anything to disgrace us? She's even had the sense to say no to the eligible men we *have* introduced to her. She's picky, that's a good thing. She wouldn't do anything silly. It's just business.'

'Don't tell me the world's changing, not again, Mother, I know it is. But it is too fast, I can't keep up with it.'

'Well your daughter has to. If she wants our business to remain successful, especially when we're gone, she has to change with it. And, unfortunately, that means mixing with people from other countries and cultures to make it work. Just look what's happening around you, Khan—tourism, global trade, a standard of living we could only imagine—and we are lucky enough to be here at the right time: we do business in the best market in Lahore with this opportunity to make a good living, better than we'd ever dreamed of.'

Khan grunted, he hadn't formulated an answer, yet he was astonished by the scale of their recent transaction, more money than they'd made all year.

Mother knew that Khan's grunt was an optimistic sound; none of what she'd said had been thrown out.

Chapter 20

The company card Melvyn gave Raihana, the one with his personal mobile number written on the back, had been a disappointing means of communication. After the first month, following his return to the UK—a few weeks when passionate texts flew back and forth—he stopped replying, and she began to wonder; why had he given it to her in the first place? But she'd kept texting. She missed him and was keen to secure further transactions and visit him in that fabulous hotel where they'd first made love. Her parents would be horrified. Raihana was a stranger to coitus, but in her imaginings the process wouldn't have been over quite so quickly. She took this as a sign of the intensity of Melvyn's love, a passion that could not be tamed. A lion unleashed.

Pap had been having treatment for his 'intensity problem' but he'd not managed to make a great deal of progress. He'd wondered if this was somehow linked to a constant dissatisfaction with the outcome of his romantic relationships.

*

Raihana, for reasons other than global trade, had made it to the UK and spent some comfortable nights in a Premier Inn, before setting out on her mission.

She looked across the damp tarmacked street toward a Mini Cooper parked outside Butts, the estate agents. A young guy got into the seat, looked in the courtesy mirror, flicked fingers through gelled hair, aligning it just right, and was about to start the car when Raihana tapped on his window. He wound it down.

'Can I help you?' he asked, smiling broadly.

'I'm looking for somewhere to live. In the town if possible.'

Raymondo looked Raihana up and down, tossing up whether he'd want to be her guide around the local properties, but decided his next appointment won. 'Go see my assistant, Brenda, she's through the office there, making coffee,' he said, jerking his thumb at the half open door. 'She'll stretch to another cup if you fancy one.'

Raymondo wound his window back up, smiled and waved as he pulled away like a racing driver off the grid.

Brenda looked up at the very pretty girl in Eastern dress who'd just stepped in.

'I think that was your boss outside,' said Raihana, closing the door behind her. 'He told me to come in and see Brenda. Is that you?'

Brenda thought it was pretty obvious, she was the only one in this morning. 'I was just going to make some coffee, would you like a cup?'

'Thank you. Black no sugar.'

'Buying or selling?' asked Brenda, as she watched Raihana checking the house prices on the flattering display of local residences.

'I'm looking for a flat to rent, short contract if possible,' she replied, walking over to the 'properties to let' section.

Brenda poured the coffee into small white mugs, gave one to Raihana and showed her details of the most desirable flats in the town centre. One she liked was above a shop and within her price range.

'Nice choice,' said Brenda. 'It's only one bedroom though, is that enough? Is it just you?'

Raihana looked sad. 'Yes, for now. I hope my fiancé will join me for some of the time. He doesn't know I'm here yet. I wanted to surprise him.' To be honest, Raihana had no idea where Melvyn was. She'd managed to find out he worked in this part of the South East at Ethical Global Logistics, but that was about it.

She'd rung the company but was disappointed. The receptionist said he was out of the country and they couldn't disclose personal details about their staff.

'Can I get him to call you when he gets back?' the receptionist had added.

Raihana didn't want to give her name or leave a message! He hadn't kept in contact as much as he'd promised, probably due to his busy lifestyle, helping everyone get rich.

Brenda sensed a subtext here. Raihana was nervous, handwringing almost. Hoping to surprise boyfriends you hadn't seen for a while, especially a man living in another country, didn't seem like a very good idea to her.

For Brenda and Raihana, this was the start of a lasting relationship and a bond they had yet to realise.

Chapter 21

Raihana's plight had upset Brenda, but when she'd found out Raihana's boyfriend was Melvyn Greenstone…Her blood boiled, her legs felt weak, she felt dizzy from the flood of images racing through her head. They say that your past always comes back to bite you, or haunt you. But surely not this!

*

Over time, Brenda, in undercover mode, and with the help of Pap's mobiles, had managed to trace several of his little secrets: women he'd left stranded, broken promises, engagements and even Angie Greenstone, an ex-wife he'd never actually divorced. Bigamy was a step too far, incurring a hefty prison sentence. She'd throw away the key. None of his past girlfriends seemed to have much idea that they were only a small part of Pap's compulsive lifestyle. They weren't going to remain ignorant of that fact for long.

Raihana must have really been in love to come all this way. Or perhaps her parents had thrown her out for daring to have an English boyfriend, which, according to the assumption that the West was seen as corrupt, must have involved sex. She'd heard that sex before marriage and inter-racial marriages were still frowned upon in many countries.

*

Brenda's sex life with Arthur had been cosy and infrequent, right from the start. On their wedding night, following consummation, Arthur had mentioned how tired he was. He remained tired for most of the honeymoon and Brenda wondered if he was ill. The act itself was quite gentle, with Arthur experiencing an orgasm similar in effect to the cramp he'd had on occasion. In fact she could never be quite sure whether Arthur actually ever had an orgasm. She'd heard of women faking it, but never men. However, it was a symptom that could only be settled by her husband jumping out of bed and hopping, like an injured rabbit, to set his bare feet on the cold bathroom floor. Brenda had never had an orgasm herself and was beginning to doubt she ever would. And if it really was like the cramp Arthur experienced, then she'd rather give it a miss.

Chapter 22

Pap had tried not to reflect on his past too much. But as the weeks went by it was inescapable. Angie, his first wife, his only wife according to law, was the first to take her rightful place in his retrospective. He'd loved her at the time, but when she'd started getting personal, rattling on about his 'lack of emotional intelligence' as she'd called it—whatever that fucking meant—his ardour waned. Intelligence? He'd got a business degree for God's sake!

He'd be the first to admit he wasn't perfect, made a few gaffes in the relationship department, meant well at the time, tried hard to correct the little practical things that seemed to annoy Angie disproportionately; leaving the toilet seat up, missing the laundry basket when he tossed his pants from the bed, prior to a night of love—then failing to pick them up in the morning.

Angie would have taken issue with 'a night of love'…

He mentally went through the women in his past. Pap always had a problem remembering the odd one or two. He'd been a travelling man most of his life, away from husbandly comforts, worldly, testosterone driven, especially when he'd nearly finished a deal and had days to spend before heading home, like a soldier or sailor away from loved ones.

The Pakistani though, what was her name? He was really sorry about her. Upset the parents big time when they'd found out he'd made advances to their daughter, then left Lahore without so much as a goodbye. Probably chucked her out of the family home, or worse. He'd heard that's what was likely to happen in Pakistan. But she was willing at the time, eager to do more business and get involved. In more ways than one.

Perhaps he'd promised too much, trying too hard to impress on her what a good guy he was; shouldn't have said he was a Christian, that was definitely a step too far. He'd got married to Angie in church and been to funerals and weddings, but that was about it. Ray... whatever her name was, had considered Christianity herself and, given his admission, may have thought him a useful source of information on the subject. She'd asked him several ecclesiastical questions for which he'd had no answers. He should have remembered the old adage: never discuss religion or politics.

'Good starter, poor finisher', one cheeky bitch had described his lovemaking. But Pap knew this was simply his overenthusiasm, due to a lack of intimacy. Everyone knew, that if a man had to wait too long, he got impatient in the plumbing area. He took care over the groundwork though, good at the chat; complimented women on their hair and dress, told them they were beautiful even when he'd considered some less than borderline. Women needed lots of encouragement before coming across. Some, usually the thinnest of them, ate and drank for England. Fortunately, he had a decent expenses allowance.

Brenda had stepped softly down the stairs and stood before him, interrupting his post mortem.

'I give up, Brenda. Just tell me what you want. I need to get out of here. I've got plenty of money. I'm sorry if I've offended anyone but there's nothing I can do about the past. Surely an apology and money will settle whatever gripe you have with me. There's nothing more I can do.'

Offended anyone? Brenda thought about going back upstairs for her list. 'This was never gonna be your call. I could tell you my plan but then, I'd have to kill you, as they say in the movies. There are worse things than dying, Pap. Ask...' She stopped herself uttering a name.

Between mealtimes, just as a reminder to keep him in check, Brenda would occasionally bring the Karcher down and stand it in the corner. Today was such a day. She wanted to see beads of sweat form on that creased brow; keep the pressure up.

'I'm thinking of Gloria now, Pap, she must be going through hell, worrying what you're up to, wondering how she's going to manage with you leaving and being out of work and all, and she won't even be able to claim alimony, 'cause you're not really married, are you?'

When Brenda had texted Angie on Pap's mobile, she'd texted back: *'What do you want? I may be your wife Melvyn, but what sort of man leaves a woman and sends her a bloody text five years later?''*

Pap said nothing, he had no defence for that statement and knew it. But he still felt that once he got out, Gloria would stand by him and Brenda would end up being a target of hate. His boss would give him his job back too, because he was damn good at it. Brenda would be exposed as a mean-minded bitch.

Chapter 23

She stopped halfway down the stairs, listening for any sign of movement. Pap's soup of the day had been placed outside the cell bars untouched and he looked peaky, pale, slack-mouthed and asleep. This was the first time he'd not eaten since his incarceration.

'What's up, Pap?' she asked, in a voice reminiscent of a line in a Bugs Bunny cartoon.

Pap stirred and wiped a trail of dribble from the corner of his mouth. 'I'm not well,' he said, looking bleary-eyed at Brenda. 'I'm off my food. No appetite. Headaches. Dizzy. I need a doctor.'

Brenda didn't need to tell Pap to stand back, he looked too weak to move from his bed. She picked up the soup carton and stepped quickly away, in case he was bluffing and had a sudden movement in mind. She was worried.

'That ain't gonna happen, Pap. You need to eat. I'll warm the soup but don't expect anything more.' Her hands were trembling as she climbed the stairs and locked the basement door. She stood with her back pressed against the kitchen wall, wondering what her next step should be.

Pap was quite pleased with Brenda's response. This hunger strike was a good idea. He'd refuse to eat at all costs, lose even more weight, throw up a couple of times. Karcher-proof. She wouldn't dare turn that ice cold jet on a man who may be dying. He smiled. This was going to be his ticket out of here.

Brenda texted Raihana and arranged to meet. Coffee 4 Us was packed. It was a cool day but they sat outside away from the crowd.

'We have a problem, Raihana. I think Pap might be ill. He's not eating and wants a doctor. Obviously I can't accede to that. Any ideas?'

'Are you sure he's not faking it?'

'Can't tell, he's capable of anything, but he looks grim. It's only his second day without food so perhaps I'm worrying unnecessarily. But I have to think ahead.'

They sipped their small batch cortados in silence. Then Raihana leaned across and whispered in Brenda's ear. She'd had an idea.

Pap was hungry. The second day had been much worse than expected. Stomach cramps kept him awake and his mouth was dry, despite the water he'd been drinking. Brenda didn't offer him soup on the third day. 'Let me know when you want your meal and I'll fetch it. I'm not traipsing up and down these stairs day after day.'

Pap almost gave in, unsure whether Brenda would ever call a doctor. Perhaps starving himself to death would seem like he'd committed suicide. That might be exactly what she wanted. She certainly hadn't shown any signs of cracking.

Pap was having hallucinations. The past came flooding back again but this time at speed, like film clips in a trailer, each showing a different scene, a different woman. Some scenes rocketed by so fast he couldn't quite make out who was in them, or where he'd been at the time. They say that when you die, your past life flashes before you. He'd always scoffed at that; had anyone ever stayed around to prove it? But where were the nice bits? There were no scenes of him doing good things or periods of him being content. He knew there had been some decent times, things he'd done for others, women he'd truly loved, but they'd been lost somehow, as if some spiteful editor had cut them out of the finished movie.

To add to the agony he'd been thinking about the therapy programme for his 'intensity problem'. It was Gloria's idea, with the promise of a more fulfilling sex life. He'd looked aghast when she'd mentioned it, felt it was an affront to his performance, but secretly he was on the point of realising it might be beneficial to make it last a bit longer. But when he went for his first visit, he didn't care much for the options, especially the self-help bit.

He'd concluded that the programme had been written by someone with a serious mental illness; an illness that could only be put right by having a proper sex life.

Was there anything else?

He'd asked about pills and was disappointed to hear that Paroxetine, the drug they'd recommended, was also used for depression. Never been depressed in his life. Nevertheless, he'd looked up the side-effects: fatigue, diarrhoea, excessive sweating, nausea and sickness. Having to stop to dash to the loo with diarrhoea and vomiting would certainly make the whole thing last longer, but was not very appealing. And the counselling was definitely out. Sex was something you did spontaneously, not had a bloody post mortem on. He couldn't imagine anything worse than talking about the mechanics of sex. It would surely kill all urges, completely.

The aroma was unmistakable. It had overpowered Brenda's perfume. A puff of moist heat rose as she opened the foil wrap, allowing Pap a tantalising view of a hot bacon sandwich. Brenda looked suddenly attractive. She'd done her hair, worn a tighter dress; shorter, figure-hugging. In another situation he would have spent a little more time enjoying the woman before him but his eyes kept wandering toward the crisp bacon peeking out from inside the soft chunky bread.

She approached the cell bars without asking him to step back. 'Before you turn this very generous treat down, Pap, I want you to know what to expect if you carry on this silly charade. Whatever you do, however ill you are, I will not get help. No doctor, ever. Understand!?'

Brenda shivered deep inside, unable to believe that she was capable of such heartlessness. But they do say, that if someone hurts us enough we are capable of anything...

Pap nodded yes before engaging his brain. His mouth was watering, he licked his lips involuntarily.

She pushed the sandwich through the bars. Pap hesitated, thought momentarily about grabbing her arm. But she might not have the key...He took the sandwich.

Brenda smiled and made her way back up the stairs, relieved that he'd taken the bait and avoided God knows what! Had he proceeded with his hunger strike, she couldn't imagine what her next step might have been.

Perhaps the hunger strike wasn't such a good idea. When Pap thought about it, how could Brenda possibly bring a doctor down here without risking arrest? Equally, she was unlikely to let him out to visit his local GP. It was impossible to guess what Brenda's long term plan might be, but he held on to the hope that she did have a release date in mind. If she'd wanted him to die she wouldn't feed him at all and certainly wouldn't have given him a bacon sandwich.

Brenda was pleased with the plan. Raihana had reminded her that one of the things Pap couldn't resist, apart from women and alcohol, was food. She'd had experience of this in Lahore. He wasn't like other Europeans, careful on the spicy food, worried about tummy upsets. He could eat or drink anything, a cast iron constitution that could take on the hottest curries, down a few drinks and still raid the hotel minibar. Because of the pride with which Pap had described his formidable appetites, Raihana took this to mean he had acquired some sort of superior standing in the community.

Poor people couldn't afford to eat like Pap so her conclusion was, he must be wealthier than she'd thought.

Chapter 24

Simon and Gloria had come to an impasse and couldn't make any real sense of Melvyn's out-of-character behaviour. On the face of it, given the surprising text, it looked as if he was about to leave his job. Melvyn was not that stupid, they'd decided. Simon knew of Melvyn's shenanigans and turned a blind eye, because the man always delivered. He'd concluded that a woman, *just a woman,* was not enough for Melvyn to risk ruining his life for. The guy loved his job, it gave him the freedom he needed to pursue his *other interests.* And he helped make Simon rich.

'We agree that something doesn't quite add up,' said Simon, sitting at his giant office desk. He was surrounded by photographs of himself and his family doing exciting things; skiing, swimming with dolphins and turtles, riding ostriches and flying a helicopter over the Grand Canyon. There wasn't a sign of them ever being still.

'He always texts me when he's away but never ignores a crisis, especially when it's about work. I told him your call was urgent,' said Gloria, noticing Simon's anxiety. He mopped his brow and tugged his cuffs, as if his shirt had started to shrink. Then he sat down, got up, walked around the desk as he spoke, checking his nails as he went.

'I'm going to find him,' said Simon. 'I know roughly where he's supposed to be. I'll check the airline to make sure he hasn't flown back. I'll try hotels too, but that might not be so easy, we have quite a loose arrangement so's he can always be where he needs to be, the right place at the right time. I have to trust him. I do trust him. Something is wrong...'

Simon didn't admit to how relaxed these arrangements with Melvyn were. They literally put pins in a well plotted map and Melvyn set off to wherever, to see what he could do. Melvyn worked well this way and Simon had never doubted his top man's ability to strike lucrative deals all over the world.

'You're welcome to stay while I make a few calls, Gloria. Would you like coffee?'

'Please. Black. Can I freshen up somewhere?'

'Through that door past my secretary's office, second left down the hallway.'

Gloria smiled at the girl as she passed. She looked as if she'd been crying. Gloria freshened her lipstick and thought she might pop in on the way back to see if she was okay.

On her return she noticed the secretary was not at her desk. She continued toward Simon's office. The door was shut but she could hear voices so she knocked loudly and walked in. Simon introduced Gloria to Margo, who stood there red-eyed, her pad at the ready, pen poised, taking notes. Margo, petite, blonde with a smart suit and tight lips, scribbled in shorthand while Simon dictated the last few words of his memo. She smiled at Gloria, without holding eye contact, then left.

Without comment Simon flipped the pages of his directory, ran his finger down the telephone numbers in front of him and rang Gatwick. The call to the airport was not without its problems. Noise and poor reception protracted the process. There was a long delay. He needed to know if Melvyn had boarded the initial flight to Tangiers, or any other destination. They said they'd check and get back to him. Simon closed his eyes.

Gloria picked up on his body language and remained silent.

Minutes later the call from the airline came through. Simon

gripped his forehead as he shakily put down the phone. He looked at Gloria.

'Melvyn never got on the plane at Gatwick in the first place. His booking had been cancelled. He didn't fly out to Tangiers—or anywhere else, apparently.'

Chapter 25

Pap's dinky mobile vibrated in Brenda's apron pocket. Incoming text. Not Gloria then, she was on his 'business phone'. Had to be one of his birds. She checked the text. From Margo: *Where the fuck are you? I'll kill you if you've buggered of with some tart.* End of text.

First time Brenda was aware of Margo. She was obviously on his contact list. New flame or old? She scanned the message history. Looked pretty new, unless some of the messages had been wiped. One was dated three days before he disappeared: *'Don't forget to book for the weekend when you get back. Can't wait. Love you xx.*

Swee-eet.

Pap was back on his favourite soup. 'There's a new text message, Pap, just popped up, from Margo. Heard of her? New bit of crumpet? She's on your list, got *sec* next to her name. Sec, short for secretary probably, but not yours, you haven't got one. Your boss's then?'

Pap twitched slightly but stayed silent, confirming, at least in Brenda's mind, that he'd definitely been having it off with his boss's secretary.

'Any good in bed? You're gonna deny it all, I can tell. Let me answer for you.'

Brenda slipped into her Bill Clinton impersonation, complete with the wagging finger aimed at an imaginary audience somewhere in the basement: '*I did not have sexual relations with that woman...*'

Pap stayed calm. No point saying anything, devil woman had the mobile, his contacts, recent message history (which he should wipe more often) plus he had no idea how many others she'd texted.

'You're blushing, Pap.'

'It's getting warm down here. Have you turned the heat up or something?'

'No need. It's a lovely sunny day, temperature's up, you should see the daffs sprouting all over the place—you'd love it out there.'

She read the message aloud, with as much vitriol as Margo must have been feeling when she'd sent it. 'I've taken the trouble to answer for you, Pap. Wanna hear?'

He didn't but he knew he had no option.

'*Hi Margo. Won't be seeing you in the office any more, I've quit my job.*

Can't stay with one woman for too long anyway, I get bored. I enjoyed your company. Really sorry. Cheers, Melvyn.'

Melvyn adopted a 'white knuckles around the bars' posture, which seemed to have the odd effect of turning his face purple.

'I'll go get more soup from the fridge, Pap, looks like you could do with some extra nourishment, and something to cool you down.'

Pap pressed his forehead against the cold steel bars, hoping to reduce his blood pressure. Brenda seemed to be taking longer than usual to take the stairs. She was watching Pap. He looked beaten, but angry not contrite. Not yet.

Chapter 26

Things were getting desperate all round. Simon had had no luck contacting Melvyn, and Margo, still red-eyed, unable to share Melvyn's latest text for obvious reasons, had been unable to come up with anything either, he'd completely disappeared. One or two contacts reported receiving texts saying he'd been delayed and might have to book another flight. So Melvyn hadn't even got on the plane. The airline had texted him when he hadn't gone through the baggage check but Melvyn (Brenda) had replied saying he'd had to cancel, change of plan due to a family crisis.

The sun was warming up in The Little Conservatory at Coffee 4 Us. Saturday morning, and an out-of-hours meeting for Brenda and Raihana.

'Gloria's texted Pap. Something's happened,' said Brenda, touching Raihana's hand across the table.

'What's wrong, aren't you nervous, Brenda?'

'No worries. I guess they're checking everything out and deciding whether it's a police matter or not. It will still take them a while to find him, if they ever do, and if I can finish what I've started before they get here, good. If not, there's still Plan B.'

Raihana looked puzzled. 'You have another plan?'

'Sure. Always have a Plan B, Raihana, something nearly as good as Plan A if possible. One thing's for sure, Pap is gonna come out of this badly. His past girlfriends might be a bit shocked at first, bound to be, but not when it's all over.'

Plan B was a lie, but she wanted Raihana to feel secure in the face of mounting pressure, particularly as Plan A was now questionable for all sorts of reasons.

Another plan? Admiration was written all over Raihana's face.

'What did Gloria say?'

'She mentioned meeting a woman called Margo, his boss's secretary. I'm feeling there's a subtext in that text,' Brenda laughed. 'Gloria's put two and two together and must have concluded he'd been playing too close to home.'

Raihana was trying to take this in. Her head was spinning with the complexity of the situation and the sheer number of problems Melvyn seemed to have created. She took a couple of deep breaths and placed her hand on her tummy

'How's the baby and the morning sickness? Can you feel it kicking?' asked Brenda, who couldn't remember the last time she'd asked anyone about such things.

'It's only four months, Brenda, it's only just starting to show, never mind kick.'

Brenda had little interest in babies and kids. She'd never wanted any and Arthur was far too busy with work and hobbies to think about such a commitment. It suited them both.

'Sorry, Raihana, don't know much about the pregnancy thing, but you look so well, perhaps I should have given it a go.' She said this without regret, just to join in the baby conversation.

'Anyway,' said Brenda, eager to tell Raihana about the current situation. 'Looks as if I'll have to bring everything forward to make sure it ends well for us, can't have you going through all that extra stress, what with the baby an' everything.'

Raihana trusted Brenda but whenever she talked about avoiding stress, Raihana became more anxious.

Changing well-thought-out plans always made Brenda

nervous. But the speed at which things were happening now, made her realise they'd have to think on their feet a bit more.

'So we need to make some changes, needn't do anything about the new people moving in, that's in our favour. Pap's recovery following his hunger strike, thanks to the bacon sandwich, is also in our favour. Means he'll last the course. The problem is the situation with Pap's boss Simon, wife Gloria and his latest bit on the side, Margo. They all know he's missing and they'll be pulling out all the stops to find him.'

'Someone might have seen him turning up at your place,' said Raihana, sipping the last of her cortado.

'Highly unlikely. He was drunk and being helped up the path at eleven-thirty at night. He didn't utter a sound until we got him inside. There were no lights on across the street, no one around. The taxi dropped them on the corner, so the driver wouldn't be suspicious or know where I actually lived. Cleo, the girl who helped him in here, was never seen again. It was a quick two hundred quid in her pocket and a free night out. I was in the house, alone. There's no way Cleo would spill the beans.'

'Do you really think the police will be involved?' said Raihana, sipping from her empty cup, waiting nervously for her friend to answer.

Brenda was thinking, turning over possible scenarios, her imagination on fast forward. The silence was making Raihana tense.

'More coffee, Brenda?'

'Good idea. My turn, same for you, Raihana?'

'I'll have a green tea please. Too much caffeine's not good for the baby.'

Brenda left The Little Conservatory and ordered. She could see Raihana nervously raking through her handbag—glancing from side to side as if she was being followed—eventually managing to refresh her lipstick. But Brenda was thinking how best to reveal what would surely happen next.

'There you go. Green tea, looks bloody awful. I should get Pap to try it, same colour as the soup,' said Brenda, grinning, trying to lighten the moment. Raihana was not smiling.

'Sorry, Raihana, I was thinking. Yes, the police are bound to be involved. From his boss's point of view the guy's disappeared and mysteriously cancelled his flight without telling anyone, not seen any of his contacts, not actually rung his wife or his boss. They'd have no choice but to involve the police.'

Raihana mentally flitted through various scenarios. There was an atmosphere of unease, a long silence, both sipping their coffee slowly, neither keen to discuss what might happen next. Distractedly, Raihana went off on a tangent and thought of Lahore.

'I'll never be able to tell my father about the baby. Fathers think their little girls are angels, never imagine them growing up. I could tell Mother, at some point, but not yet. I will never be accepted back in Lahore.' Raihana was close to tears.

'Don't think too far ahead, you'll drive yourself crazy. Do you wish you'd stayed at home?'

'No way, made my bed and all that. I had silly dreams about becoming a UK citizen, doing well, eventually getting my parents' approval. How stupid could I be?'

'You won't be the first or the last to be in this situation. Not helpful but true. Think of the escape you've had. Imagine being tied to Melvyn Greenstone for the rest of your life!'

Raihana started to feel a little better.

Chapter 27

Simon's office seemed crowded. Detective Sergeant Barker and Constable Smithy sat to one side of his desk while Margo and a couple of senior staff sat opposite.

'We're treating this seriously, sir, I can assure you. But it all seems rather strange. According to those who saw him last, Mr. Greenstone seemed perfectly fine before he left on his trip,' said Barker.

'Perfectly fine,' echoed Simon, 'in high spirits as far as I can remember. He usually is. Melvyn likes his trips, enjoys his work.'

'If that's so, why would he send a text giving in his notice?'

'We've had time to think about it, and without being overdramatic, we don't think he sent it.'

'Then who did?'

There was a knock on the office door. 'Who is it?' shouted Simon.

'Gloria—sorry I'm late.'

Simon rose from his desk and beckoned her in.

'Thanks for including me in the meeting. Not sure how much help I'll be, it looks like we're all in the dark.'

'Take a seat, Gloria, we've only just started. We're talking about the texts, how we think something's wrong, not enough contact from Melvyn. He's usually so good when it comes to work.'

'Not always so good when it comes to *his wife*,' added Gloria, sharply. 'We only text while he's away, unless one of us has a crisis. I said that this *was* a crisis, but he never rang. Not like Melvyn at all.'

Simon turned to Barker and Smithy. 'My apologies, I need to introduce Melvyn's wife, this is Gloria.'

The two officers nodded. 'Pleased to meet you, Mrs. Greenstone, you were next on our list anyway, you've saved us a journey. We'll need to search your house at some point, the earlier the better. We can get a warrant if you want to make it official.'

'Not a problem. Melvyn took some clothes for the trip, but I haven't moved anything of his. What are you hoping to find?'

'Nothing in particular, but it's standard procedure when someone goes missing, first port of call. Helps us get the feel of the person, helps the investigative process and sometimes provides information that you may not think relevant,' said Barker. He avoided adding that spouses were often under suspicion when their partners disappeared.

'We've checked the airport in case he'd taken another flight. He's not on their CCTV system. So as far as they're concerned, Mr. Greenstone never entered the terminal...'

'Was he planning to drive to the airport?' asked Smithy.

'His car's in the garage,' said Gloria. 'He usually takes a taxi if he's flying somewhere'.

'Do you know which company he uses?' asked Barker.

'No idea. There's a number on his mobile, he just presses a button and someone turns up.'

'Black cab or private?' asked Smithy.

'Don't know. The driver usually gives a blast on the horn when he arrives. We don't wave each other off,' she said, colouring slightly as if she'd admitted to a minor parking offence.

'We'll need to check his bank accounts and credit cards. Can you get all the paperwork together for us, Mrs. Greenstone? We'll see if any money has been withdrawn, either by him—or his captors, should abduction be the case. Do you have joint accounts?'

Barker knew this was an important question in a missing persons case. Gave an idea how the marital finances were handled and who had access to what, should there be a sudden clearing of funds from an account.

'Yes we do have one, to pay the mortgage, monthly direct debits and such, but we have our own personal accounts too. Melvyn gave me an allowance, so I could be independent.'

'So, let's sum up what we have. A man who, apparently, throws in his job but informs the company by text! That doesn't feel quite right, does it? No one knows where he is. No one's seen him for weeks. He's financially comfortable but not stacked with money so, presumably, if he's been kidnapped, it can't be for financial gain or you would have received some sort of ransom demand by now. He could have left the country, so we'll check every port and airport. It'll take time. Unlikely he's had an accident, otherwise a hospital would have rung you, Mrs. Greenstone. He had his mobile with him, I presume?'

Gloria and Simon were looking a little shell-shocked. The worst case scenario was dawning on them. Things looked bad. Very bad.

'Presumably he took his passport and a case?'

Gloria nodded. 'Tan leather soft top. Not big, he travels light and usually gets his laundry done at the hotel or somewhere local while he's away. He takes his passport everywhere.'

'So he could be absolutely anywhere,' ventured Smithy, who'd remained silent until now.

'Sorry to ask this, Mrs. Greenstone...'

When someone apologises for something they are about to ask, it's usually worth listening to. Smithy cleared his throat. All heads turned toward him. Gloria and Simon, maybe Margo too, had some idea what was coming next.

'Did you ever suspect your husband of being unfaithful?' They could all so easily have jumped in with a resounding, *yes of course, everybody knows that*!

Gloria spent some moments working out how to answer. Nobody moved. Breath was held and let out as Gloria delivered her reply. 'Melvyn has always been faithful…to me.'

Margo reached for a tissue and blew her nose, hard.

A suppressed snigger, cunningly disguised as a cough, came from Simon. Barker and Smithy made a mental note of these distractions.

Chapter 28

Barker and Smithy had worked together before. In fact they considered themselves a capable and highly motivated section of the force. In all their time chasing missing persons, neither could think of an odder case. Someone had been missing and remained unreported for weeks! Usually people panicked after twenty-four hours and, unless it was a child or vulnerable person, were asked to give it a bit more time before filing an official missing persons report. This wasn't some tramp or homeless person sleeping rough and off most people's radar. This was a respected member of the community with a mortgage, a decent job…and a lying wife. It hadn't taken them long to find out that Melvyn Greenstone was a serial womaniser who kept most of his brain in his underpants. The rest of it he used to earn a pretty decent living, by most standards.

The Association of Chief Police Officers' (ACPO) definition of a missing person is "anyone not at a place they are expected to be but the circumstances are out of character or the context suggests they may be at risk of harm to themselves or others."

Barker always spoke in a quiet voice, almost a whisper. He'd developed this low key approach following a virus which he'd picked up while travelling abroad. Unexpectedly, he discovered that a quiet voice amongst the shouted orders given by some of his colleagues often had more impact. He'd Googled this phenomenon and found it was also a technique used by actors to command attention in certain situations. Smithy sometimes had difficulty hearing what Barker was saying, which occasionally resulted in the message not quite getting through.

'The trail's gone cold. The only possible lead we have so far is the taxi driver, but we don't know where he came from. Even if we did, it won't be easy to remember a fare he'd picked up over a month ago; couldn't really expect anyone to manage that. By the looks of it, Greenstone would have appeared normal, carrying his tan leather bag like any other commuter off on a business trip. He'd have paid his fare in cash with hardly a glance from the cabbie, maybe the driver hadn't even clocked his appearance.'

Smithy scribbled a note. 'I'll make a start. It's all we have to go on at the moment.' His skinny fingers wrote down the names of the cab companies he needed to check. Some drivers were legal, but some muscled in on their territory; fearless immigrant entrepreneurs in leather jackets, with dark stubble and heavy friends.

Barker tried to clear his throat, a habit he'd adopted when making a special point. This often produced a clearer, louder, sentence or two. 'Perhaps we need to check Gloria's movements a bit more closely. She obviously knows about Greenstone's philandering. Did you see her look down at her hands when she denied it, Smithy? That could be interpreted as a body language sign that she's lying. In which case, she may be lying about other things.'

Smithy had already worked this out for himself, and speaking to Gloria again was on his list of things to do. Smithy had learnt, over his years in the force, that lies never came alone. His mind moved to a worst case scenario; that Gloria, or one of his mistresses past or present, had done away with Melvyn Greenstone.

Melvyn Greenstone's house was a fine one. Not magnificent, but well outside Smithy's budget; a detached modern job with a landscaped garden, perfectly mown lawns and freshly painted exterior. Gloria, who greeted him at the door, was also well maintained. Her hair was freshly styled, and she had neat, expensive clothes and green eyes that flicked nervously from left to right along the street as if she were about to let her lover in.

'Please come in, Constable Smith,'

'It's Smithy, Constable Smithy. Everyone makes that mistake. Thanks for agreeing to see me. We want to find your husband as quickly as possible, Mrs. Greenstone. We think we might have missed something, so we're double checking.'

Gloria led Smithy into a brightly lit kitchen that looked out onto another perfect lawn. 'I'll make a drink, tea or coffee?'

'Whatever you're having.'

'Better not while you're on duty,' she said. 'I've got a G and T going. I'll make some coffee, black or white? Sugar?'

Smithy wondered about the lack of photographs, none of Greenstone or his wife. No shots of kids. And it hadn't escaped his notice that Gloria was drinking, at ten-thirty in the morning.

Gloria placed the coffee and two Hobnobs next to Smithy's mobile on the kitchen table. 'How do you think I can help?' she asked, her glass topped up ready for questioning.

'You mentioned he was wearing a navy tweed jacket and pale blue shirt. Anything else you can add to that?'

'I've already been through this,' she sighed.

'The picture you gave us seems out of date. Six years ago according to what's written on the back. Do you have a more recent one?'

Gloria felt slightly ashamed that she didn't really have much in the way of photos of Melvyn.

'There's one of him at the firm's party taken a couple of months ago.' She went to a drawer and riffled through some papers. She took out a photograph of the office where Smithy and Barker had interviewed Simon. People were raising glasses. The glasses were high, at the end of their toast. In the shot, Margo was looking at Greenstone, affectionately, Smithy thought.

'Can I take this, Mrs. Greenstone? I'll give it back of course.'

'Melvyn would probably like to keep it. I'm not a one for photos myself.'

So I've noticed, thought Smithy.

Gloria turned away and looked fixedly across the garden. Smithy picked up on her sadness and decided to follow her gaze.

'Nice lawns, Mrs. Greenstone.'

'Present from my husband.'

'The landscaping?'

'No, the sit-on lawnmower,' replied Gloria, without smiling.

Smithy couldn't help himself. He covered his mouth and coughed gently until his smile faded. In that brief moment, he got a clearer picture of the man they were looking for; a chauvinistic womaniser who left his wife at home, alone for far too long, and expected her to hang around twiddling her thumbs while he swanned about all over the world.

'Do you have any paperwork details related to your husband's mobile phone, a service contract or anything like that?'

Chapter 29

'Message from Gloria, Pap, they've called the police in.'

Pap was looking forlorn. Brenda's plan included letting him go at some point, but when? Lots of shit hitting lots of fans out there, he imagined.

'Would you mind reading me the full message?' asked Pap. Sometimes the polite approach got a civil reply.

'My pleasure. Word for word?'

'That would be nice.'

'Did I hear a bit of sarcasm there, Pap? Not good tactics for a prisoner. Anyway, here goes.' She gave a dainty, throat clearing cough and lifted the mobile to eye level as if about to read a long text. 'Here it is, in full. *They've called the police in.* End of message. No, *Hi Melvyn, Dear Melvyn*, not even *Melvyn* and no, *Love Gloria*, at the end. No point.' Obviously everything was going pear-shaped and this was a last shot at getting some reaction from Pap or whoever was using his mobile. They'd have thoughts about that too.

'Worried or relieved, Pap?'

He was now optimistic about being found. The text from Gloria must be a warning. Nothing in there to show she believed he was answering her messages because he'd failed to ring in an emergency, and that was something that had never happened before. Emergencies, business or pleasure, were his forte. He always responded.

'Game's up, Brenda. They'll all be looking for me now.'

'*All*? The whole police force looking—for you? Can't believe you're that important, Pap, but I'll change my plan, just in case.'

Brenda sealed the two mobiles in a Jiffy bag and drove to the airport. She slid the bag across the counter of the lost property office while the attendant was distracted, then left. She knew about triangulation for tracing mobiles. Best be on the safe side. She drove back from the airport smiling. Despite a few hiccups, the plan had gone well.

Chapter 30

Gloria had raked through Pap's office and found the service provider's details for an iPhone which she'd given Barker and Smithy.

They watched in fascination as the technician began the laborious process of triangulation and got bored pretty quickly when he explained, in techno speak, what he was doing: 'I'm using cell phone towers to approximate the location of Mr. Greenstone's phone; the accuracy, depends on the density of cell tower population. That's the key.'

The technician checked the paperwork provided by Gloria. 'I'm using the IMEI (International Mobile Equipment Identity) number taken from Greenstone's phone contract...'

Smithy stifled a yawn and Barker made an excuse to get some coffee.

Pap's photo at the office party appeared in many of the next day's papers. There was a ring drawn around his face to show which one of the group he was and an inset photo showed an enlarged detail of his face in profile, blurred, but unmistakable to anyone who knew him.

UK BUSINESS MAN MISSING FOR ONE MONTH:
POLICE SUSPECT FOUL PLAY

*Anyone seeing this man, Melvyn Greenstone, over the past month should contact the police without delay. Mr. Greenstone is five foot ten in height, with sandy coloured hair and slightly overweight. He was last seen wearing a navy tweed jacket, light blue shirt and carrying a tan leather case. Mr. Greenstone was due to fly abroad over a month ago but police investigations show that he never left the country. A check of hospitals and hotels have drawn a blank. Police have been unable to trace the taxi driver that picked him up from his home on the day of his disappearance. If you have any information, however small, or if you are the taxi driver who remembers picking this man up, please contact Detective Sergeant Barker...*Followed by the station number, address and email in bold font.

Triangulation had pinpointed Pap's mobile, and police were on their way to the airport. Barker and Smithy showed their identity to the lost property manager who passed them the opened Jiffy bag with the two mobiles.

Smithy and Barker looked at each other. Two mobiles! Things were getting complicated. 'Is there any paperwork? Could you describe the person who left them?' asked Barker, checking to see if any CCTV cameras were visible. There was, just one.

'Did you try any of the numbers?' Smithy asked the manager, 'Someone might have picked up and saved us a lot of time.'

'I'd considered it. The bag wasn't sealed but I thought it might be confusing if someone thought I was the owner of the mobile,' answered the manager. 'Didn't want to say I was from the lost property office at an airport, they might have got worried. Plus my fingerprints would have been all over them.'

'Very good point,' said Barker, something he'd almost missed himself. 'Do you have the CCTV tapes for the past month?'

'We do, sir. I'll get them for you. We can replay them in the back room. Give me twenty minutes or so. Why don't you grab a coffee? There's a Costa's over there,' he said, pointing across the concourse.

'Give us a wave when you're ready,' said Barker.

They didn't need second bidding. Smithy paid for the coffees before taking a corner seat where they had a clear view of the lost property office.

'Looks promising,' said Smithy. 'If they've got the tapes we may have our man.'

'Not necessarily. Whoever placed the phones could be a courier, or some kid paid to drop them off. I didn't know there were two.' In the excitement, Barker forgot about gloves, took the phones out of the Jiffy bag and handed one to Smithy.

Barker checked the pay-as-you-go and tried to access the contact list. 'Greenstone's a busy man, looks like all women's names on this one. What's on yours?'

'Seems normal; wife, business and mates by the look of it,' said Smithy.

'Someone wanted us to believe Greenstone had taken a plane, otherwise why bother to leave the phones here?'

'He's either with another woman or dead,' said Smithy.

Barker was reserving his judgement. They finished their coffee in silence and looked toward the lost property office.

'Let's check the messages,' said Barker, tapping the message icon. 'Hey, there are a few recent calls Smithy, how about yours?'

'Some here too.'

'We're going to have to trawl through every bloody contact and search the message history.'

'Might be a problem, sir. Looks like someone's done a lot of editing to confuse us: left some of the questions people have messaged, but wiped the answers. And vice versa, by the look of things. If there were addresses and email details, they've wiped those too, apart from business stuff, companies and reps. It'll take time to check the lot.'

The manager waved them over. Smithy and Barker stepped into the tiny back room. They watched the tape play back.

The CCTV was concentrated on the broad centre of the counter where most of the business was done, the ends cropped by the camera's limited range. Many people came to and from the office. They'd almost seen the whole of that day's tape when the right hand corner showed the Jiffy bag being slid onto the counter.

'Only the arm, coat sleeve and part of a headscarf,' said Smithy. 'Waste of time.'

'Not quite,' said Barker. 'At least we know it was a woman, and we have the clothes to go on. The picture's good, so let's get some analysis done back at the station.'

Chapter 31

Before she'd dropped Pap's mobiles off at the airport, Brenda decided to actually send the original text to Gloria: the one that informed his wife he'd met someone else. She removed the name Pap, replaced it with Melvyn and pressed, *send*.

It was a moment of mischief. Then she edited most of the message history on both phones, leaving just enough recent texts to confuse the bigger picture.

Gloria and Simon had already been suspicious about the text, the one giving his job in, so when this particular message arrived, it didn't have quite the impact Brenda intended.

But despite her reasoning and Simon's reassuring logic, Gloria couldn't quite rule out the nagging uncertainty that Melvyn might actually be ditching her. She had sleepless nights and anxious days.

The text wasn't really from him, was it? He seemed quite happy with his life. The marriage wasn't made in heaven but it worked, after a fashion. Melvyn had the work ethic, did well, strayed a bit, so rumour had it, but unproven as far as she was concerned. If she had known with absolute certainty that her husband had been truly unfaithful, a proper affair: hotels, restaurants, love texts, the smell of perfume, too much aftershave etc., then she would have reconsidered.

All her life she'd seen how gossip ruined friendships and marriages. This seemed particularly true when couples spent a significant time apart. But Melvyn had this job when he married her. She knew what to expect, knew there were times when she'd be lonely. Eyes open from the start.

They'd had sex before they got married so she knew the score there too; disappointing but tolerable. Not the best lover but probably not the worst either. At least he got straight to the point and didn't want anything exotic; no *Joy of Sex* manual for him! He had simple tastes, probably following in his parents' footsteps. He wanted the lights on at first but changed his mind when Gloria insisted on keeping her eyes closed throughout; said it put him off.

With all that time on her own, Gloria had learnt to take care of herself, preferred sex with no one else in the room. She was faithful, apart from the imagined sessions with George Clooney or Denzel Washington, and this was certainly the case when Melvyn had kept the lights on and her eyes were shut.

She had to admit that three years wasn't long to be wed, but she counted her blessings and had no desire to draw a line under her marriage.

The phone rang. Gloria picked up before it switched to answerphone. 'Mrs. Greenstone?'

'Yes, who is it?'

'DS Barker. You wanted to be kept up to date with our news. Your husband had two mobiles. We've traced them to the airport and we're trying to find out who handed them in, but there's not a lot to go on.'

'Two mobiles, you say?'

'Didn't you know he had two? One you gave us the contract paperwork for and the other a pay-as-you-go.' Barker wished he'd waited 'till he met with her face to face.

Gloria couldn't think of a response. Her chest tightened.

'We wondered if you could help us sort out some of the information and contact details. He seems to have had calls—and answered them. All recent,' said Barker.

'Who to?' she asked, trying to blot out the truth. Melvyn had more secrets than she could possibly imagine.

'Better if we meet up,' said Barker.

'I'll come straight over.'

Chapter 32

'Thought you'd like to know, I've got rid of the mobiles, Pap,' said Brenda, taking the old disposable boiler suit and replacing it with a new one. She wore rubber gloves, just in case, didn't want to risk catching anything. He wasn't keeping himself that clean, a bit smelly to be truthful, despite the soap, flannel and towel. Might have to resort to the Karcher again.

Pap didn't respond. He was trying to work out what getting rid of the mobiles meant, in terms of his prognosis. There'd be no more texting back and forth, no more contact at all, in fact.

'It was fun, but I have to be one step ahead, Pap. That's the secret of success. Time's getting on and you're nowhere to be found. My guess is the police will have questioned your boss and your wife and started tracking down your mobiles.'

'Where are they?' asked Pap, without expecting an answer.

'Don't mind telling you, Pap, they're at the airport, the very place where you should have taken off for Morocco. That last night boozing with the tart was not a good idea, Pap. I guess you realise that now,' she grinned, pointing towards his pathetic bedraggled figure. Pap didn't think it was funny.

'You'll be on CCTV, they're all over the airport, they'll catch you in no time, Brenda. You'll see.' Pap smiled sardonically, but without a great deal of confidence.

'Have you thought what might happen when your wife finds

out you have two phones, Pap? And when she gets a chance to start ringing round those contacts, oh boy, I wouldn't like to be in your shoes. You're safer here for now. But when I do let you out, not long now by the way, two words spring to mind; shit and fan.'

Pap slumped onto his bed. He'd had it. He was going to be free, at some point, so that was something. He couldn't think of a thing to say, still having trouble making any sense of what she was supposed to be doing. He'd been imprisoned, humiliated, starved, threatened and Karchered. It looked like she was the only brain behind this farce, yet he'd never done more than put his hand up her jumper; bit of an over the top reaction by anyone's standards.

'I'll be off soon, Pap. The house is sold, new people moving in a week after I leave. You'll never see me again. You'll be able to start a new life. Probably not in this area, maybe not even in this country, but a new life, I can definitely guarantee you that.'

'When are you actually going?' ventured Pap, realising that he would be a bit of a shock to the new residents, unless she had plans to let him out before they arrived.

'Can't tell you that, but you'll know ASAP. There'll be no more soup then, so you might have a day or two without anything. You'll survive.'

Chapter 33

Gloria was staggered to learn that Melvyn had a second mobile; a secret one, with contacts completely unfamiliar to her. Barker read out some of the names on the list. All women. There was only one she recognised, Margo, and that must be business, she was Simon's secretary. But, as Barker pointed out she was on Melvyn's contract phone too.

Gloria had already started to smoulder. A slow burn that would, at any moment, burst into a firewall of fury. After three years of marriage, she finally realised that the gossip was true. Her husband was a serial womaniser. Global, it seemed. What other possible reason could there be for his secret phone and secret list? And all this time she'd defended him against the bitchiness that prevailed in her neighbourhood.

'The phones are charged,' said Smithy. 'We'll have to check all the contacts out. Anyone special you think we should try first?'

Apoplectic pause...

'Margo. She's on both for some reason. Try the pay-as-you-go first. Switch to speaker so I can hear everything.'

Barker pressed the speaker button with some trepidation.

The phone rang and Margo picked up. '*Where the fuck are you, Melvyn? Funny way to treat someone you love. I want to know where you are. Now! You're not gonna mess me about like that other poor tart.*'

Smithy switched off the phone and looked across at a very pale Gloria who'd heard every word. 'Sorry about that, Mrs. Greenstone. Your husband obviously had other reasons for using this mobile.'

Gloria started to sob quietly into a Kleenex. The man she thought she knew was someone else, a secretive bastard who had another life; one that she'd taken no part in. Smithy wanted to put his arm around her for comfort, but given the sensitive nature of the situation, thought this might be misinterpreted.

Gloria didn't cry for long. She blew her nose hard and threw the Kleenex in the bin. She pulled out another and dabbed at her smudged mascara before leaving for the public rest room.

'Bloody hell,' said Smithy. 'I wouldn't like to be in his shoes if she ever gets hold of him.'

Barker looked grim. 'Ring all the numbers on his pay-as-you-go, Smithy. See if he's with any of those women. Set up interviews, if you think there's a lead. I'll check his contract phone and see how many messages are genuine, if any.'

Barker and Smithy had already worked out and concurred, telepathically it seemed, that Melvyn Greenstone was with one of the women on his contact list. Or dead! How good were these women at keeping their secret arrangements with Greenstone? If they picked up calls, did they give anything away: a tremor in the voice, any sign of nervousness or a phone switched off suddenly?

If Barker and Smithy ended up with lots of voicemails they might need to go down the laborious route of finding out who owned each phone. All the numbers were mobiles. This might not be as easy as they first thought. But for now, at least they had Margo to question.

Gloria came back to the office freshly made-up, with just a residual redness around the eyes. 'I'm going now, Sergeant. Let me know if you have a lead or anything new for me. I'll have a think about what to do next.' Her lips thinned to an unforgiving line of determination as she picked up her coat and left. 'Thank you both for your help. We *will* find him,' she snarled.

Barker and Smithy glanced at each other as Gloria clacked down the corridor apace. They'd both picked up on, 'we *will* find him', and wondered if they ought to be keeping a closer eye on Gloria Greenstone.

All the other contacts were women who'd known Greenstone. How intimately, was difficult to say. Most were aware that he was on the news, captive somewhere, but probably didn't come forward because, a) some were married with husbands who were unaware of their wives' association with Greenstone, or b) they hadn't heard from him and saw no point in putting themselves in the firing line for no good reason.

So they were left with Greenstone's recent relationship history, including Gloria and Margo from the office and someone with the initial 'R', plus some odd calls they could only interpret as Melvyn Greenstone *touching base*.

Chapter 34

The time to leave was drawing ever closer. Brenda tried to tie up all the loose ends at Butts. Raymondo had taken time off but was now back, preparing for Brenda's leaving. The team worked well under a bit of pressure. Brenda's house had sold, box ticked, contracts signed and buyers ready to take possession as soon as they got back from holiday. Pap's release would be carefully synchronised.

Before taking Pap's phones to the airport, she'd copied his contacts onto a new pay-as-you-go. She might need to make some calls or send a few texts before she left for Australia, tidy things up. Hadn't quite worked out what she'd write, maybe a round robin type of thing, but what'd be the fun in that? Some texts required a bit of creative writing. And without getting too emotional, some of her missives needed a sympathetic touch.

Raihana had yet to hear of Brenda's *finale*, or the full extent of Pap's dodgy past, but in due course, all would probably be revealed. Raihana's baby was flourishing and she was approaching a critical time. She could still have the abortion and maybe even return to Lahore and try to patch it up with her family. Unlikely. Mother had the capacity to forgive and forget, of that she was sure, but her father never would. Neither would the neighbours. And Shalmi market would be agog with the scandal. Plus, aborting the baby, even though from a man she didn't love, was not in her heart.

Chapter 35

Margo was an attractive woman but right now she wasn't looking her best. Barker and Smithy were interviewing her, asking lots of questions about Greenstone and waiting between sobs for some of the answers. They were patient men but they needed responses.

'How long have you known Melvyn Greenstone?'

'A few years. Met him when I started here,' she said, inhaling deeply, attempting to recover a professional manner.

'So you knew him before he married his wife Gloria?'

'Yes,' she said, pulling a tissue out of the box, holding it ready.

'Did you have a relationship with Mr. Greenstone before or after he got married?'

Margo hesitated, gripped the Kleenex. 'We went out a couple of times before he got married...' Her answer trailed off.

'What do you mean by that? Was it a sexual relationship?'

'We did it a couple of times, if that's what you mean.'

'If 'did it' alludes to sexual intercourse, then that's exactly what I mean.'

Margo nodded.

Smithy sighed, couldn't understand why admitting the bloody obvious was such a big deal. But this was the nature of interviews, people rarely answered directly. They'd spend an inordinate amount of time trying to make their tricky situation less incriminating. It rarely worked.

'What finished it? You did finish it, didn't you?' offered Barker.

'He met Gloria.'

'Was he upfront about that?'

'Not exactly, I caught them coming out of a restaurant.'

'It could have been his sister, a relative, or a friend.'

'They were holding hands. They got into a taxi and started kissing, passionately. I was shaking like a leaf. I was just across the street, for Christ's sake! I texted him straight away.'

Barker could only imagine what Greenstone must have felt when he picked up the message and then had to face Margo at work the following day.

'Did he reply?'

'Not immediately, but he did later, apologised, said he'd wanted to tell me but didn't want to hurt me.'

Barker and Smithy were experiencing another telepathic moment—*a woman scorned*. A suspect was beginning to emerge.

'We stayed professional at work, but it was all over.'

'Really? How about since then? Before you answer, I have to tell you we have Mr. Greenstone's mobile and his message history.'

Margo used the Kleenex to full effect. *Genuinely upset*, thought Barker.

'We started seeing each other again,' she said, glancing nervously at Barker then Smithy.

'What about Gloria?'

'Melvyn said it wasn't working out. He'd made a mistake and would get a divorce as soon as possible.'

'Did you believe him?'

'I wanted to.'

This is some bastard, thought Smithy. Gloria seemed perfectly happy. They weren't the most loving couple, he'd seen their text messages and looked around their grand but rather sterile home, but nothing indicated they were not a decent couple.

'Are you still seeing him?' *Obviously not*, he thought, *the guy's done a bunk*, but he still wasn't sure what Margo knew about Greenstone's whereabouts.

'I saw him not long before he...' A fresh Kleenex seemed to be waiting just for this moment, ' ...disappeared.'

'So you've no idea where he is now?'

'The bastard could be anywhere.'

Smithy tried not to react. Barker stayed cool. 'That's all for now, Margo. If you think of anything that might be helpful, please give us a ring. Here's my card. If I'm not around, ask for Smithy here, same number, different extension, but someone will put you through.'

'Will Simon need to know about this?'

'We'll be as discreet as possible. But if anything comes to mind, any ideas at all, of where Greenstone could possibly be; names of friends, colleagues or family you might have met. Anything. Please call, day or night.'

'He's probably' (sob) 'with another...' she cried, then broke down, taking a bundle of fresh Kleenex and soaking them in no time at all.

Barker and Smithy concurred without saying a word, that another woman, not Margo, seemed to be the most likely reason for Greenstone's disappearance.

Chapter 36

Angie, Melvyn Greenstone's first wife, his only wife according to law, was sitting in her sunroom overlooking a small garden, miles from where her husband was imprisoned in Brenda's basement.

Angie was Melvyn's only true love. She'd convinced herself of that and couldn't understand why he'd left. They'd got on pretty well, more or less. He hadn't ever talked about divorce, maybe because he had no grounds. She would have had some, but then she didn't want a divorce. So when the phone rang and Barker asked if she knew Melvyn Greenstone, she was shocked.

'I'm his wife,' said Angie, affronted.

Barker was in shock now. He'd only seen Angie on Greenstone's pay-as-you-go, but no surname. He'd been ringing around, trying to get information on his whereabouts. This was going to be trickier than he thought.

'Have you seen him lately, Mrs...' he hesitated, didn't want to put his foot in it by questioning their marriage. '...Greenstone?'

'Not for about five years. He left me, you know?'

Barker was not surprised. 'I guessed that was the case. Are you divorced?'

'No. I didn't want one and he didn't bother. I was seriously depressed for the first year, we hadn't argued and neither of us had talked about splitting up,' she said, her eyes misting over as she held back the tears. 'That's worse you know, when there isn't a reason and someone disappears out of your life, much worse, no closure. Like they'd fallen off a boat, their body never found. Not knowing whether they're dead or alive.'

So the bugger is a bigamist. Well, well. No wonder he's done a disappearing act. 'Has he contacted you at all during that time?'

'I got a weird text recently, but didn't believe it was from him. Not after five years without an explanation. I texted back, just in case, but that was the end of it. No more contact. Somebody playing around, I guess. Anyway, at the time he left, he didn't even worry about his share of the house. It's paid for and I'm working, so I don't have a grouse with that.

'How did you find me?' she asked.

'Your name is listed as Angie on one of his phones. We didn't know you were his wife until we rang.'

'One of his phones? How many has he got? What's he been up to?'

'We don't know, but apparently he's been missing for a month.'

'Why didn't you contact me sooner?'

'We've only just found his phones. They were handed in to lost property at the airport. His boss didn't worry about his absence at first. Your husband is more or less left on his own to do his business deals, unless there's a problem.'

'He's always worked abroad a lot, weeks at a time. A woman gets lonely,' she said, wistfully. 'That's why his leaving wasn't quite as bad as it might have been. Got used to him not being around, I suppose.'

'We've checked with his boss, he didn't take his flight. No one's seen him,' said Barker, realising that this was a dead end, but at least Angie was someone he could cross off his list of potential suspects. She didn't sound suspicious, no sign of bitterness or anything, not like she was out for revenge. Barker wondered if he'd have the heart to tell her about Gloria. Not yet. No point, she needn't get mixed up in it all. *But she's going to want to when we find him, human nature when there's a mystery, especially when it's a dearly beloved, albeit once removed.* He smiled at the irony.

'If he does contact you, here's my number. By the way, do you know of any pals or family he may have contacted? People he knew when you were together. There's nothing much on his contract phone.'

'He's an only child. Has a few pals, none that I can remember him being that close to: best man at the wedding, couple of work pals. Ask his boss, he should know. Simon, wasn't it?'

'By the way, have you seen the news or the papers regarding his disappearance?'

'I don't have a television and never listen to the news, too depressing.'

'Thanks for your help, Mrs. Greenstone. Our apologies for putting you through this, we'll let you know if anything happens.'

Angie was not like Gloria, Melvyn's 'second wife'. A different relationship altogether, fewer treats—no sit-on mower for a start—but they'd been through leaner times. He was just getting up to speed with his business then. Angie was calmer, less possessive and probably more in love with him; backed him all the way through those early years. She knew he was absorbed in his work and put his slightly odd behaviour down to business pressure, never to his secret life with other women.

Angie hadn't seen him for years. Barker wondered why Greenstone had bothered keeping her number on his secret mobile; sentimental at a guess, guilt for leaving her in the lurch too, perhaps.

The media exposure of Greenstone's disappearance had created interest but no leads as to his whereabouts. Reporters had talked to Barker and Smithy who'd been accused of dragging their heels over the case in some of the tabloids. They'd interviewed Gloria and pestered Simon at Butts but all to no avail. There was a taxi driver out there somewhere, a guy who'd probably choose to remain anonymous.

The media had obtained more pictures of Greenstone, taken in various parts of the world, working mainly, attending seminars. He'd been featured in newspapers, talked about on TV, Facebooked, tweeted and even mentioned in a public debate about the growing number of UK citizens reported missing, never to be seen again.

Chapter 37

Brenda picked up her tickets from the travel agents and tucked them into a plastic folder with her passport. *Good to go,* as they say. As far as the trip was concerned, everything was in place. She'd found somewhere to stay, temporarily, on the outskirts of Melbourne. Her UK house was sold. And she'd got nearly everything she needed to finish her plan for Pap. One thing she hadn't quite decided on was whether she wanted to be around to watch the fun. It might make things complicated, but what a great exit—for her and for Pap!

She hadn't really needed to leave Pap's mobiles at the airport, but wanted to lay as many false trails as possible. Diversions that would involve a lot of work, checking. Red herrings were important because in the end, it would all add to the dramatic impact of her game plan.

Barker had received a whole load of calls, people claiming to have seen Melvyn Greenstone in several parts of the country and abroad. The police had a limited amount of manpower and they knew, from past experience, that when someone went missing, a lot of publicity seekers and cranks crawled out of the woodwork to join in the fun and cause as much confusion as possible. But the media loved it, speculating at every turn, making the most of it and raking up as much of Greenstone's past as they could lay their hands on.

Not that Pap would have any idea what was going on, but Brenda was concerned that Raihana might, at some point in the not too distant future, be pursued by reporters.

Brenda had employed *Big White Van Man: no job too small,* to take most of her furniture to sell off or give to charity. She just needed a bed, chair and table, until she left. The house looked so bare. She was sad to be leaving. She and Arthur had spent most of their married life there; it hadn't been the best of marriages but it had ticked along, both had been faithful, hardworking and in many ways, had kept their independence: no restraints on Arthur's hobbies or on Brenda's desire to work hard and meet friends.

In many ways it had made his leaving the planet easier. Arthur's euphemism for anyone dying: *another one's left the planet,* he'd say, like they'd been catapulted off a rocket launcher. So there had been times when she could, quite easily, have imagined herself a single woman.

Chapter 38

Pap had been making slow progress with the lock. After weeks of fiddling he'd heard a tiny click and felt a small movement inside the mechanism, a tumbler or whatever, doing its work. The handle had given a tad, so when he gave the bars a push the lock seemed a little less secure, with a bit of play. He remembered watching lock pickers in crime dramas. Usually one click followed another when the tool was positioned at a slightly different angle. That was the problem, the awkward angle he had to work at. But he was encouraged and time was on his side.

He'd noticed there'd been some activity upstairs, furniture moving around, distant scraping. The room was too soundproofed to detect voices but something told him there were other people in the house. He thought that rattling the bars of his cell to make as much noise as possible was worth a try. Within seconds Brenda appeared with the Karcher and plugged it in. 'Do that again, Pap, and I'll use this while you're still clothed. It won't be as much fun as last time, you might get pneumonia and die. That would be a shame because at some point, as I've already told you, I am going to let you go; patience, Pap, patience.'

Pap slumped back on his bed and turned on his side to face the wall. His mind was playing tricks now. No fags, no booze, no telly or radio, no work, no sex, no books. He was virtually a monk. He'd heard about meditation, thinking really, and didn't rate it highly.

As far as Pap was concerned it just gave you time to worry about things you never worried about before. Perhaps some people needed stress. He'd met a few who seemed to spend most of their lives fretting about something or other. He had to admit though, that being locked up here with all the bizarre stuff that crazy bitch Brenda was doing, was enough to trouble anyone. And yes, he was troubled.

Brenda realised that Pap must have heard the movements upstairs. Probably felt, more than heard, as the floors were connected by beams and ties and plaster and stuff. She remembered the *feel* of Arthur's opera, resonating through the floor, the only indication that he'd switched on his CD player—especially if she stood barefoot in the kitchen—a mild tickling sensation at the soles of her feet. And that's what had happened when Pap shook the bars, she felt this rattling vibration through the kitchen floor, like a mouse nibbling at the joists and guessed immediately what it was. Never once did she expect Pap to be simply lying on his bed for the duration, without him trying to think of a way out. She'd thought of most of them herself, but rattling the bars? She hadn't expected that futile gesture. When she'd last checked the cell, the bars wouldn't budge, never mind rattle or make a sound. She wondered why this should be. The lock was secure, otherwise he'd have been up and away. She'd check it again.

   Pap was beginning to regret shaking the bars of his cell. They'd made more noise than he'd expected.

Chapter 39

Although Pap hadn't worried unnecessarily about stuff, he'd now had time to reflect. Gloria had wanted kids but he hadn't. They were both in their late forties when they got spliced, they'd missed the boat, so he could absolutely understand that she'd be lonely with him away all the time. Gloria said no to adoption and made it quite clear that she was not happy with Melvyn's alternative: a rescue dog, particularly the one that he'd seen and loved, a needy German Shepherd with a dubious history.

He was fond of Gloria, wanted her to be happy, but once out of the country he kept his mind on the tasks in hand. He had a keen eye for spotting a business in trouble, not that a company was selling inferior products, but because they needed to tighten up their workforce and get the best man for the job. Staff heavy, profit light usually. So Melvyn's eye in spotting this opportunity, providing the product was good, helped make lucrative deals.

In his experience, particularly if it was a family run business, loyalty kept the various relatives employed for life, often overpaying them for no other reason than they were genetically linked. No one ever got sacked, even if they couldn't do the job they were being paid for. Profit was lost. In fact it was a non-profit making certainty.

When Melvyn met these families and got them round the table, telling them exactly what they needed to do, it didn't usually go down well. He was a stranger rattling the family cage and upsetting everyone. They were suspicious of his motives, as if he were there solely to split the family and cause ructions. Someone sent by the competition maybe.

When he suggested that they needed to cut out the dead wood and employ people who could actually do the job they were being paid for, the family would often protest and get angry, preferring to keep the family together rather than go down the route he suggested.

This was his dream moment. At the point when the family was worried about the survival of their business but unable to see the truth, he was ready to make them an offer they couldn't refuse. He'd be in for the kill and give them a generous pay off; a lot less than the company was worth but more than they would ever get bumbling along the way they were. Simon would sanction the purchase and Melvyn would set about employing an efficient staff to run it properly. Usually, Simon's company got their money back in a year or two and profits would rocket. Melvyn was good, well worth the wages and bonuses he'd had over the years.

One of the problems for Melvyn was the social aspect; too much restaurant food, plying clients with alcohol and being invited to their homes, where they felt confident about clinching the best transaction. Plus the added headache of wives trying to influence the outcome of a deal behind their husband's backs—*you can't blame a girl for trying,* he supposed, *and you can't blame a man for being sympathetic to such negotiations.*

Chapter 40

Pap heard the door to the cellar open. There was a lot of clattering and banging. Brenda came clonking down the stairs, carrying something, but not the Karcher, no yellow flash appeared at the corner of Pap's eye. But the basement became much brighter than usual.

'Mornin', Pap. How are we this sunny morning?' Brenda was taken aback by how ill he looked in the new lighting, pale as a ghost. He'd not seen daylight for weeks and his one-size-fits-all disposable orange boiler suit made him look even more pathetic.

Pap viewed this sudden cheerfulness with trepidation. He wouldn't know about the morning outside, but it was certainly brighter down here. The extra light was hurting his eyes.

'This is a big day for you, Pap. You're about to become a movie star,' she said, setting up a robust tripod in the centre of the floor outside Pap's cell and getting it spot on by using an integral spirit level. 'Not looking your best, are you? But perfect for the part.' Unrecognisable. She hardly recognised him herself, in this light.

She wasn't a complete technophobe but she'd tested the camcorder and edited sample clips on Windows Movie Maker.

Pap stroked his straggly beard and self-consciously ran fingers through his hair.'

'Don't fuss, Pap, I want you in character. The makeup artist won't be arriving anytime soon.'

He didn't like the look of this. He watched Brenda attach a camcorder to the tripod and then pull a small mic out of her pocket. 'Wireless,' confirmed Brenda, noting Pap's increasing interest. 'You're going to be adding some dialogue, Pap. No script, you can ad lib, wing it, like you do in real life: flying by the seat of your pants kind of thing.'

'What's this about, Brenda?'

'YouTube, Pap. You've had quite a bit of publicity out there.' She waved casually toward the door of the basement, as if press and TV crews had been sitting there all along. 'But a video would be a great addition. No one's actually seen you in captivity yet. People need to know you're alive and kicking. Well, alive at least. I'm the director, and here's what's going to happen. You can say whatever you like. Obviously you can't say where you are, because you don't have the foggiest idea. The only rule: you mustn't mention my name. If you do I'll edit it out of the final movie. I'm the editor and sound technician too.'

'I can say anything I like, apart from your name?' he asked, unable to fathom out Brenda's motive.

'Yup. Want a moment to think about it, Pap? You've got thirty seconds.'

His brain was going into overdrive. Having seen a fair bit of YouTube, he knew it was most likely to be a short video. They're the ones that tend to go global and get the most hits. He needed a sound bite or two. Quick, quick. He could see Brenda counting the seconds down on her watch.

'Lights, camera, action!' shouted Brenda, swinging her finger in an arc toward Pap, like a seasoned film maker. She switched on the camcorder and moved alongside it holding the mic out toward him, careful to keep herself out of shot.

Pap gripped the cell bars as if about to protest, then faced the camera.

Gripping. Nice touch, thought Brenda.

He dropped his head forward, like a beaten dog, a look that

might create sympathy amongst YouTube viewers. 'My name is Melvyn Greenstone,' he mumbled. Then remembered this was his chance to say it like it is—to God knows how many people. Clearing his throat and in a stronger voice, he resumed his monologue. 'My name is Melvyn Greenstone. I've been kept in this cell, against my will, for over a month. Even my best friends may not recognise me. My wife will be worried out of her mind.' Pap tried to bring tears to his eyes but failed. The result was a weird screwing up of his face, like a short-sighted man trying to read small print.

'The texts people have been getting recently, are not from me. My captor sent them, trying to make my life even more of a misery. The woman who's imprisoned me in this awful basement has not given any reason as to why I'm here. This is a violation of my human rights,' he shouted, gripping the bars even tighter, trying to remember what his human rights actually were. Something about not being detained against your will was one, he was sure of that. 'I don't know if people are searching for me, but if they are, thank you, from the bottom of my heart.' Bowing his head again, as if trying to collect himself. 'Please find me...' he paused for dramatic effect and had another go at the eye screwing, tear producing technique, but failed for the second time, '...before it's too late.'

He looked nervously at Brenda as if in danger of being Karchered on camera. But she looked pleased. 'That's fine, Pap, we'll do a sympathetic fade at the end of that shot. Don't think I need to edit any of that performance. Oh, maybe the bit about texts, might not want that info out there just yet. Of course, I might decide to add my own monologue to yours. Plus a bit of outside broadcasting, shot somewhere miles from here, send them on another wild goose chase like the airport trick. No music though, maybe a bit of voiceover on a couple of scenes.'

Pap couldn't work out what she could possibly say that wouldn't incriminate her. Surely she wasn't going on camera! If so, why was he forbidden to mention her name? Looking on the positive side, he'd got the idea that his disappearance was now very public, that the police were *really* looking for him, so this YouTube thing might hurry things along.

'Nice work, Pap,' said Brenda. 'You won't see the finished video. At least, not this side of your release, unless I change my mind. But rest assured, the whole thing will still be around when you get out.'

Pap viewed this revelation with mixed feelings.

Brenda disassembled the camera and tripod, tucked the mic in her pocket and clacked back up the stairs smiling. She couldn't have scripted Pap's performance better, it was exactly what she wanted.

From her captive's point of view, Brenda smiling was never a good sign.

Chapter 41

The police station was busy, there were other matters to deal with. Smithy was occupied with a couple of local break-ins and Barker was going through his mail following a meeting with the Chief. He prioritised the morning batch of paperwork into the usual: in, pending and out trays, but kept a couple of items back for scrutiny. One caught his attention, a handwritten envelope with just the name Melvyn Greenstone written in the top left-hand corner.

'This looks interesting,' he called across to Smithy. 'Make some coffee and we'll take a look.'

Smithy put the kettle on and dropped spoons of instant into a couple of mugs. They'd not progressed far with the missing Greenstone case. The media publicity had only resulted in cranks or leads that went nowhere.

Barker had read the letter by the time Smithy returned with the coffees. 'Very interesting, looks like we have a lead at last.' The letter was handwritten in pencil on lined paper torn out of a spiral notebook. He passed the letter to Smithy:

I saw this man's picture in the paper. I dropped him at the corner of The Avenue and Blackstone Road about the time he was supposed to have disappeared. The man looked drunk and needed help. He was with a good looking woman who seemed keen to get him in and out of the car as quickly as possible. She didn't say much but gave me a big tip, the biggest ever.

Smithy turned the paper over, hoping to see a name or contact number, but that was it. No signature and no indication of where the letter had come from.

'Has to be from *the* taxi driver who doesn't seem keen to get involved, in which case, why leave a note at all? Notice he says car, not taxi. But we can do a door-to-door search of the area. Someone is bound to have seen something if we show them Greenstone's picture and describe a drunk being helped out of a car by an attractive woman. The Avenue doesn't usually witness such late night shenanigans.'

'Supposing it's another crank?' asks Smithy.

'Could be, but this is the first bit of logical intelligence so far,' said Barker. 'My guess is the taxi is operating outside the system and the driver doesn't want the publicity. But let's get going on the house-to-house. One of the others can help and meanwhile, I'll try and find out who the taxi driver is.

The writing was unusual, scrawling, not fully formed. Not much to go on but it was a start. Barker tucked the letter and a photo of Greenstone in his pocket and set off to the local taxi ranks that employed more casual labour than was lawful.

Smithy pulled up at the corner of Blackstone Road and The Avenue. Their business was not rated as an emergency, so no sirens. It was six-thirty pm, when most people would be home from work, kids back from school and the best chance of questioning whole families. He'd chosen Constable Jane Buffet as his partner. Good cop, sharp, fearless and pretty.

'You take The Avenue and I'll take Blackstone,' said Smithy.

Buffet took the photo of Greenstone and the leaflet Barker had given her, with the words: 'Have you seen this man?' Followed by, time of disappearance, approx. drop off point and a reminder that he'd been seen with a good-looking woman. And at the bottom, mobile contact numbers to get straight through to either Barker or Smithy.

For people who were not at home the leaflet could be put

through the letterbox. They had a check list. Those who failed to respond would get another visit.

Buffet had no trouble getting doors to open and neighbours to show interest in the missing man, but none had seen or heard a thing around that date. She knocked at Brenda's door. There was no car in the drive. No answer. She knocked again then left a leaflet.

Brenda turned the corner into Blackstone, just as the two officers returned to their car. She felt another spin around the block might be the best strategy. By the time she'd done the circuit, the police had gone. She wondered why they were calling. They couldn't possibly know Pap was being held there. If they had they would have sent a team in with Kevlar vests and one of those metal battering ram thingies. She did some deep breathing before opening the front door.

She looked at the photo on the handout. Not quite the man she had downstairs. Not now. She was concerned, that the police had managed to get this far. She'd been so careful. Cleo, the girl who'd brought Pap in, wouldn't have spilled the beans, but the taxi driver? Surely he wouldn't want to be discovered either, Cleo was certain he'd been moonlighting.

Brenda didn't want the police calling again. Too risky, so she decided the only way was to call in at the station, a Victorian building just off the high street, no distance at all. She had taken extra trouble over her appearance: tight, smart dress, well made-up, smiling, with extra perfume that she'd used like an air freshener, leaving a trail of womanliness wherever she walked. Barker had caught her scent, sucked into the room by the sudden draught of the swing doors, as they opened then closed behind her.

'Good morning. Are you DS Barker?' she asked.

He rose from his seat, trying not to breathe in Brenda's womanliness too deeply. 'I am. Can I help you?'

'I live in The Avenue. This was put through my door. Unfortunately I was at work when you called but I don't want you to waste another trip. I've read about this man in the papers but I'm sorry, I can't help with your enquiries. Hope someone else can,' she said, about to leave.

Barker wondered why she hadn't rung the station. 'Not familiar at all then?'

'Not at all.'

Chapter 42

The video needed a little tightening up before putting it on YouTube. Brenda ran it on her PC video editing programme, enhanced the sound quality, and cut Pap's hangdog scenes to a minimum. Didn't want too much sympathy out there! She edited out the bit about Pap denying the texts were his, and trimmed the moment when her mic hand had moved in front of the camera. Someone might spot a tiny detail that revealed too much: nail extensions, sleeve of her jumper, or some other clue that a forensic eye might pick up on. She added a title, *The Prisoner*, and left it at that, deciding not to add her voiceover or anything else. The quick rush of the final edit lasted just over two minutes, short but sweet .*The Prisoner* would come up nicely on search engines, so max exposure on YouTube, Facebook and Twitter.

Brenda had done her research and knew how to put the clip on YouTube anonymously. Simple, just a user name, no real moniker required. User name: Papillon.

Before releasing it, she wanted Raihana to have first viewing. Brenda took her laptop and met her friend in the small park just across the road from Coffee 4 Us. Mid-morning, Greenacres Park was empty, kids at school, adults at work.

Raihana gasped when Brenda clicked open *The Prisoner* file and revealed Pap gripping the cell bars, looking as if he was on death row. 'I don't think that's Melvyn,' she said, 'It can't be.'

'Hope it's not too distressing for you Raihana. It's him alright, of that you can be sure.' She pulled out a photo taken when she'd first locked him up. He looked younger, tubbier and better groomed then.'

'That's incredible, Brenda. Aren't you worried? He looks so awful.'

'Believe me, Raihana, he'll be fine. It's nearly over and then he'll have to face the consequences. That weight will go back on in no time. It'll be worth it, you'll see.'

Brenda logged on to the YouTube site again, typing in the title of her video and adding tags—*prisoner, captive, womaniser*—to help people trawling Google and other search engines. Then came a description: *man held captive in secret cell*, intriguing but not giving too much away. She declined to fill in exactly where the video was taken, so put, *At home* and added the date. Then just a click of the mouse on the publish button and the film started loading. It took its time. Brenda knew that YouTube had the right to reject certain content, but if terrorists could get their stuff on there, why not her? The video disappeared into the ether. Nothing came back to censor her efforts. Soon, more or less anyone in the world would be able to see it; on their mobiles, tablets or computers—or someone else's.

Brenda went online to see if there were any hits. Ping, ping, ping... Yes, coming in, twenty already and counting. She texted Raihana: *Go online and type in, The Prisoner, on Google or YouTube.*

Raihana held her breath. This was the man who had wrecked her life. *Did he really?* Raihana was the one who'd ignored her parents' advice, who'd betrayed the Muslim faith, who'd brought shame on her family and caused so much gossip in Shalmi Market that her parents were having to put in a lot more effort to make the business work. It was she who...Thoughts of what her parents might be thinking trailed off as *The Prisoner,* in bold text, travelled diagonally across the screen. Melvyn appeared ghostly on Brenda's clever fade-in. Nearly a thousand hits already. She watched as the camcorder zoomed in on Melvyn's knuckles tight around the bars. She listened to his words. They seemed hollow despite his predicament, and in that moment, all feelings for Melvyn Greenstone evaporated. Any hope of a link to his impending fatherhood, washed away like dirt down a drain.

*

Mother and Khan were surprised when someone who'd been avoiding them since Raihana's episode with Melvyn Greenstone, called them into the computer repair shop in Shalmi to show them the latest YouTube phenomenon. 'Who is it?' they asked as *The Prisoner* title came up and Melvyn, unrecognisable to the Khans, stood ready to make his plea. 'Listen,' said the trader, a diminutive Kashmiri native. They did.

'*My name is Melvyn Greenstone...*'

The Kashmiri spent a good part of his time surfing the net, YouTube especially. He'd never known life outside Lahore and marvelled at the odd goings on in the world. Women imprisoning men seemed as fantastical as it could get, and try as he might, he couldn't work out how it could possibly happen. He'd seen Greenstone doing business with the Khans—the market was alive with the biggest deal in Shalmi's history—he knew the name but would never have recognised him from the video.

The Khans gripped each other tightly, something only permitted in a crisis. 'What does this mean? Who is the woman that devil's talking about? Who imprisoned him?' Khan racked his brain: Raihana was in the UK. Was there a connection? Surely not. Against their wishes she'd gone to find Mr. Greenstone to complete more business with his company. This was bad news.

The trader though, was smiling, seeming to enjoy the Khans' protracted suffering, the result of their daughter's disgraceful behaviour.

The Khans soon let go of each other, smoothing their clothing of invisible creases.

The Kashmiri quickly saw them out of his shop. His fun with the Khans was over and he wanted to share his glee with the other traders. Perhaps he could charge a few rupees to let them watch *The Prisoner* in his shop while giving them the lowdown on the Khans' obvious distress and a few juicy titbits about Raihana's argument with them. Some of the traders only had mobiles, so to see Greenstone on a bigger screen would be a bonus.

Chapter 43

Brenda had failed to anticipate what her venture into the world of YouTube would mean. The hits were piling up. People were sharing it on Facebook and Tweeting comments across the globe. By now, many of the women from Pap's past would have seen it, as had Gloria, and Simon too of course.

Barker and Smithy had also seen it, within the hour. They hadn't expected anything like this, not imprisonment, that was serious stuff. Kidnapping carries a very long gaol sentence. Without any demand, financial or otherwise, neither of them could see the point in taking such a risk.

Once they'd got over the shock, they began to realise that, along with the taxi driver's note, this turn of events narrowed the search somewhat. The press were pestering the station for news on Greenstone's whereabouts and all this prompted the team to put up a whiteboard, like those you see in TV cop dramas, with pictures and leads and connecting tapes pinned like a web across the surface, annotated with a black marker pen.

'Right, Smithy. Let's have a look at what we've got. I'll call out and you write and pin.

'Picture of Greenstone, date of reported disappearance, approximate date of alleged disappearance, interview with Gloria Greenstone, interview with Margo, interview with Simon and the staff at Ethical Global Logistics. Way up in the left-hand corner, shots selected from the scenes on YouTube with the cell background, shot of The Avenue and Blackstone Road, roughly where he was dropped off. Taxi driver's note.'

Smithy continued to write and pin until the board looked amazingly like things were at last coming together, especially as Greenstone's boss had phoned to say he was offering a reward for information leading to Greenstone's whereabouts.

'Coffee?' asked Barker. Smithy didn't need persuading.

'Let's look at the video again,' said Barker as Smithy brought in the coffee and digestives. He sat in front of his computer and clicked on the saved link. *The Prisoner* clip came into view.

'It has to be a basement or garage,' said Smithy. 'The floor has been screeded with cement. And look at the walls—they've been soundproofed with that egg boxy stuff, like a radio station.'

'I don't think it's a garage,' said Barker. 'It's not so easy to soundproof a garage door and if it was bricked up it would draw attention. Has to be a basement. We can assume it's somewhere in this country because, as far as we know, he never left.'

'Let's look again at the place where Greenstone was dropped off with that woman. There can't be that many houses with basements in the area. We'll get someone to check,' said Smithy, dunking his biscuit, unable to stop a good half dropping into his coffee.

'Greenstone mentions a woman in *The Prisoner* video. Could it be the same one who helped him out of the taxi? Unusual for a woman to imprison a man, but not beyond the bounds of possibility. She may be in a gang of course, but that doesn't quite fit, gangs tend to make demands of some sort, mostly money, and shortly after the kidnapping. So let's assume that whoever she was, she managed to lure Greenstone down to the basement, maybe drugged. It seems the whole sorry business now has to be given full-on publicity, everyone on board: press, posters, media—especially local TV and radio—anything we can think of to attract some feedback.'

'Could there still be a demand?' asked Smithy.

'I doubt it, it's well over a month now. So possibly a woman on her own, someone he's treated badly. But why keep him for so long?'

Chapter 44

Gloria was crying. She'd got it wrong. Melvyn wasn't out there philandering, he was being tortured in a prison cell by some demented woman. Any texts would have been a set up; he wouldn't be allowed to use a phone, not if he'd been kidnapped! She wanted him to come home, wanted to feed him up and get him back to being the cuddly man she'd had a life with only weeks ago. She kept logging on to see Melvyn on YouTube and took a fresh tissue out each time. She called in to see Barker at the station, to find out if there was any news.

He'd had his suspicions about Gloria, even suspected her of being in it up to her neck at one point, but not anymore. 'Anything happened your end?' asked Barker. 'No demands or threats? In our experience it's usually the wife or husband who gets contacted first.'

'Nothing,' said Gloria. She noticed the board set up in the room behind the glass partition but it was too far away to read. Smithy was pinning something to it and she guessed they were putting together all the information about Melvyn's disappearance.

'We have more information. There are some comments on YouTube that we're looking at, but they may not be genuine. People tend not to check these remarks. Research shows we watch video clips and move quickly on. But we've checked them all. Someone posted a comment saying she's his wife. Was he married before?' Barker was fishing, wanted to play the innocent as if he'd yet to find out about Angie.

'Definitely not,' she said angrily. 'I'd have known. Melvyn would have told me.' Gloria had obviously not bothered to read the comment section on the site.

Barker had to admit that most of them were quite silly, things like: *This must be the terrorists*, or *Let's get a petition together to free Melvyn Greenstone*, but obviously the police had to check each one.

'Did she leave a name, this woman who claims to be his wife?' asked Gloria, not really wanting to go there.

'Angie Greenstone,' said Barker, not inclined at this point to reveal anything else he knew about her.

Barker gave a statement to the media following the YouTube publicity and the early tabloid newspaper article came out, hot off the press. They loved this stuff. The headline was in dramatic font that took up much of the page.

RELEASE MELVYN GREENSTONE NOW!

*We are appealing to the gang or persons holding Melvyn Greenstone, a British citizen. Please release him now and save his wife and friends from suffering any further from this terrible ordeal. (*There was a picture of Melvyn gripping the bars of his cell, taken from the YouTube clip but, for maximum dramatic effect, purposely blurred to look as if ISIS or Al Qaeda might have him imprisoned somewhere, and next to it, a photo of Gloria crying into a Kleenex.)

Greenstone is five foot ten tall, with sandy coloured hair and, prior to being kidnapped, slightly overweight. He was last seen wearing a navy tweed jacket, light blue shirt and carrying a tan soft leather case.

If anyone has a planned demand for his release, please contact DS Barker at the number below, who will ensure your request is fully considered by the appropriate parties. A reward for his safe return has been financed by his employer. A petition demanding the release of Mr. Greenstone is currently being circulated and the number of signatures are growing.

The police have intensified their search and would like anyone who has information about the whereabouts of Mr. Greenstone to come forward. He was last seen being dropped off at the junction between The Avenue and Blackstone Road, Chipperford. House-to-house calls have been made in the area. No witnesses have yet come forward.

The police are not ruling out the possibility that Greenstone has been moved and is no longer in the vicinity. Ports, airports and railway stations have been alerted.

Typical *Daily Moon* reporting, all this talk about gangs and abuse of British citizens, to up the drama. Despite the mention on YouTube, Barker was surprised the press hadn't brought terrorists into the equation, not yet anyway.

He was pleased that Gloria's response fitted in with his plan. She agreed to an interview and to the video getting maximum exposure on TV. Crews had already appeared outside her home and technicians with woolly microphones and zoom lenses were hovering close by when she stepped out of the front door. Barker stood behind her, authoritative but silent.

'Do you think he's still alive?' asked a young reporter.

'You've seen the video,' said Gloria, 'Of course he's still alive.'

'That could have been taken anytime. The date it was put on YouTube may not be the time it was filmed.'

Gloria reached for a Kleenex. Perhaps they had made the video—then killed him. A wailing sound and snuffling sobs followed.

Barker stepped into camera shot. 'Nothing is certain in cases like this, but we are of the opinion that Mr. Greenstone is alive. We are following new leads suggesting that, apart from his obvious distressed appearance, he's in reasonable health. A police medical team took a look at the video and declared him fairly fit for someone held captive that length of time. So he must have been fed. Not huge meals but enough to keep him alive.'

A fluffy microphone seemed to rise on its own, hovering close to Barker. 'How close are you to finding him?'

'The net is closing, but I can't give you information that might alert his captor to our strategy.'

Gloria was still thinking about Melvyn being filmed and then possibly murdered. She was in no condition to take any further part in the interview.

'That's all for now, gentlemen, ladies. I'll update you tomorrow at the station.'

There were a few groans as Barker brought the meeting to a close. He'd avoided mentioning Greenstone's real wife, Angie. But he couldn't do that for much longer. Angie wouldn't stay secret for long and neither would the others. Since the media exposure and the inclusion of Barker's contact details, a number of women had called claiming to have had a relationship with Greenstone, engaged even. In an odd way this removed them from suspicion. Why would anyone who'd imprisoned Greenstone ring up to say they'd had a relationship with him? It wouldn't make any sense at all. Nevertheless, Barker might be compelled to question every last one of them.

Chapter 45

The news was on. Gloria was first up, then Barker, being interviewed along with his Chief and Smithy. Brenda was surprised at how quickly things had happened. By now everyone on Pap's mobiles would be texting and ringing like nobody's business. She wondered how many thought they'd been Pap's exclusive property and how many suspected he was a pig all along. It'd be fun to run a survey.

From where she was sitting and despite the media coverage, they were no closer to finding Pap. Not many days to go before she flew off to Australia. She'd have been quite happy for Raihana to join her. But that would be impossible, now that she was pregnant and without a visa or permission to do anything but return to Lahore.

The reporters at the *Daily Moon* had also been going through the comments on YouTube and decided that Angie, the woman who'd been claiming to be his wife, was worth checking out. They rang Barker for some feedback. He was tempted to say 'no comment' but that's what criminals say when they know the answer but intend to keep quiet.

'Yes, we have noted that message and we are investigating, going through the site with a fine-tooth comb,' said Barker, giving nothing further away.

'Does his present wife Gloria know anything about this Angie?'

Barker didn't want to reveal too much at this juncture. 'Not to my knowledge, but at some point she'll find out—*if* it proves to be true. We don't want her upset unnecessarily. It may be someone trying to get publicity. Can I suggest you keep out of it, until we've investigated?' requested Barker, aware that this would present a challenge to any hard-bitten journalist. He had a dilemma; should he alert Gloria before the reporter got to her?

By the time Barker had arrived at Gloria Greenstone's house, Kev Strong the *Moon* reporter, was already standing at her front door accompanied by a press photographer and a TV news cameraman. Barker was furious but no one had yet answered the door.

'I asked you to leave this alone for the moment,' said Barker, trying to contain his fury.

'I'm a reporter, this is what we do.'

'How about co-operating with the police occasionally?'

'Sorry, Sarge, but this is too good to miss.'

'It's DS Barker, if you want your report to be accurate. Let's make a deal. You're not going in there, not negotiable, but if you let me have a word with Greenstone's wife, you will have first crack at what comes out of it. Deal?'

'Deal.'

A curtain at the bay window moved slightly and Barker caught a brief glimpse of the very person he wanted to interview. He rang the bell. Gloria appeared in a dressing gown.

'Have they gone? Come in,' she said, stepping aside in the dark hallway. It looked like every curtain in the house was drawn, until she led Barker to the conservatory.

She was anxious for news, good or bad, wanting him to stay a while. 'I'm making coffee, would you like a cup?'

'Thank you, black no sugar.'

'Have you got some news? Something's happened, hasn't it?

Is Melvyn dead? Why are you and the media turning up at this ungodly hour?'

Nine o'clock in the morning was far from ungodly as far as Barker was concerned. 'You've seen the YouTube video. Have you read any of the comments since we last spoke? And if so, any thoughts about some of the claims?'

She bowed her head, trying to put the memory of Melvyn held captive on hold while she answered the question. 'Only the first few: nutcases by the looks of them.'

'You are now aware of the message left by someone calling herself Angie?'

'Yes.'

'That's why I'm here, wanted to chat before reporters questioned to you.'

Gloria frowned, forgetting about the coffee; two spoons in the cafetière, electric kettle about to switch off, was as far as she'd got.

'We've been investigating the claim that she's your husband's ex-wife,' said Barker, realising this might sound ridiculous.

Gloria gave a mocking laugh. 'She can't be, the whole thing's a farce. She's a crank. I've been married to Melvyn for three years. He's told me all about his past and he never mentioned this Angie person.'

Barker, pencil in hand, looked down at the blank page of his notebook.

'When you find Angie, whoever the fuck she is, I want her charged and behind bars,' said Gloria, waving her finger threateningly at Barker.

He didn't respond but shifted uncomfortably in his seat, surprised at Gloria's robust response to what he'd hoped would be a collaborative moment in his search for Melvyn Greenstone. Barker didn't feel that this was quite the right moment to press home the fact that Gloria was not Melvyn's one and only wife. The law would be on Angie's side.

By the time Barker got back to the station, Smithy had contacted the authorities who'd provided a scanned copy of Angie and Melvyn Greenstone's marriage certificate. There was also a copy of a certificate of marriage to Gloria, but no evidence of a divorce between the two marriages. If Gloria truly believed Melvyn was her husband she was in for the biggest shock of her life. Barker, however, was not so sure that Gloria was as innocent of this fact as she appeared.

The phone rang in a pleasant house overlooking a river. Angie picked up. 'Angie here.'

'Is that Mrs. Greenstone?'

'Who wants to know?'

'We're looking for your husband.'

'Who's we? Everyone seems to be looking for him.'

'I'm from the *Daily Moon*. Your name was on the YouTube site, you left a comment following the clip of Melvyn Greenstone…I traced your number through the directory, it's not a common name in the UK…' Silence. The reporter didn't want to lose her. 'We can get your message out there, Mrs. Greenstone. Say whatever you like. We'll pay...'

Angie slammed the phone down. It rang again. She picked it up and smashed it back down. She wasn't going to have some tabloid crowd forensically examining her life. No way! It rang again but she had a retort ready. 'Just listen here, you parasite...'

'DS Barker here, Mrs. Greenstone.'

'Oh, I'm so sorry, Detective Barker. Have you any news?'

'Not of your husband's whereabouts I'm afraid, but we do have proof that Melvyn remarried, after he left you.'

'Don't believe it!'

'We're waiting for a copy of the marriage certificate right now.'

'Who the hell do you people think you are? My husband disappears and instead of finding him you trawl through our lives and come up with this rubbish. That certificate is a fake. Anyone with a computer and scanner can make one. I bet you haven't got the original,' she spluttered, breathing oddly, in choked gasps, the air sucked out of her as she was trying to speak, 'I—KNOW—MY—HUSBAND,' she shouted.

Barker felt a sudden fatigue wash over him, the tiredness you feel when you know the truth, and the person who most needs to believe it, is in denial. But he had to say, before he rung off, 'The certificate will be with us shortly. When it arrives I'll ring you.'

'*If* it arrives,' she said defiantly. 'And while you're digging up all this muck, going all out to wreck our lives, ask about *my* marriage certificate. And if you want to take a look at that—it's right here in my bedroom drawer!'

Barker knew it was pointless trying to talk things through with Angie now, and what with the Margo connection, he didn't hold out much hope for a reasoned interview anytime soon.

Chapter 46

The trouble with Brenda was that she knew exactly what she was doing. What she didn't know, of course, was what everyone else was doing. She didn't know Pap was trying to pick the lock, though she'd heard some extra rattling of the cell bars but assumed it to be frustration. She didn't know about the Khans' knowledge of Pap's incarceration and she certainly didn't realise that, right at this very moment, Kev Strong, roving reporter, allied to the *Daily Moon*, was already taking steps to bring Gloria and Angie together for his biggest scoop of the year.

That said, she'd set out her strategy well; only days 'till she left and no one was anywhere close to finding Pap.

Brenda called at Butts to check that all was okay. Raymondo led her into the office, turned on his computer and typed *The Prisoner,* on Google. Pap appeared at the cell bars. Brenda swallowed hard and clutched her handbag. 'What's this?'

'Everyone's talking about this, haven't you seen it? '

'Well yes, but what's it to do with us?'

'You may not recognise him but don't you remember the name, Greenstone?'

Brenda frowned, tried to look as if she was doing some serious thinking. Didn't quite get round to scratching her head, but almost.

'Nope, can't say I do.'

Had Raymondo turned the heating up? She was feeling awfully warm; a bead of perspiration travelled down her back before stopping, dammed by the tight bra strap.

'He was at that networking convention, way back. Arthur was with you. I think Melvyn took a shine to you.'

'Don't recall the name. Doesn't look like anyone I know. Are you sure?'

'I can look back through the records, might even have some photos of the event. It was a pretty big affair, I seem to remember, everyone drumming up business, free lunch, free booze. He's big news, Brenda, worth checking. We may be able to help.'

'Well I'm off soon, so won't be around to find out,' she said, eager to leave the office.

'Hang on.' Raymond pressed a button on his computer and used the mouse to select a file folder. He trawled through the documents and located the event. 'Here it is, guest list with photos.'

Brenda groaned to herself but realised this shouldn't be any big deal. So what if anyone found out she'd met Greenstone briefly a year or two back?

A picture of Greenstone came up in a group photo of about twenty people. He was standing next to Brenda, Arthur the other side. Gloria was not in the shot. Melvyn was looking at Brenda, she was gripping Arthur's arm and staring straight ahead.

Brenda remembered that moment well. Just before that was taken, a well pickled Melvyn had pinned her against the wall of the corridor leading to the loos and clumsily tried to kiss her while slipping his hand under her jumper. She'd pulled away sharply, totally in shock, as more people came to use the toilets. The picture she'd just seen was taken minutes later. She'd been trembling and having a problem holding it together.

'You look shell-shocked,' said Raymondo. 'Were you pissed?'

'Might have had a couple, didn't we all?' She hated Melvyn for that unforgivable episode. He'd embarrassed her, been more aggressively intimate than Arthur had been during the whole of their married life. The sheer arrogance of the man, pissed or not, to think he could do whatever he liked to whoever he liked. Unforgivable. Unforgettable. Traumatic. Humiliating. Devastating.

'But that can't be the man on YouTube, doesn't look anything like him.'

'But the photo in the papers does. Haven't you seen it?'

'Haven't had time to read them, too busy getting ready for Australia,' she lied.

Chapter 47

Kev Strong, roving reporter, also had wind of the house-to-house search by the police. Not exactly secret, in fact there had been a bit about it on the local news. It had proved fruitless. What wasn't public knowledge was that someone called Brenda had called at the police station the day after the search. He'd had a tip-off from a girl he knew at the station who was not quite as discreet as her bosses would have liked. Her job on the front counter had been useful to Kev in the past with the advantage of being first contact for the public entering the station. Brenda's name and where she worked were passed on to Kevin. But that was it. Brenda had been immediately referred to a senior officer.

So Kev had Brenda's name and where she worked, but no idea why she'd offered to assist the police. She seemed to be worth keeping an eye on. He'd found out she lived in the area where Melvyn Greenstone was last seen and close to the estate agents Butts, who employed her. He'd Googled their website and found her picture and CV on the *meet our team* menu. Not a bad looking woman, in a blowsy sort of way.

Kev followed Brenda from Butts and turned up at Coffee 4 Us just after her friend arrived. He sat with his back to them in the Little Conservatory and was able to pick up snippets between in-house music and mostly inaudible conversation: Brenda was moving fairly soon and something about *Pap*. Her friend's father? Short for *papa* maybe?

Kev felt this was a dead end, that Brenda was about to leave, and that pursuing her any longer might be a waste of time. But perhaps the Asian woman was worth talking to.

Brenda and her friend hugged and then parted outside the coffee shop.

'Bye, Raihana, see you tomorrow.'

Kev wrote down the name and followed Raihana back to the bus stop. He boarded the same bus and got off at her stop, keeping well back. She approached a small entrance to a couple of flats above a shop and disappeared into the flat on the left, number two. He made a note then went back to his office wondering what the hell he was doing. He sat there thinking, clicking a pencil against his teeth. A reporter's nose can be wrong, but he was missing something.

He checked the latest on the media. Ten thousand hits on YouTube, Tweets flying everywhere, Facebook friends sharing YouTube stuff and the other scraps of news posted by well-meaning but ill-informed members of the public. People's junk mail folders were filling up with emails from unknown sources. Not one of them actually seemed to know Melvyn, but hey, what's a world without a cause?

The 'Free Melvyn Greenstone' protestors were gaining momentum, five hundred online members and rising. They sent out *membership* forms to draft in more sympathisers, posted petitions to raise even more awareness. Fly posters were appearing, some copied off the web page clips showing Greenstone in his cell and some put up by the police with the photo of him in chubby good health, the way he would have looked the day he disappeared. Confusingly, the two images looked like completely different people. Kev guessed that much of this publicity was manna for professional protestors, those who seem to pick up a cause at the drop of a hat. And Melvyn Greenstone, held in a cell somewhere, was too good to miss.

Brenda wasn't born yesterday. She'd been super careful never to mention Greenstone by name, wherever she was, even to

Raihana. She'd spotted Kev with his back to them. He'd more or less followed them in but made the mistake of sitting too close, when the whole place was virtually empty. She didn't like her personal space taken up by a stranger. Later she watched him leave to follow Raihana and wondered why. She took out her mobile.

'Hi, Raihana. It's Brenda. Best not say too much in case our phones have been tapped, but someone is following you. I took a pic' of him (attached). He was sitting on the next table in Coffee 4 Us, then he crossed the street and followed you onto the bus. Don't say anything now but we'll meet as arranged tomorrow.'

Raihana looked at the picture of Kev Strong and wondered what he was doing. Obviously not police, otherwise they'd have been round for an interview. Reporter most likely, but how on earth? Perhaps her parents had sent someone to keep an eye on her. That would make a bit more sense as they would be the only ones with an obvious interest.

Chapter 48

Margo was not dim either. It was evident that Melvyn Greenstone was a serial womaniser. But then she never wanted a commitment in the first place, at least not until she'd spent some very nice weekends being spoiled rotten. It was addictive. She remembered thinking, *I could get used to this* and she had. She'd been without a boyfriend for over a year before she took up with Melvyn; he was persuasive and not that unattractive. He wasn't married then. They'd got up close and personal at work and it just happened.

They did call it off once, when she'd found out Melvyn was getting married. Despite that rocky episode, their relationship started up again. He'd promised to leave his wife, because it hadn't worked out. It was a lie!

Margo had spent considerable time making a banner for the protest, due to take place in front of TV and media in the centre of town tomorrow. FREE MELVYN GREENSTONE: RESPECT HUMAN RIGHTS. The banner was made with a split white sheet about ten feet long and two feet wide. The letters were in dark green marker, chosen especially. Margo thought this added something to the look of the message and visually associated the green with Greenstone.

Simon knew he had a good team and that Melvyn and Margo had been close, so wasn't surprised to learn that Margo had happily joined the campaign to free Melvyn Greenstone. She'd got others in the office to sign the petition. Simon signed it too, but drew a line at standing in the middle of town waving a torn sheet. He wouldn't be accompanying Margo to the protest. He also wondered just how effective a campaign could be, given that no one knew where Melvyn was. The reward he put up had not been responded to, no one had made any demands, and it had been impossible to discover who his captor might be.

Kev Strong had put the protest meeting in his diary, wondering if someone in the crowd might be a source of interest. Perhaps he was thinking of the movies where the killer turns up at the funeral before disappearing into the landscape, or watches the goings-on from a car with tinted glass. He didn't know that Brenda had spotted him previously and had alerted Raihana to his stalking. Nevertheless, he made a second visit and sat innocently in Coffee 4 Us for most of the morning, hoping they would come in. He was about to leave when a barista came across and placed an envelope on his table. He opened it. Five typed words.

'*Why are you following us?*'

Kev turned to scan the coffee shop but was disappointed. He approached the barista. 'When did you get this?'

'It was put on the counter while I was making coffee.'

'Did you see who it was?'

The barista shook his head.

'How did you know it was for me?'

'Someone rang, must have been watching the place. They asked me to give it to the man in the green jacket, sitting by the plant in the conservatory. You were the only one like that,' said the barista, clearing the dirty crockery.

Kev started to leave but stopped at the door. 'Any idea who the two regulars who sit in the conservatory might be? One Asian lady; young, pretty. The other woman slightly tarty, big...' He stopped himself saying tits and resorted to cupping his hands under his chest and lifting them slightly.

The barista grinned then smiled as Kev passed a ten-pound note across the counter. The tenner helped his memory.

'They're regulars yes, always whispering. Brenda and Rya something, weird name.'

'Know much about them?'

'Only that Brenda told me she works at Butts the estate agents, been coming here for a while, no idea where she lives though. Don't know anything about the other one, she's fairly new.'

Kev already knew about Butts and the Asian girl's address. 'Any chance you could give me a buzz when they come in again?'

'I'd rather not. What are you up to?'

Kev now had to play the intrigue card which worked well most of the time. 'Undercover reporter onto a big story.' He stressed *undercover*, whispering it with his hand alongside his mouth as he spoke.

The barista perked up with interest.

*

Pap was playing with his carton of soup, hungry but not hungry, wanted something to eat but not broccoli. Brenda came downstairs with her laptop and set it up on the old chair which she pulled in front of him. Not too close.

'Thought you'd like something to watch, Pap, changed my mind about not sharing stuff with you, felt a bit mean... First, the little video we made. You're quite a celebrity by the way, look at the hits you've got.' He saw the title, *The Prisoner*, followed by two minutes of his star performance. Number of hits; over twenty-five thousand. He was stunned but felt a sense of pride that his little clip had gone global. Yes it was him, but had he been shown it by anyone other than Brenda, he wouldn't have believed it.

'Ready for the next part of the show?'

Pap grunted dismissively, with thinly disguised interest.

It was a news clip. Couldn't tell what day, but hundreds of people were in the town square shouting at no one in particular.

There were a few police there, passive, just standing around as if a minor dignitary was about to arrive, no one in need of protection, only a show of solidarity; a demo.

Gloria was there with her pal waving a bloody great banner. He felt a surge of love. She was swirling the banner and shouting: *Free Melvyn, Free Melvyn, Free Melvyn.* He remembered, with affection, that Gloria had a tendency to repeat herself. But soon the others joined in, pulsating and moving as one, like a murmuration of starlings. He felt heartened at all these friends turning out to protest for him.

Brenda saw the look on his face. 'Don't kid yourself, Pap, they're not your friends, just a bunch who do this sort of thing at the drop of a hat. A kind of rent-a-crowd without payment involved. They'll be throwing stones at something next, looting shops and burning cars.'

He squinted at the screen trying to spot faces he knew: there was Gloria, her pal and...*Well it was damn good of them to turn out*, he thought, unable to recognise anyone else in the crowd, the laptop too far away to focus on those hovering in the background. *Ah, there's Margo with her even bigger banner*—size matters: *I was the last one in bed with Melvyn Greenstone,* it seemed to say.

All in all it was looking good for him, a lot of sympathy out there. When he was released he'd give interviews, be selective of course, not the local rags, make a few bob from selling his story. Get a ghost writer to rustle up a book. Maybe a film...

Something not quite right about Brenda showing him all this stuff, it wasn't done to cheer him up, goes without saying. So what the hell was she up to now?

Maybe this was the end game. She just wanted to give him a few weeks of payback for finding out about his past. There was nothing more she could do, not really. None of it warranted a prison sentence. At least, that was his take on it. As far as he could tell, from the stuff Brenda had shown him, the world was most definitely on his side.

Chapter 49

Kev Strong walked boldly in-to Butts and asked for Raymond, confident that first name terms would disarm Brenda's boss. Unfortunately, Strong had decided on a last long drag of his fag, before grinding the half smoked stub into the spotless pavement, bang outside the entrance to the estate agents. The tobacco residue lingered, seeming keen to invade every corner of the office.

'How can I help?' said Raymond, from his office door, breathing in deeply and coughing exaggeratedly. Kevin Strong had already become Raymond's least likeable person of the day, even though it had hardly started. 'This is a non-smoking establishment,' said Raymond. Kev was about to state his case when he exhaled. A rogue puff of smoke rose to the office ceiling, so he decided against it.

'Sorry about that, I thought I'd left it all outside.'

Kev ignored the disapproving look, smiled and gave Raymond his card: *Kev Strong, Reporter, Daily Moon*. 'I'm doing a story on the disappearance of Melvyn Greenstone. Do you know him by any chance?'

'What led you here?' asked Raymond, wanting to throw the guy out, but continuing before Kev had time to respond. He put the nicotine-contaminated office issue to one side. The only possible reason he could think of for the reporter's visit, would be something to do with that business seminar.

'I met him at a networking event some while back, but don't really know him. Can't be much help sorry,' said Raymond, coughing again for added effect.

'Seen him since?'

'No.'

'Was there a record of the event, photos, list of guests— anything at all?'

Raymond wasn't sure how to play it. All the staff appeared in the photos. Did he want them being bothered by this parasite? Surely none of them could be implicated in Greenstone's disappearance? He decided to play for time.

'There may be. I'm far too busy right now but leave it with me. I'll check our records and get back to you.'

Kev drew a ring around the mobile number on his card and gave it to him. 'Much appreciated. Today would be fantastic.' He nodded at Raymond, before smiling and winking at the girl he suspected might be doing the spadework.

'By the way,' said Kev, 'you really ought to do something about that cough.'

Brenda walked into Raymondo's office and noted the excited buzz of the place. They were talking about Kev Strong's visit and his enquiry into Greenstone's disappearance. And discussing the networking event and photographs.

'Hi, Brenda,' said several voices in unison.

'Hi, everyone. Can I have a word please, Raymond?'

He put a hand on her shoulder and guided her into his office.

'Could you do me a small favour?' she asked.

'What's up, Brenda? This is a first, you never ask for favours.'

She felt nervous and coloured slightly.

'Well, the photos... Nothing to worry about I'm sure,' she said, uneasily. 'But this guy's a reporter. He'll want to start interviewing us, wasting our time. You've got a business to run and I've got a plane to catch.' She knew it didn't sound right but

Kev Strong would start to piece it together; the picture; the covert meetings with Raihana and to cap it all, the note: W*hy are you following us?* He was gonna be like a dog with a bone. 'But could you hang back from giving him any photos...'

Raymond was baffled.

'...Save me hanging around waiting to be interviewed. I've got stacks to do,' she said.

Raymond didn't like the feel of this. Surely she just needed to say she didn't know the guy, tell the reporter she'd just met him the once, at a firm's gig. The interview would take two minutes max and in any case, Raymond, a respectable member of the community with a reputation to consider, was keen to help do what he could to narrow the search for Greenstone.

'Sorry, Brenda. Not happy with that,' replied Raymond. He imagined being arrested for holding up investigations that may eventually involve the police. After all, he'd already delayed showing Strong the photos.

Her buttocks clenched involuntarily. It was inevitable now, that once Kev Strong spotted her in the photo next to Greenstone with her staring into the abyss as if she'd been struck by lightning, he would be on the case. Plus he'd spot Greenstone's leering look, grinning like a Cheshire cat as if something of an intimate nature had occurred between them. Strong would follow that up by spying on her, or getting someone else to do it. Then he'd no doubt try for an interview, which would be tricky. Brenda was pretty sure of one thing though, Strong would be unlikely to tip off the police until he'd got a scoop in the bag.

Once the police got hold of the Kev Strong take on things, she'd be sunk. They'd remember her voluntary appearance at the station following the house-to-house and link her to Melvyn in the photo. Then they'd send a dozen cops in Kevlar vests to kick down her front door at night, with laser lit guns and dogs with a strict sense of duty.

Chapter 50

Barker and Smithy were at a bit of an impasse. Or they were until they heard that Kev Strong, investigative journalist, was making enquiries at Butts. Since Strong contacted Barker, fishing around for titbits for his story on Greenstone, he'd had someone keep an eye on the young reporter.

Raymond, following a sleepless night considering the possibility of appearing in the *Daily Moon*, and being linked precariously to the missing Melvyn Greenstone, had decided to phone Sergeant Barker and tell him about Strong's visit. Some people might have thought this a bad move: the police could be all over the office carrying out a far more thorough search than Strong would have had the authority to do. But it was too late. Raymond had made the call at six am. As the church clock struck seven, he was opening Butts early for Barker and Smithy. Raymond fired up the computers, logged on to his account and searched for the picture that now seemed as important as the evidence against O.J. Simpson.

They scrolled through several shots of the networking event before arriving at the photo in question.

'Stop it there,' shouted Barker, unnecessarily as it turned out.

'Can you focus on Greenstone and the woman he's looking at?'

Raymond clicked the editing menu and chose 'crop'. With the two faces isolated he pressed 'save a copy' and enlarged the revised picture.

'Can you let me have details of your staff and the other firms at the networking event?'

'I'll check it out. We usually keep a record of the day: events, talks, participants, etc. We all tend to get together, firms intermingling to show how friendly and global we are. You'll see arms around people we've never even met before. You probably know about this corporate stuff; get close, smile for the camera, the results splashed across company magazines, websites, Facebook and all that social media stuff.'

'Do you know the woman next to Greenstone, is it one of his girlfriends? I've seen her before,' offered Smithy. 'At the station.'

'She works here,' said Raymond, 'but she's certainly not one of his girlfriends. I'd stake my life on it. As far as I know this is the one and only time Greenstone and Brenda have ever met.'

'Who's the guy standing the other side of her?' asked Smithy.

'Her husband, Arthur. He's dead now.'

Barker leaned closer. 'Can you print a couple of copies, both the cropped shot and the bigger picture? Is she due in today?'

'Not sure, she's leaving the company, tying things up before moving away.'

'Where to?'

'Australia.'

'Shouldn't you know whether she's coming in today or not?' asked Smithy.

Raymond bristled slightly. 'She's almost done here, so we want her to feel free to get everything sorted before she leaves. She's on the end of the phone should anything unexpected crop up. So Brenda may or may not turn up today,' he snapped.

In no time at all, Smithy and Barker telepathically had the same recall. Brenda was the woman who was out when they'd organised the door-to-door. She'd apologized at the station for not being in when an officer called.

'We should have details from when she visited the station, but can you confirm her address and phone number, just in case?'

Raymond flipped through his employment file and drew out a document with a picture of Brenda in a smart suit and crisp white blouse. Her name and address were at the top.

'Save me taking notes, can you photocopy this? Then I'd like to ask you a few questions. Your office might be best.'

'But the staff won't be in for at least another hour,' piped up Raymond, adding Brenda's home telephone number to the copied document.

'Office, if you don't mind.' Barker knew that the best place to ask a man delicate questions was not down at the station, or at home, but comfortably ensconced in his own office with the door tightly shut.

Barker sat down before Raymond had a chance to offer him a seat. Smithy followed them in, but stood at the half glazed door with a clear view of the entrance to Butts.

'Coffee?' asked Raymond, as a diversion. He needed a moment to think about this.

'No thanks. We hope this won't take long,' said Barker, taking out his notebook and pencil, oblivious to his own irritating habit of licking the lead before setting down anything on paper. Smithy told him once that he risked lead poisoning. But Barker, with the conviction of the man who's right much of the time, told Smithy that he'd been sucking pencils for twenty years and hadn't dropped dead yet.

'How long have you known this woman?'

'She came to me, with excellent references, six years ago.'

'No reservations about taking her on then?'

'None at all.'

'Why's she leaving?'

'Had enough she says, time to start a new life.' Raymond regretted those words immediately. It might give the impression she wanted to escape something.

Barker wrote *starting a new life* and underlined it. Anyone who was starting a new life was worth keeping an eye on. He reckoned that Brenda was no longer as innocent as he'd first thought with regard to this whole affair. She may well be implicated in the disappearance of Melvyn Greenstone.

*

Brenda had decided not to pop into Butts until later in the day. Not much to do there, a simple case of tying up a few loose ends and alerting Raymondo and the staff to any transactions pending. As she left home for the bank, to organise the closing of her accounts, she saw Barker and Smithy turn into the street in an unmarked car. They were busy looking right, probably trying to locate her house. She was on the opposite side of the road, driving slowly away from them. They were still looking right as they passed each other. She looked in her rear view mirror, saw Smithy get out of the car just outside her property, and drove on.

Smithy rang the bell. No answer. He rang again. Barker walked through the rear gate to the back of the house. He looked at the neat garden, peered inside the summer house and shielded his eyes to reduce reflection as he squinted through the back windows of the house. He tapped on the glass panes as he went. Not a sound from inside.

He returned to Smithy. 'Anything?'

'Nope,' said Smithy, giving the bell an extra hard push and rattling the letterbox.

'She must have gone to work after all. Give her boss a ring, see if she's there now. If not, tell him to let us know if she arrives and not to mention we've been looking for her.'

Chapter 51

The Khans were about to make the biggest decision of their lives. They'd never left Lahore, let alone travelled abroad, and had spent many nights talking about the situation, agonising what to do about their daughter. One thing they'd agreed on: neither of them could live without seeing Raihana again. Despite all the advice from family and friends—to cut her out of their lives—they simply could not do it. The consensus of the neighbourhood was that the sins of the daughter should not be tolerated. Some would even have had her physically punished, beaten, and then cast out.

Khan thought he might be losing it. His world was small but his concerns were big. Although his parents and his grandparents had believed in the long tradition of severe punishment for daughters who'd *disgraced* their families, Khan winced every time he heard what had been done to some of these girls.

How could a husband and wife create such a lovely human being, only to reject her forever, just for one sad mistake in what otherwise had been an exemplary life? He'd blamed his softening approach on the particularly strong bond he'd felt for Raihana. Not only had he watched in pride as she grew into a beautiful woman, he'd taught her everything he knew about trading in Lahore. She'd grasped the concepts quickly, as quickly as Khan would have expected of a son, if he'd had one. She was fearless in her bargaining and sometimes took her negotiating skills to levels that

Khan had secretly admitted were cleverer than his. To him Raihana was the son he never had. And if he ever had the courage to admit it, she was as good as any trader in Shalmi Market, possibly in Lahore even!

Another factor that had influenced Khan's opinions was the internet revolution. He'd been against mobile phones and computers, but as traders started to use them and his daughter had demonstrated their usefulness, he'd softened. He was by no means computer literate, but used a mobile to make calls and watched in awe when the man in the newly established computer repair shop trawled through subjects of interest from all over the world. Khan knew that the trader would eventually try to sell him one of the damn things and offer to repair it, for a fat fee, when it needed attention. So Khan, through his gradual exposure to the World Wide Web, had become enlightened as to how the rest of the world carried on. He could see how people in the West treated their families, how liberated they seemed to be from some of the strict practices of the East. Gradually, the new generation growing up in Lahore were beginning to rebel against the ancient and sometimes brutal traditions of the old cultures.

It was not easy for the Khans to get visas. Fortunately they did have passports, still in date, which they'd never used. Raihana's earlier plans, to encourage them to travel, never materialised. Business always came first.

They had to make an online appointment with the visa application centre in Lahore, something the Khans needed a lot of help with. They were asked to get the completed documents and accompanying letter printed off, then were instructed to turn up fifteen minutes early for their appointment.

At the visa centre they collected a token and waited until their number was called. They were given a receipt, enabling them to collect their document pack. All supporting paperwork was then given to the enrolment clerk. It went on and on for most of the day. It was exhausting!

But they'd been patient and now they'd booked flights to London Gatwick and were due to leave for the UK in two days' time. They would find Raihana and refuse to go back to Lahore without her.

Another first for Khan, was the tricky situation of asking two cousins to take over the business while he was gone. They weren't the brightest of sparks but worked hard, though not always productively, as they liked to play hard too. Where Khan feared they might not come up to scratch was when bargaining. He'd found out, quite early on in his life, that when people looked after money that wasn't theirs, it appeared to have less value. But what else could he do? Well he could establish guidelines: don't make a quick decision, the profit is fifty percent of the mark up, so never bargain below that, unless it's old stock. These items are marked with a small star clipped to the garment or stuck on a product. They can be sold for less, but not without a bit of bargaining, go for the biggest profit possible. And don't forget to be pleasant. Smile, bow a little, make tea, if the customer looks wealthy or appears indecisive. Watch how they walk past other stalls. Are they picking up and dropping items quickly or are they examining, thinking about things, weighing up whether they should try and bargain? Watch other stalls for pickers and droppers; shoppers who move stock around, make a mess, then leave—they are not worth spending energy on. Of course the cousins should know all this, but Khan was nervous enough about leaving them to look after his business as it was, without taking a chance on their ability to incorporate good common sense.

Chapter 52

Angie had to accept that Melvyn was a bigamist, that the police were on his case and that reporters were snooping around, looking for juicy stories to add to their bottomless pit of other people's dirty washing. But she'd be damned if, after all these years without him, Melvyn was going to wreck her peaceful life. She'd been faithful, waited for his calls and even looked forward to him coming home at first—despite the fact she'd had time to think about what he might be getting up to.

She prided herself on being a calm person, a little turmoil inside at times, but mostly peaceful in her daily goings on. *Angie's armour* her mother had called it, her daughter's ability to button up her emotions and get on with things.

Melvyn, on the other hand, had always seemed on his way to somewhere else. She took this personally at first, but over time realised he was like it in any given situation, twenty-four-seven, whether at work or socially engaged, he was always glancing around, a magnet for the next distraction.

When they'd been married for a while she'd brought this to his attention. He didn't seem offended. 'Sorry, Angie. Been like it all my life, some genetic thing. It's in my DNA. Dad had it. It's one of the reasons I got this great job. My boss liked the way I was never still, said I took in more information than all the rest of his guys and gals put together. Can you see that? When he sends me on a job I never miss a thing. I can spot a situation, weigh up the people I'm about to do business with and cut a quick deal. Sorry,' he said again, smiling, waiting for Angie to compliment him for having the same traits as his father.

She had to admit to being disarmed by that statement, particularly the word sorry at the beginning and the end of his response. An apology always disarms. People should say sorry more often, she'd decided. So she wasn't being left out or ignored, she was simply—she tried to think of a way to describe it—simply, married to Melvyn Greenstone, husband and nemesis as it turns out. But now, if Melvyn had the word sorry tattooed on his forehead, she'd be hard pushed to find any forgiveness left in her heart.

She showered in her favourite jojoba gel, dried her short dark hair and slipped into a pair of snug fitting jeans and a long sleeved tee shirt. She put on her light waterproof jacket and stepped out into the early morning rain.

Chapter 53

Gloria, on the other hand, had not so easily accepted that Melvyn was a bigamist. She was tanked up, been drinking most of the day trying to get the perpetual pictures of other glamorous women, including Margo, out of her mind. Especially the most beautiful woman she could imagine, which she'd conjured up from nowhere and called Angie. Easier to hate something when you can put a name and face to it, albeit an imagined one. But she was damned if anyone was going to let these tarts win. She'd made it clear to Barker; no future interviews with the media unless he was there to keep an eye on things. He'd already warned her about the paparazzi's approach to this kind of story. They were ruthless.

She poured another gin. Not counting. It was late afternoon and her migraine was starting to kick in: part stress, part gin. She'd been warned about her drinking but with Melvyn away for so long and most of her pals keen to indulge her, there was little chance of escaping the merry-go-round. But if she and Melvyn survived this, got to talk things over and make some changes, they could still be happy. Might even be able to adopt a couple of little 'uns, take them on holiday, something she'd been totally against before. They could be like a real family. She'd stop drinking.

She looked out of the bay window onto the street. It was quiet. She moved the net curtain to see if there was anything going on. A man was standing alongside the pillar box, twiddling with something. As she moved the curtain he raised a camera, with a telephoto lens by the looks of it, and took a shot of her before she had a chance to step out of range.

She ran down the hall and opened the front door. Kev Strong took another shot of her coming toward him. He noticed she was angry, then as she got closer, swaying slightly like blasts of wind were striking her from different angles, he realised she was drunk. He started to run but wasn't quick enough. Gloria tugged at the camera strap around Kev's neck, and his face bordered crimson as the thin leather tightened then snapped. He missed grabbing the camera as it fell to the ground, but free of its encumbrance, continued his flight.

Gloria didn't need encouraging, she booted the camera like a football, running after it as if to give it another kick and head for a goal further up the street. Instead she stamped on it and smiled at the pleasing sound of breaking lenses and cracked casing. All sorts of bits and pieces burst from the expensive Nikon. Kev Strong was furious, but frightened. Gloria's success in demolishing the camera had given her the confidence to go after him with the intention of doing harm.

'You unfeeling bastard, aren't you ashamed of how you make your living? I'm an innocent woman. My husband might be in the hands of maniacs being tortured and water-boarded, yet all you can think of is getting a picture of his poor wife for your pathetic rag.'

Kev moved behind a parked car. 'I'm doing my job. Trying to get to the bottom of all this. People want to know what Greenstone's leaving in his wake. They want the human side. They'd love your story, Gloria, there's loads of sympathy out there—much better than waving banners and shouting. You could give me a proper interview; tell me your side of things.'

Gloria picked up the shell of the camera case and threw it hard in Kev's direction.

'Parasites, leeches, merchants of misery.' She'd heard *merchants of misery* somewhere, Shakespeare probably, just the place to use it.

'You'll hear from my solicitor. You can't go around destroying property just because someone's doing a job you don't like. And being drunk as a coot won't help your defence. Not one bit,' uttered Strong in a falsetto response.

She couldn't find another object big enough to throw with the intention of hurting, so she ran at him, no plan, just temper; some kind of grab and wrestle she imagined, a bit of scratching maybe. But Kev reached his car before she got hold of him, operated the child lock and reversed back down the street until he could do a wheelie and shoot right past her.

Gloria sat on the pavement exhausted. People were coming out of their houses to see what was going on. They'd heard shouting but had never seen their neighbour in such a state. She was obviously drunk and they could see she was mad. Once they'd reviewed the situation, they crept back indoors. Everyone except Joe, the only one brave enough to enquire about her predicament.

Joe from number twenty-three had known Gloria and Melvyn since they'd moved in, and knew what was happening in Gloria's life. Still fuming, she let Joe take her arm. It was nice to have someone helping her up and holding her as she walked back to the house.

'Shall I make us some coffee?' said Joe, noticing the nearly empty gin bottle.

'Yes please, black. Everything's in the corner cupboard; coffee, cafetière, cups. Spoons in the drawer.'

Joe watched her through the serving hatch as he boiled the kettle and tossed three spoons of Italian style coffee into the cafetière. While he was waiting for it to brew, he called through the serving hatch. 'Any sugar, Gloria?'

'No thanks, just straight and strong, I need to sober up. There's biscuits if you want, Joe, same cupboard, next shelf up.' Her voice had a shaky quality now; she was trembling from the physical effort spent chasing Kev Strong, and the fury with which she'd demolished his camera.

Joe came back into the lounge with a small tray; he'd found the biscuits and held one in his mouth as he walked in. He set the tray down on the coffee table, took a bite out of the biscuit and smiled. 'You'll feel better after a nice cup of coffee. Put your feet up and I'll pour.'

Gloria reached for the Kleenex and the floodgates opened.

Chapter 54

Pap was frustrated. He felt dirty and desperate. Was this how a homeless person might feel? He'd seen a few, tucked into filthy sleeping bags across the city of Brighton when he'd been there for a seminar. He'd had little sympathy then but now he'd be happy to be in their place.

He hadn't had a proper erection for a month, just a twitch one night when he'd woken from a heavy sleep to smell Brenda's perfume and seen her vague shape in the half light. A state of flaccidity had quickly followed.

He'd washed daily and brushed his teeth but nothing came close to the feeling of cleanliness from having a shower or bath. The flannel, now rougher than ever, was probably good for the circulation but a devil for the skin, especially around the nether regions. The small towel, about the size of an antimacassar, the ones used in first class train carriages to keep greasy hair off seats, was not much better. But there was a reason for its skimpiness. It was Brenda's idea, to deter the prisoner from hanging himself.

His hair, washed in Simple soap, had the texture of wire wool. He'd almost given up trying to get the tiny plastic comb through it. There wasn't a mirror, so he'd no idea what he looked like and had no desire to find out. Not yet anyway.

He itched all over, scratched his beard and various other places and almost wished he had the courage to ask Brenda to

Karcher him on the soap programme. But he knew that any request would be refused on account it would be something he might find vaguely enjoyable. His memory of how much it hurt at the time had faded. He'd read that some women saying 'never again' after childbirth, changed their minds to 'let's have another baby' once the memory of pain had abated. He felt a connection.

If loving women was a crime then he was guilty. Obviously it had its downside, that's why he was here, according to Brenda. But he'd never forced himself on anyone. Always treated women well, a gentleman, a generous person, never asked for commitment. He felt himself grow with this positive self-analysis which seemed to exonerate him from all guilt and made him really wonder about Brenda's motives.

He'd had time to reflect on the occasion when he'd groped her. He had to work hard to bring the scenario to mind but remembered trying to kiss her and didn't think she was totally against it. She'd looked a bit wide-eyed but hadn't pushed him away, not until he'd grabbed her breast. Too late. But surely that wasn't what this was about; revenge, just for a quick feel!

He hadn't thought of it before. But he was worried as hell now. It never occurred to him that while trying to locate the keyhole with his lock-picking tool, he would end up scratching the surrounding metal. The bars and lock were obviously new, so any marks would show up easily, especially as the whole construction had been sprayed with dark grey paint. It was impossible to see the outside of the lock from inside the cell so he felt with his fingers, drawing blood as his fingertips touched the sharp metal swarf, peeling from the deeply scratched surface of the unyielding lock. Brenda would surely notice it, if she hadn't already. There was a possibility that with the poor lighting it would remain in shadow. As long as she didn't decide to direct another brightly lit YouTube documentary, he might get away with it.

He suddenly felt relief and celebrated by having another go at the lock. A bit late in the day, but he tried to be more careful this time. Within minutes he'd found and located one of the levers and heard a healthy click as a bit of mechanism gave up its resistance. He moved the pointed tool further in. Having passed the first cam, it was harder to move, the ring-cum-lock-pick was a bit short. It seemed ages before he felt another shift; a small rocking movement, as he wiggled the tool back and forth. The lock was responding! His arm ached so much he pulled it back and cradled his aching joints and muscles.

The end of one of his fingers started to bleed profusely, it was hard to stop.   Drips of blood spattered the floor. He staunched the flow with some toilet paper and tried to wipe up the rest with the remaining handful of tissue. The result was a series of muddy brown streaks across the cement work. Dampening the tissue, he managed to lighten the colour at the expense of enlarging the patch.

The surface was now dry but stained, a sample fit for a forensic pathologist's master class. A bit more scrubbing didn't change things, except the smear had acquired speckles of white toilet paper as if it had suddenly started to snow. The cement around the patch had become lighter, producing a halo like effect. Pap stood back to survey the result, scrutinised it like a judge at the Turner Prize Exhibition, and decided he'd have to leave it, tell Brenda he'd thrown up or something.

Chapter 55

Brenda had noticed the scratches around the lock. She'd seen the desperate markings as a sure sign of Pap's frustration at being unable to pick the lock and make a bolt for it. She excused herself the pun.

Brenda wasn't that daft. She knew the only thing strong enough to deal with the task would be something metal. There was nothing. Had been nothing. That is, apart from Raihana's ring which seemed to have mysteriously disappeared, she was never convinced that she'd thrown it out with his dirty clothes. The engagement ring was cheap, not up to the task and certainly not up to dealing with the five lever job she'd had fitted. He'd reach two levers at best. He wasn't going anywhere. But her confidence was waning; a niggling unease. Was she missing something? The uncertainty was working on her subconscious, especially at night, taking up too much time in her nocturnal thoughts.

Not long to go now, but Brenda was starting to crack. At first a few sleepless hours, night sweats, anxiety that showed up at odd moments throughout the day, forgetting things and making too many mistakes at work. She plunged into a deepening depression. She'd been there before, worked it out with a little help after a while and got through it. But this was such a critical time in her life. *Please, not now*, she prayed, to a God she didn't believe in. She needed help.

*

Dr Scrant was not unsympathetic.

He got Brenda to step on the scales, and checked her pulse and blood pressure; it was on the high side but not critical. Patients often had elevated blood pressure when first entering the surgery. He'd check it again before she left. He listened to her heart, checked her lungs with a stethoscope, tapping her back and chest to elicit any tympanic clues to an underlying problem.

He took her recent history, listened to her explanation and went through her past health record. Nothing remarkable: bronchitis as a child, mild heart arrhythmia around the time Arthur died, one notable period of depression around the same time—not medicated, she saw it through with a bit of NHS counselling. Type 2 diabetes diagnosed a couple of years ago and slightly overweight, but not a cause for concern. There was an old reference to some mental health problem when she was a teenager, before moving to Surrey, a rough note in a physician's handwriting that denied him access to what actually happened. Brenda didn't mention it and he didn't see the point in bringing it up now. Might make things worse, reminding a depressed person that they have history.

'It could be the thought of moving,' she started. 'It's one of the most stressful things you can do. I Googled it, it's in the top ten.'

Scrant nodded and pretended interest, as if hearing this explanation for the first time.

He made a note.

'I'll send you the link, if you like,' said Brenda, thinking Scrant's note was a reminder to check Brenda's analysis.

His note said; *Moving! Prescribe AD (antidepressant)*.

'Moving from a home you've loved is enough to cause an episode of depression. Anything else bothering you?' asked Scrant. If she brought up the teenage episode he'd question her further.

The image of her basement prisoner flashed through her mind. An uneasy feeling caused her to place a hand on her chest, unconsciously betraying a *what have I done?* moment, and maybe causing Scrant to suspect a heart issue.

'Well I'm starting a new life the other side of the world, that makes it even more stressful,' said Brenda, shakily continuing her self-diagnosis. 'I'll be leaving friends, a job I've been in for years, my husband is buried here.'

Scrant nodded sympathetically at each revelation. 'Would you like me to prescribe something, a little pill to settle things down?' he suggested.

'Not keen on pills, what have you got in mind, are there any side-effects?'

'All drugs have side-effects but short term use of this particular drug will get you through the move at least.'

Brenda said nothing. Scrant took this as a sign of assent and started writing a prescription for Prozac.

He smiled and handed it to her before glancing at his watch. 'If there's anything else I can do, just book an appointment. Tell the receptionist it's urgent because you're off to Australia.'

Brenda went to the pharmacy next door. The heavily made-up chemist, whose scraped back hair displayed a line of white roots, said there'd be a twenty-minute wait, so Brenda texted a message to Raihana: *Coffee, asap x.*

The response from Raihana was not immediate. An hour had passed. Brenda was home Googling the side-effects of her new drug, when the mobile buzzed. Text from Raihana: *Something awful has happened. Meet me straight away, I haven't got much time.*

Coffee 4 Us was virtually empty. Raihana looked much paler than usual. Her eyes were red. She was sniffling and drawing breath in pants like a child trying to stop crying. The cortados were waiting. Brenda had ordered and had sat down in the Little Conservatory. They were alone. She'd checked for signs of Smithy, Barker, or Kev Strong; there were none.

Raihana sat with her eyes closed as if opening them might release another bout of tears. She sipped her coffee before looking at Brenda. They held hands across the table.

'What the hell's happened?'

'Mum and Dad are here. They rang from the airport and want to know where I live. I think they want to take me home to Lahore.'

On the face of it, Brenda didn't think this was such a bad plan. There seemed little point in Raihana trying to start a new life here. Obviously Pap wasn't going to feature much in her future. But she didn't want her leaving yet. She wanted closure, revenge, trial and retribution for all concerned.

She decided that now was not the time to mention her visit to Dr Scrant.

Brenda didn't like the sound of the side-effects of the antidepressants Scrant had prescribed. She'd made a brief memo of her symptoms: *feeling anxious, troubled, nervous*, before looking up the side-effects of *Prozac* (*Patients may feel agitated, nervous, shaky)*—exactly the same symptoms she was being treated for! Plus; anxiety, depression, suicidal tendencies, fatigue, stomach pains and difficulty obtaining orgasm (never had one, didn't want one). She thought of Arthur's cramp.

She Googled Yellow Pages for a mind doctor, psychiatrist or psychologist, she wasn't quite sure of the difference. There were a couple of local men in the same practice, with loads of letters after their names, specialists in dealing with *life crises:* depression, anxiety, phobias, OCD (whatever that was). She'd go private. Didn't want her dirty washing aired at the Health Centre.

She rang the number. A woman with a pleasant voice answered. 'Good morning, Janine speaking. Can I take your name please?'

Brenda gave her name and told Janine that she was about to move to Australia, going through a period of anxiety and depression, but didn't want to take pills.

'We have two consultants here. Our psychiatrist tends to prescribe medication.'

'What does the other one do?' asked Brenda.

'Mr. Starkey's field is Cognitive Behavioural Therapy, he teaches people how to handle a crisis situation. He uses various self-help techniques that really suit patients keen to be in control of their condition rather than taking medication with all the risks of side-effects.'

'No antidepressants then?'

'He doesn't prescribe medication at all, so can I refer you to him? He's our psychologist.'

Brenda had never heard of this cognitive therapy stuff, but she liked the sound of Starkey. 'When can I see him? It's urgent, I'm off soon.'

Janine covered the mouthpiece and called out to someone in another room.

'Dr Starkey can see you at four.'

'Today?'

'Yes. Please bring a list of any medication with you and wear loose clothing. You need to feel as relaxed as possible.'

Brenda thought she could already feel Starkey's therapeutic influence drifting over the phone line.

Chapter 56

Pap was feeling optimistic. His mood brightened, with the realisation that he *was* actually going to be let out. There were signs, something in the atmosphere had changed. He'd noticed Brenda getting quite anxious. She was forgetting stuff: toilet rolls, soap, a new disposable overall when he'd started to smell a bit, even had to remind her about his broccoli soup a couple of times. She fiddled around more, seemed less sure of herself.

His mind was working overtime. He lay on his bed and imagined what the process might be, following the release of Brenda's videos. He knew she'd shared them on YouTube, Facebook and Twitter. The press and TV news would be adding their bit and his guess was that people, seeing this poor wreck of a prisoner, must still be rooting for him. Not everyone of course, a few exceptions, the odd woman or two, perhaps a peeved husband. But he knew about people: show them a man in a cage and they'd want him out, especially as he'd done nothing wrong, well, not killed anyone or anything like that.

'Pap?' shouted Brenda from the top of the stairs.

'What?'

'Are you decent?'

Pap smiled. In all the time he'd been there, Brenda had never worried about his state of undress, another sign that something had changed. He felt it in his bones: Melvyn Greenstone's internment was entering its final stage.

'Another week or so and I'm going to let you go. Well, not exactly me, I've nominated someone special for that pleasure. I'll be up in the air and far away.'

Pap couldn't work out what this was all about. He could understand that Brenda wouldn't want to be around when her 'caged animal' was let loose. Maybe she thought he might make a dash for her and do some serious damage. But still, what *was* the fucking point of it all? She'd looked after him like any dedicated prison warder should, talked a lot about nothing of consequence to him, meted out a bit of punishment, rattled on about other stuff, probably gathered snippets from contacts she'd texted. But that was nothing, it really wasn't. Mentioned crimes against women more often than necessary. He'd got what she was driving at but they weren't crimes. They were all about bitter women having a moan.

If there was one thing Melvyn Greenstone hated, it was a moaner.

'What's been happening with those videos?'

'Shared them. I told you. They went viral, loads of hits, Pap, you're famous. Here's your soup.' She handed it to him without getting him to back off. Weeks earlier he would have grabbed her arm, given her a few Chinese burns 'till she passed him the key. But he knew, now, because she'd told him; Brenda never carries the key into the basement, it was left in the kitchen, *just in case*.

Brenda padded back upstairs, seeming forlorn, a plodding step rather than the confident one he'd got used to. She wasn't enjoying the scenario now. Pap took this as another positive sign, perhaps a realisation that she'd gone too far: dug a hole and forgot to stop digging. He guessed maybe the media coverage and police involvement had brought too much unwelcome attention. A jigsaw was being put together by his pursuers and Brenda was in the background, like a piece of landscape that didn't quite fit, until most of the picture had been completed. Then she'd drop straight in, completing the puzzle and ending the search. Unless he was let out before that happened, which would be a shame in some ways. He'd like the story to end with him the long suffering hero and Brenda banged up for kidnapping, mental and physical torture, theft (his mobiles), libel, impersonating him, giving his notice to quit to Simon. He could go on.

He lay supine on the bed, knees up to ease the ache in his unused back muscles, and rested his head on his hands clasped behind his neck. He stared at the ceiling.

He didn't care now, it was nearly over and when he got out he'd write that book and she'd get hate mail. He knew a few people in the publishing business; it would be his story, not hers. He was thinking that Brenda had unknowingly been his publicity agent. If the man in a cage video really had gone global, the end result would only prove positive once he was out. He'd look the victim then, whatever Brenda said. He'd use it in the promo video for his book. What should he call it? *Prisoner of Brenda* came top of the list. He'd remembered an old film starring Stewart Granger, about some king, kidnapped on the eve of his coronation to prevent him being crowned. *The Prisoner of Zenda.*

So a play on that title then, *Prisoner of Brenda* would be perfect. He thought it clever and amusing. It would stand out on the bookshelf in Waterstone's. A cover, maybe with a frame taken from Brenda's video, of him gripping the bars looking like, dare he admit it, Papillon. And way down in the corner, a small, very small pic of Brenda scowling.

He fantasised further, a film would be great. He could play the star part himself, 'specially now he'd lost weight. Who'd play Brenda? He didn't want her looking attractive. Pap had someone like the cruel Annie Wilkes in mind, the character played by Kathy Bates in the Stephen King film *Misery*, about a woman who kept a famous author captive, tying him to a bed and torturing him. Perfect. She'd scare the shit out of the audience.

Chapter 57

The reception at Starkey's was just as Brenda had imagined. The pleasant voice was a pretty girl in a smart suit, seated at a business-like work station. She smiled and stood up, offering Brenda her hand. 'Hi, Brenda, I'm Janine, the practice manager, pleased to meet you.'

Brenda took the tiny soft hand and tried not to crush the delicate fingers. 'Hi, Janine, pleased to meet you too,' she said, quietly impressed by the friendliness and comfort of the place. 'I didn't ask what the charges were.'

Janine handed Brenda a sheet, itemising treatment fees: First visit, one hundred and eighty pounds, follow-ups one hundred. Brenda thought this a bit steep but Janine, as if she'd anticipated her thinking, added, 'You'll be with Dr Starkey for about an hour and a half.'

Brenda sat in a comfy wrap around chair, picked up a copy of *National Geographic*, skipped absently through the photos of the Yangtze River and the Taj Mahal, and thought about Raihana. Brenda had given her opinion; Raihana should tell her parents exactly where she lived, welcome them, let them have their say and then talk through the options. Brenda reminded Raihana that she had the advantage, regarding a final decision. Her parents would be nervous, being in the UK for the first time, they'd need a bit of support too. They obviously didn't want to lose their daughter, so some sort of solution was on the cards. Brenda could be there for backup if needed.

'Dr Starkey is ready for you, Brenda,' said Janine, 'second door on the right, just give a couple of knocks and walk in.'

Brenda grunted as she eased herself out of the chair which seemed to have her in a fairly tight grip. She was ever so slightly nervous as she walked toward Starkey's office. She tapped the door gently.

'Please come in, Brenda.'

She hesitated. The voice was deep and slow, how she'd imagined a hypnotist might speak.

Dr Starkey was sitting in a wingback chair looking out of the window across a small garden. His profile displayed a high forehead and large nose with a shallow dip halfway down like a miniature ski slope. He was fairly young, forty at a guess.

'Don't you just love birds?' he asked, pointing to a couple of finches taking off from a nearby tree.

'Yes,' she said, unsure how much she needed to reveal of her interests in nature at this particular juncture.

He turned to face her. *Flesh tunnel*! He had a hole in his ear big enough to put her pinkie through. She was thrown, imagining one of Arthur's Black and Decker special attachments drilling through Starkey's flesh, prior to the stainless steel ring being fitted. His image had taken a dive, psychoanalyst to punk rocker in a few seconds. But he had a good face, broad smile, neat teeth, a trim beard. Brenda tried to stop staring at the hole in Starkey's ear.

'Please take a seat. I try to avoid saying, 'How can I help?' I find it quite irritating, don't you?'

She did. In fact it was something that made her want to smack people in the face. 'Yes I do,' she said. 'Same as people saying 'to be honest' or using the word 'like' at every conceivable moment.'

He nodded vigorously, grinning widely in agreement. Already soul mates and they'd only just met.

'Most people come to me for therapy because, one: I avoid taking them down the drug route and two: I want to see them through a particular crisis in their lives and teach them how to handle similar situations in the future. It's more fast track, because they play a big part in their treatment; a shared responsibility rather than giving out pills to cover up the real issues.'

She wondered what Starkey's drug-prescribing partner would think of this rather undermining comment.

'Pills have their place, of course, but I get the impression you're the sort of person who needs to understand and solve issues, rather than risk unpleasant side-effects or an addiction to antidepressants.'

It was Brenda's turn to nod vigorously.

'There is no doubt in my mind that what we are about to go through together will be invaluable. Please tell me why you're here,' said Starkey. He steepled his fingers and rested his chin on the tips of them. He stared unblinkingly at Brenda.

'Well, I er, um, not quite sure how to start...'

'Take your time.'

'My husband died a little while ago. I've coped well so far, but now I'm about to leave everything I know, to start a new life in Australia. I've given up my job, the home I've lived in for the whole of my married life and am about to say goodbye to all my friends. Suddenly I'm starting to get stressed, anxious, can't sleep.'

'You shouldn't be surprised, Brenda, but what's troubling you most?'

'Everything seems to be happening at once. Overwhelmed, I suppose.' But she wasn't overwhelmed by the things she'd just mentioned, she was handling them well. The problem went beyond that, the Pap problem. The net was closing before she was ready to leave. Too many people were searching for Pap and caring about him as if he were a poor lost soul in the hands of terrorists or kidnappers, too many people getting close to finding out about her involvement. She shouldn't be here lying her head off, what was the point in that?

Starkey gave her the spiel. He didn't want to delve into her past, unless there were particular things she felt were pertinent, didn't want to know about every little problem she had, just to teach her some coping strategies for getting through her life right now; some deep breathing exercises, relaxation, some tips on living in the moment; concentrating on things, when the mind starts to get bogged down with stuff.

'Are you in a relationship?' Starkey queried.

'Not right now. Not since my husband died.'

'Does it bother you? Is there someone waiting in Australia; family or a new man in your life?'

'Yes.' Uncle Fred who lived in Australia didn't count in the way Starkey had meant, but she would be seeing rather a lot of him.

'Is sex important to you?'

'Yes,' she lied.

Starkey smiled as if he'd mentally hit the right button: attractive lonely woman, deprived of intimacy and making big life decisions, a recipe for a breakdown.

'I think you'd benefit from hypnosis. Have you tried it before?'

Brenda's buttocks twitched and after feeling so relaxed her whole body tensed up. She'd seen stage hypnotists getting people to do stupid things and talk in funny voices. Then she imagined spilling the beans, about Pap being held captive in her basement.

'It's not what you think it is. The way I use it ensures you are in control the whole time, you won't say anything you don't want to say, you'll just find it easier to talk, more relaxed.'

'And you're bound by law to keep everything secret?' asked Brenda, needing assurance.

'Of course. Nothing will go outside this office,' confirmed Starkey.

'What about Janine, your assistant?'

He hadn't been asked this question before. 'She only fronts the office. All files are only accessed by me. They're locked away in that cabinet,' he said, indicating a spot outside of Brenda's view.

Brenda turned to look at the tall cabinet with its steel drawers, checking, as if she doubted it was capable of holding her intimate revelations securely.

'I'll be awake and in control the whole time?'

'In control, yes.'

'Supposing there's something I'd rather not talk about?'

Starkey wasn't surprised at this. He never quite understood why patients wanted all the help they could get for their mental health but held back on what he considered the most likely catalyst for their condition, the unspoken problem.

'That's up to you. But don't you think it might be more helpful to talk about anything that comes up and not limit yourself? No pressure, but let's see how we go. Let me explain the process first, demystify it. Then you can decide. Remember, you are in control and we can stop whenever you want.'

Starkey explained the process. It wasn't like the stage version at all. In fact Brenda felt that hypnotism with Starkey would be no more than a bit of relaxation with a question and answer session thrown in. And she could pass on some of the questions, if she so wished.

Starkey asked Brenda to sit in a fine-looking chair. It moulded to her body, supported her back and neck, holding her hips and thighs in check like a comfortable corset. She was looking out toward the small garden. Birds pecked at a feeder. Her eyes felt droopy before he'd started.

'You look relaxed already, Brenda. But let me take you through the process.' Starkey took on the air of total calm. 'Close your eyes, if you find it easier. Breathe in deeply but smoothly, hold for a few seconds...then let the breath out slowly. Imagine all the tension is leaving with the breath. Then picture yourself in a pleasant scene, anywhere: a beach, a forest, a place you like to relax in. You could even use the scene you are looking at right now, outside this window. Thoughts will interrupt at first but don't hold on to them, let them pass through your mind like a fast forward film.'

Brenda kept her eyes open at first but there was a problem. She ended up staring at Starkey's flesh tunnel. She closed her eyes. First image was Pap, eating his broccoli soup, then Arthur in his workshop, then Starkey's ear, then a beach in Australia; an image she held for several seconds before other memories took over.

Surprisingly, she started to remember her kiss with Pap, just before he groped her. She could feel herself colour and hoped Starkey hadn't noticed. That kiss from Pap was her first with another man since marrying Arthur. Pap was drunk of course and she'd had a couple of drinks too, but when he groped her, *bam*, horror of horrors. She'd imagined it was the prelude to a rape, that moment when the man loses control and turns from a persuasive date into a monster. She'd never forget that moment in her life. It had scarred her more than anyone would have thought possible.

'Are you alright, Brenda? You're breathing a bit too hard, try to slow the breath to an easy rhythm. Now, very gently, open your eyes and we'll talk.'

Brenda felt hot and embarrassed, imagining that Starkey had read her images. Maybe she'd said things out loud, she couldn't think straight. The effect was like waking from an interrupted dream and only remembering a very small part of it.

'Tell me a little more about yourself. What do you want most from life, right now? What's stopping you achieving it? What are your greatest fears?'

She only had a problem with the last of these questions, her greatest fears. Brenda said nothing. Starkey was always ready to accept a silent patient as a sign of buried problems. Secrets.

'What set your breathing off just now? My guess it was something deep inside suddenly remembered. It's common in these circumstances, perfectly normal, healthy, a sign of progress. Don't be embarrassed. You don't have to talk about it, but if you do, I guarantee it will help. Freeing the mind in this way usually brings up important stuff hidden in one's memory. Sometimes for years...'

Starkey sat back in his chair, touched the stainless steel ring supporting the flesh tunnel, scribbled a note and asked Brenda if she needed a break.

She didn't. Starkey had hit the nail on the head without knowing it. He'd got her to stop and think, really think. This revenge against Pap was not just about other women. It was about her. Brenda's streak of self-imposed celibacy since Arthur's death could have ended badly with Pap, if he'd caught her completely alone. She'd felt violated.

'Let's carry on. I need to get sorted. I think I dozed off. Did I say anything?'

Starkey didn't want to reveal too much at this point. She'd rambled on about something, words missing but obviously distressing.

'You mentioned Arthur. Was that someone you know?'

'Arthur was my husband. He died...'

'Do you want to talk about him?'

'Not really. It was a good marriage. A bit dull, some might say, but Arthur was a good man...not romantic or anything.'

'Did you have a reasonable sex life?' queried Starkey, feeling this the right time to ask. Usually sex or money came somewhere in the cause of people's unhappiness.

Brenda felt a mild flush. 'Occasionally. Didn't set the world alight. He wasn't that keen, Arthur, obsessed with his hobbies.'

'But you did have sex, now and again?

'Rarely.'

'Did you find that a bit frustrating?

'Sometimes.'

'Were you attracted to other men?

'Never thought about it much.'

'Did your husband have a nickname?

Brenda had problems making any sense of this question. She frowned. No.'

'Then who or what is Pap?'

Chapter 58

Kev Strong, Barker and Smithy were now in bed together. Not literally of course, but they were collaborating, piecing together information that bound them as surely as lovers sharing their most intimate secrets. They collaborated on the Angie/Gloria connection, factored in the scarlet woman Margo, and knew there were more. A lot more, if their combined instincts and gathered evidence was anything to go by. They agreed that Brenda, who'd acknowledged living in the area where Greenstone was dropped off, had become an irritating itch somewhere in their thinking. On reflection, Barker and Smithy concluded that the photo of her at the seminar took on a different hue when scrutinized further.

'She looks a bit shocked, don't you think? And he looks like the cat that got the cream. We agree that Greenstone's a bit of a lech. Maybe something happened between them?'

Kev Strong was certain something had gone on. Every picture tells a story. And if you're a hard bitten journalist, something he considered himself to be, then it was obvious from their expressions that Brenda knew a bit more about Greenstone than she'd let on.

'I think we should speak to her again,' said Barker, 'might be a good idea if you approach her first, Kev.' The Greenstone case had granted them the intimacy of calling the reporter by his first name. Barker and Smithy though, had kept to their stock monikers.

'It would be less threatening than the police turning up,' added Smithy.

'How do you want it played, or do you want to leave it to me?' asked Strong.

Smithy and Barker connected telepathically, they didn't want him taking too much control.

'Just say you heard a taxi had dropped the missing man in the area. The police wouldn't reveal much about the house-to-house, so you're trying to get an article together, talking to people, assuring them he's not dangerous. Play it easy, just looking for a comment or two. She'll play dumb, of course, but you might pick up on body language. Get inside the house if you can.'

'Might go pear-shaped,' said Kev, unusually pessimistic.

'Then we'll bring her in for questioning. We need to know when she actually intends to leave the country too. Check that out please, Smithy,' said Barker.

Chapter 59

Raihana decided on a baggy cardigan and shapeless coat for her trip to the airport, because her pregnancy was now evident. She'd parked in a hurry and hadn't remembered where the bay was. Her parents had come through passport control and customs. Mother had smiled broadly when she saw Raihana, but reduced it to a half smile when Khan nudged her in the ribs. Khan was not smiling. His face didn't change nor did he utter a word as Raihana spent twenty minutes locating her car, going from floor to floor clicking her remote button until the headlights flashed recognition, halfway down a distant aisle.

Khan claimed the front passenger seat and looked around the inside of the car as if he was about to buy it but had spotted several defects. He grunted. Raihana felt claustrophobic, her parents seemed to have taken up every conceivable space in the vehicle. Mother talked about the trade in the Shalmi Market, how everyone missed her, how business was picking up again after a period of calm, doing well, but not as well as when Raihana was running it. Khan spoke, but only to correct Mother on a few points.

Raihana took off her coat but kept the baggy cardigan on, holding back from the inevitable revelation. She was sitting opposite her parents in the tiny flat. The atmosphere was grim. Khan was waiting for hospitality; for his daughter to offer some refreshment after his long journey.

'I will cook some food, then we can talk.' It was hard for Raihana to take the initiative but she couldn't bear the thought of them all going to bed without discussing their plan. Tomorrow was not an option.

Khan refused the mint tea that Raihana offered and asked for water.

'Is it safe to drink?' he asked.

'Safer than anything you've ever tasted, Dad.'

'A small glass then, just in case,' said Khan.

Raihana ran the tap and half-filled a tumbler, placing it on a coaster next to him.

She held back a smile. This fussiness, from a man who drank contaminated water at home; there were high levels of arsenic in Lahore city water. He was going to make his visit as difficult as possible.

Raihana was getting hot. There was never going to be a good time to announce her pregnancy. She took off the cardigan and stood directly in front of her parents. Mother's eyes went straight to the spot. Raihana made no attempt to soften the blow.

Khan took in the swollen belly then looked away, as if doing so would erase what he'd seen. If Khan was to make a single facial expression encapsulating anger, fury, disgust and helplessness in one go, this would be it. His eyes filled and seemed to bulge. He raised both fists as if about to strike his daughter, before dropping them limply to his side. His whole body sagged, like a man who'd survived a terrible beating.

The doorbell rang, and rang.

'I've come to help,' whispered Brenda, after giving Raihana a hug. She walked into the silent room and picked up on the tricky atmosphere.

'This is Brenda, my best friend in England. She helped me find a place to live here.'

Khan, looking half the man he was ten minutes ago, stayed put but gave a cursory nod toward Brenda. Raihana took this as a positive sign, concerned that he might have ignored her friend completely. Khan sniffed his water before sipping it gently, like tasting a new medicine that had yet to complete its trials.

Mother, not deigning to look at Khan, rose and gave Brenda a gentle hug. Brenda hugged back.

'Is there anything I can do to make your stay more comfortable?' asked Brenda.

'We don't intend to stay long. Where is the man who did this to my daughter, is it that monster, Melvyn Greenstone?' asked Khan, pointing rudely to Raihana's stomach.

Raihana and Brenda were stunned by his sudden directness. Raihana looked pleadingly at Brenda and let her eyelids fall, long lashes touching her cheeks.

'Yes, he's disappeared, nobody knows where he is,' said Brenda, aware that Raihana might crack, and spill the beans.

'Have your parents seen the video then, Raihana? The one of...' she just stopped herself saying Pap, '...Melvyn Greenstone?'

'Yes, they saw it in Lahore. They knew who it was. Melvyn's video is all over the world.'

'Exactly! Then why haven't they caught this criminal? We heard the British police are the best in the world. They must have found him by now. Even the Lahore police could have caught him,' said Khan. 'We want him to pay for what he's done before we take my daughter home. She can't stay here. She will never be able to afford it, what with a new child and no husband. She will be on the street and have to beg for the rest of her days,' he said, looking as if all life had drained out of him.

'We love her. We want Raihana home,' pleaded Mrs. Khan.

Khan frowned at his wife. Admitting to love someone by actually speaking the words was against his religion. Well, his principles at least.

Brenda reasoned that Raihana would fit perfectly into UK life. She was bright, her English was excellent. She'd have no problem getting a job and Pap would be dealt with, one way or another.

They could get help with the baby. But now was not the time. Anyway, she had no idea whether the Khans could persuade Raihana to go back with them. That's what they seemed to have come for. And if she was to be totally honest, Lahore was probably the best place for her. Raihana's friends, family and work were there. She had a thriving business and a loving family. But the expected hostility from the locals could push things either way.

Brenda sat on the only empty chair and let out a long sigh. The Khans turning up was not part of her plan. But in an odd way, they were going to be helpful. All she needed to do was keep them here for a few more days.

'I'll prepare some food,' said Raihana. 'I don't need help, sit and talk to my parents,' she added, looking pleadingly at Brenda.

Brenda felt awkward. Khan looked permanently fierce and Mother made weak attempts at concealing the fact. 'He's had a long day, a tiring journey, he's not as young as he used to be,' she said, covering his hand, which failed to respond. Brenda guessed that even on a good day, Khan would still look a daunting prospect.

He grunted at, *not as young as he used to be*, a sign of disagreement.

'I've never been to Lahore,' said Brenda, 'What's it like?'

Khan clearly didn't want to talk about Lahore. The history of the British Raj stuck in his gullet, so coming to the UK was seen as a step too far for this particular Pakistani.

Mother smiled. 'It is like a whole country squashed into a city, over six million people live and work there. We have hundreds of temples, mosques, churches, shrines, and a big tourist industry. We are getting more modern all the time.'

Khan fidgeted in his seat, feeling uncomfortable about Lahore becoming modern.

'One day soon, we expect to have a metro, like your London tube,' said Mother, looking at Brenda for a response. To Mother, a metro was the height of sophistication in a modern city. To Khan, it was a slippery slope to God knows where.

Brenda smiled, realising that Mother was trying to show similarities between Pakistan and the UK rather than the differences.

'Sounds wonderful, is it beautiful? Is it safe?'

'Very beautiful and quite safe, no gangs.'

Brenda thought of the news reports coming out of Pakistan; Al-Qaeda, ISIS and terrorists, sprung immediately to mind. But what did she really know about this distant country? She decided not to bring up this darker side.

Raihana called from the kitchen, 'I'm bringing the food in. Could you give me a hand, Mother?'

Mother was up and in the kitchen before you could say Melvyn Greenstone and definitely on a mission. She half closed the kitchen door. 'Raihana, are you coming back with us? I need to know, your father is expecting an answer and I am expecting one too. Reassure me now, then we can all relax,' she said, wringing her hands.

'I need a few days, Mother. Father should speak to me, and soon. I hate his overbearing silence. It doesn't help, it won't solve a thing. Problems have to be discussed!'

'Try to understand, Raihana. You've no idea what it took. Your father has proven his love just by being here. Look at the history of his family, his culture, his religion and you will see this situation is unprecedented.'

Raihana felt a huge surge of love toward her father. She'd lived in Pakistan long enough to know how strictly culture and religion were observed. Underneath it all she knew her parents wanted her happiness and were keen to try and understand Western ways. They needed to, as in the modern Lahore, business was global now and some pretty ambitious characters were appearing on the trade horizon.

Her expectations of Melvyn Greenstone ever being part of her life had been reduced to nothing. But Pap needed to know he was the father of her baby. He should pay for the child's upbringing. Right at this very moment, she had no idea how she was going to achieve that.

Chapter 60

Kevin Strong didn't like the new camera as much as his old Nikon, the one that Gloria had dismantled on the street. This one was undoubtedly more powerful, with a decent range of lenses, trillions of pixels and an infinite capacity to store all his shots, but it was too complicated.

He was after an interview with Brenda and with a bit of luck a photo opportunity—she was on his list now. Plus, Barker and Smithy were beginning to put together a file they'd promised to share with the *Daily Moon*, providing they had some editorial control of any article that came out of it.

The reporter waited up the street until he saw Brenda park her car. He wanted to catch her before she bolted the front door and refused to come out. Something she was entitled to do, especially given the interview he had in mind.

Brenda looked toward Strong, saw the camera swinging in front of his chest and slammed the boot hard. Strong twitched, then waved.

She wanted to play it cool. This was going to be difficult. She smiled.

'Kevin Strong, *Daily Moon*,' he said sticking his hand out for Brenda to shake.

'I know who you are, Mr. Moon. I've seen you around.'

If Strong hadn't been a reporter, he might have blushed. 'It's

Strong, not Moon. *Moon* is my paper! I wonder if I could have a word,' he said.

She ignored Strong's correction. 'Is this about the house-to-house, the hunt for Melvyn Greenstone?' Brenda surprised herself. But best get in first, he wouldn't expect that.

'Yes. Just a question or two really, the police are getting nowhere, this is roughly where he was last seen, wasn't it?'

'I think we both know that, Mr. Moon, it's hardly a secret. I don't want to talk out here, where's your car?' she asked.

'Blackstone Road, round the corner,' he said, lacking the courage to remind her she'd got the name wrong again.

Brenda put the shopping back in the boot and walked toward Strong. Reflexively, a *déjà vu* moment, he put the camera in his bag and zipped it tight. 'We'll talk there,' said Brenda, keen to take control of the situation.

Strong was disappointed but he could hardly force his way into the house. He should have waited 'till she'd got through the front door, and rung the bell after all. But hey, he was about to get an interview!

Brenda was gathering herself for the grilling. Moon couldn't have too much of a clue or the police would be all over the place.

Strong opened the car door for Brenda, then moved a pack of cigarettes and crumpled anorak off the passenger seat, before sitting next to her and placing his camera behind. He wouldn't be taking a pic here. Then he pulled out the photo of *that* seminar from the glove compartment. She'd guessed it was coming. Mentally she'd run through as many possible scenarios as she could dream of. This was high on the list.

'Do you remember this picture?'

'Sure, big seminar but not that recent, that's Greenstone,' she said, sticking her finger roughly in the area of Greenstone's left eye.

Strong drew breath mentally. He wasn't expecting such compliance. 'Did you know him well?'

'Only met him once, at that seminar, seen him on telly of course, kidnapped by terrorists they say.'

'We don't think so, rumour has it a woman from his past might be taking revenge.'

'Well don't look at me,' said Brenda, surprised at how calmly the words came out.

Strong pointed to the photo again. 'He's looking at you as if he knows you.'

'You must have heard, Mr. Moon, that Greenstone likes his booze and is a known womanizer. Public knowledge. He was drunk at that seminar and tried it on with every woman there. I was just unfortunate enough to be standing next to him for that photo. My bad luck, as it turns out.'

'Any idea if your neighbours know him?' he said, changing tack.

'Doubt it. Ask the police, they did the house-to-house, they would know, wouldn't they?'

'Suppose so,' Strong nodded. He'd already asked Barker and Smithy and they'd assured him that no one had ever heard of Greenstone. Not until they'd seen him on the news, caged up.

'Can I ask you a question, Mr. Moon? Why did you spy on me and my friend?'

Strong was caught out. He didn't expect this either. 'I found out you'd called in at the police station, saw you in the picture with Greenstone, courtesy of Barker and Smithy, and heard you are going to start a new life, Australia wasn't it? A reporter would think that's a good enough reason to follow the link. Who's your friend by the way?'

'None of your business really, but she's from Lahore. I helped find her a place to live and we hit it off.'

'She doesn't know Greenstone by any chance?'

'No way. She's from Pakistan, first time here.'

'Why did she come?'

'Are you sure this is necessary? She's just looking at business opportunities. She's a successful business woman and like the rest of the world, keen to go global. Check her out. She's nothing to do with Greenstone.'

Strong made a mental note. He'd certainly check her out, and ask Greenstone's boss if he'd ever done business in Lahore.

'Thanks for your time, Brenda. One last question.'

'Fire away.'

'Does your house have a basement?'

She tried to swallow the constriction in her throat and coughed. 'The four houses on my side of the street do, the older properties, they've all been filled in with rubble and concrete to try and stop the rising damp.'

She wanted this interview to end, now. 'Is that it?'

'Yes, thank you. Can I give you my card?' he said, thrusting one directly into Brenda's hand.'

'When do you fly out by the way?'

'Next week. Lots to do, so please excuse me.'

Strong dashed round to open the passenger door for Brenda. He smiled and thanked her again. Brenda had some trouble walking normally, her legs starting to buckle. *Deep breath, walk straight, don't look back.*

Strong had pulled his bag across to the front of the car, taken his reporter's notebook out and made some entries;

- Find out more about Brenda's friend from Lahore.

- Visit Simon and find out if Melvyn had connections to anyone in Lahore.

- Check council records to see if all the basements mentioned had been filled in: building regulations required, reports of rising damp etc.

- Remind Barker and Smithy that Brenda is going to fly out next week. Suggest they check the basement situation at her house, use one of those drug raid door bashers you see in crime dramas. No necessity for Kevlar vests or guns, but they might need a warrant or something.

Kevin Strong had not been able to trace any other link between Greenstone and Brenda. Maybe she was telling the truth. But his reporter's nose kept twitching like a detectorist's bleeper hovering over buried junk or treasure.

Chapter 61

She put a call through direct to Emirates. They had single seats in economy and business class left, flying out in three days' time on the 13th of May, nearly a week before Brenda had originally planned. They'd hold the seat for a few hours. She'd no intention of cancelling her original Virgin flight, because she'd had an idea. Her boss knew the exact day she was due to go and what with the press and police sniffing around, they'd get it all wrong and she'd have flown the coop a week earlier. But there was lots to do. She didn't mind sacrificing a grand for a flight she'd never take. The situation was that dicey.

Barker and Smithy checked Brenda's Virgin flight, due to leave on the 19th of May, and were relieved to know they had nearly a week to check things more closely. Strong popped into the station with news of his interview.

'She's a cool one, I'll say that for her, didn't bat an eyelid when I talked about Greenstone. I threw in a question about the basement.'

'What do you mean?' asked Smithy.

'Asked if she had one, she said it'd been filled in.'

'We can check. Not sure if she needed permission to do that. Ring the council office, Smithy, ask for Building Control, see if there's been any application to fill in a basement from Brenda Brown at number twelve.'

Smithy went off to his desk. 'What else did you find out?' asked Barker.

'Not too much, you know most of it. She's leaving for Australia soon, says she never saw Greenstone before that networking event. But she was too cool for my liking. Doesn't feel right.'

'Well there's certainly no evidence she knew Greenstone, apart from that one snap of her at the seminar.'

'Either she really didn't know him and doesn't bother to look at the news or there's a whole lot more than she's telling.'

'There's no other person to follow up. No one's come forward, no one's asked for ransom money. Although Greenstone seems to have had a lot of woman trouble, none of them have exactly threatened to kill him. We've checked the two wives, I'm happy with their interviews. I don't think they're involved.' Barker tapped a pencil against his teeth.

In no time at all, Smithy came back from his call to the local council. 'No regulations needed to fill in a cellar boss, it's part of the inside of the house, you don't need building regs or any other application. So the basements in The Avenue may or may not have been filled.'

Strong looked at Barker, Barker looked at Smithy.

'Brenda Brown said all four basements on her side of The Avenue had been filled in,' said Strong.

'Get your jacket, Smithy, call on Brenda's next door neighbour. Make up some cock and bull story. Say you're from the council, concerned about the water table since the heavy rains or something, ask if they've got rising damp or whether they've filled their basement in.'

'That won't tell us whether Brenda's filled hers in,' said Smithy.

'But if her neighbour hasn't, she must be lying: that means they haven't all been filled,' said Strong. 'And that alone will be reason enough to pay Mrs. Brown another visit.'

Brenda was at home when she saw Smithy call next door. She wasn't too bothered, the neighbour only knew what he'd seen on the news. Nothing Brenda had done so far could have had alerted him to anything. Or had she missed something? But why wasn't Smithy in uniform? He was holding a clipboard. A plastic name tag was pinned to his lapel.

'Good morning, sir,' said Smithy holding his fake council tag up high, for Brenda's neighbour to see. 'Can I take a few moments of your time?' Smithy's clipboard displayed an official looking questionnaire: five questions quickly cobbled together for the occasion and printed on paper headed, *County Council Damp Survey: rising water table levels in rural England.* The neighbour invited Smithy into the hallway.

'What's this about?'

Speaking with some authority on a subject he knew nothing about, Smithy responded. 'You may have heard, sir, that water table readings for the area have risen due to the season's high rainfall. We're making sure that houses with basements have not been unduly affected.'

'If we had, you'd be the first to know,' said the neighbour, smiling. 'We don't have many problems here. The houses are well built. Proper builders in those days,' he said, tapping the door frame as if it were irrefutable proof of his claim.

Smithy had no idea when *those days* were. 'Can I take it you have no rising damp in the cellar, no mould or anything like that?'

'None at all, in fact we filled ours in years ago, snug as a bug, we are.'

Smithy's heart dropped. 'Do you know if any of your neighbours have filled in their basements?'

'Being council, you probably know there's only a few with basements in The Avenue, but I couldn't really say how many are filled in, you'll have to ask the neighbours. Brenda next door is in, give her a ring?'

Smithy didn't want to do that. She'd recognise him and that would really put her on alert. 'Thank you, sir, you've been most helpful. I need to call the office first.' He walked down the street to his parked car. The neighbour waved him off and closed the door.

Was Brenda watching? He hoped not. The building control surveyor had been helpful. Smithy now had a list of the houses with basements and the phone numbers of those residents, so instead of knocking, he phoned the neighbour the other side of Brenda. He introduced himself, said they could check with council offices if they wanted authorisation (but hoped they wouldn't) gave the same spiel he'd given before, then asked the critical question. 'Have you filled in your basement?'

'No need to, we keep all our bits and pieces down there. Dry as a bone.'

'Has anyone filled theirs in?' he asked, knowing damn well there was at least one.

'Only the old boy the other side of Brenda Brown, as far as I know.'

'Thanks for your time,' said Smithy.

Smithy felt a surge of optimism. Brenda had lied, quite unnecessarily if she was innocent. That meant she'd lied for a reason. He couldn't shake off the idea that her lying about filling in the basement when she hadn't, could only mean one thing; Brenda Brown was holding Melvyn Greenstone prisoner there.

Chapter 62

Gloria and Angie had yet to meet. But Kev Strong was determined that this should happen quickly. He wanted to step up the ante on the publicity, put the pressure on Brenda by waylaying her friend from Pakistan and generally create an air of tension.

He'd approached the 'Free Melvyn' protesters and found most of them to be professional complainers with no real connection to Greenstone. The reporter had wasted a lot of time getting nowhere and time was running out. He was now thinking the unthinkable; of breaking into Brenda's house himself. Within minutes, he'd know whether Greenstone was there or not. He'd take a camcorder and when his story was out and the prisoner freed, his breaking and entering would be seen as heroic.

Strong followed Brenda at a distance. He'd vowed never to disguise himself in order to acquire news, but was about to break his own rule. He stuck on a false beard with some disgusting adhesive. For the first time in his adult life he wore trousers with a sharp crease and borrowed a tweed jacket from his brother, an accountant in the city. To complete his charade, Strong bought a pair of glasses, off the shelf in Boots, and topped it all off with a peaked cap.

He watched Brenda leave her house and make her way into town. Sitting opposite Coffee 4 Us he saw her friend turn up with two older people, Asian presumably, possibly the girl's parents.

They looked solemn. Even disguised, he wasn't taking the risk of following them in-to the coffee shop, so he watched and waited patiently.

Raihana sat opposite Brenda with her parents either side. Khan surprised them all by ordering espresso and a glass of water. Mother had the same as the girls, cortado. The Khans had warmed to Brenda, she'd been keeping an eye out for their daughter, been kind, welcomed her into the family home, just like people did in Lahore, even though Brenda didn't appear to have a family as far as they could tell. This was the first time they'd ventured outside Raihana's flat since their arrival two days ago.

Kev Strong's beard itched like mad. He couldn't see well through the specs either, hadn't bothered to check they were for reading only. Removing them, he peered across the street, and waited. It would be tricky, once they came out.

They left Coffee 4 Us and Strong followed them to the end of the street. He wasn't sure if they were travelling by car; his was close by just in case. But they walked to Raihana's flat, said goodbye to Brenda and went inside. Perfect. Brenda walked on to Butts.

Kev decided now was the time to check out Brenda's property. Wouldn't take long, he had a decent set of lock picks which he'd used on a previous mission for the *Daily Moon*. Not sanctioned or legal, of course, but all he needed was a quick peek at Brenda Brown's basement.

He parked in Blackstone Road and walked casually round the corner toward the house. The Avenue was quiet, everyone at work. He made a pretence of knocking gently at the front door, aware that no one was in, but a neighbour might be watching. Holding a small parcel, to give the impression he was about to deliver something, he looked up and down the street. No curtains twitched so he walked up the side path and around to the back of the house.

The neighbour Smithy had previously tried to get information from, watched Strong from his side landing window on the first floor, before pressing the start button on his iPhone video recorder. From this position, he could observe the whole of Brenda's sideway. Anyone below would find it virtually impossible to spot him; people rarely looked skyward when they were up to no good.

The neighbour tracked Strong as he moved to the rear of the house, and watched him testing Brenda's kitchen door. It didn't appear to budge, so the trespasser pulled a bundle of metal implements from his pocket, removed his glasses and proceeded to fiddle aggressively with the lock. All on camera.

Strong heard a police siren a long way off; *someone in trouble*, he thought. He carried on picking the lock. The siren got louder, the police car sped down The Avenue and stopped close by with a screech of tyres. He panicked but walked as calmly as he could down the sideway—straight into the arms of a police officer. They searched him, confiscated his press identity card and removed the lock picks from his jacket. The officer told Strong he'd been spotted trying to break into Mrs. Brown's property. He read Strong his rights and informed him he was being arrested for attempted burglary and that, by the way, his beard was coming unstuck just below his left ear. Then he handcuffed him.

The neighbour stood at the front door smiling and suggested the video clip be sent to the station for evidence. However, being caught in the act seemed proof enough. Strong tried not to look like a sneaky burglar, but what with the handcuffs tight around his wrists, his false beard coming adrift and a bunch of burglary tools being deposited in an evidence bag, he failed.

Back at the station, Barker and Smithy were not amused. Kev Strong, as if this was a perfectly normal situation, casually removed the remainder of his false beard.

They copied the video for station use. Strong, picking Brenda Brown's lock, appeared on Smithy's computer screen. It was shot from above and not that clear, but an expert witness would have a field day. They digitally enhanced the video to prove, in no time at all, that the criminal was indeed Kev Strong.

'What the hell were you doing?' said Barker.

Smithy opened his mouth to ask virtually the same question—ruling out more suitable four-letter expletives as unbecoming to a respectable police officer.

Strong tried to think of the best way to explain his disguise and plan. 'I wanted to prove once and for all that Brenda Brown was hiding something. Hopefully Melvyn Greenstone. But now it ain't gonna happen.'

'You're right, it ain't,' confirmed Barker. 'She'll sue the pants of you, Strong, and I for one won't blame her,' said Barker, slamming down the wedge of paperwork. 'The neighbour's insisting we formally charge you. I have no choice.'

'I still think she's hiding something,' said Strong, weakly.

'Not enough proof to enter the place. We'll never get a warrant either, not on the evidence we've got so far.'

'And if the papers get hold of this, you'll be front page news in your own tabloid,' added Smithy, unhelpfully.

'So can I go?' asked Strong.

'Not yet, we need to fill in the paperwork for the record, but there's no real reason to keep you banged up. I don't want to have to apply for a restraining order, Strong, so you need to promise you'll keep away from The Avenue until we say so.' This turn of events had compelled the officers to revert to addressing him as Strong, just in case they were seen as being too friendly with a petty criminal.

'I promise,' said Strong, already planning to speak to Brenda's friend. She must have visited Brenda at some point, they seem close.

Two hours after he'd left the station, Strong stood across from the entrance to Raihana's flat: a solid green door, set back on the left hand side of a small mini-store. He didn't have to wait long before two elderly people came out, followed by Raihana who locked up before leading them toward the local park.

Chapter 63

Brenda had left Starkey's clinic in rather a hurry after he'd mentioned Pap. But the psychoanalyst was already piecing together fragments of what she'd told him and a story he'd heard on the news over the recent days, one that seemed to be having a disproportionate amount of air time: the disappearance of Melvyn Greenstone. While under hypnosis, Greenstone was one of the names Brenda mentioned. Nothing revealing, but Greenstone wasn't a common name, her appointment had been urgent and she couldn't wait to get out of his clinic, once he'd mentioned Pap.

'Don't be put off, Brenda,' he'd called, as she'd bolted from his office. 'It's not unusual to react like that when something triggers a memory. Make another appointment. I really think I can help...'

Brenda had passed Janine, who'd stood smiling but said nothing, as Starkey's latest patient, flushed and tearful, headed for the street.

Brenda thought she'd blown it, said too much, but once she'd got over the shock of hearing someone else mentioning Pap's name and remembering that Starkey was sworn to patient confidentiality, the tension eased. She remembered that lovely feeling, sitting in his clinic, slipping into a state, not unlike the anaesthesia when she'd had her hysterectomy. Suddenly, she wanted to talk to Starkey again. Reaffirm that her revelations would not leave his file and share the heavy load she was bearing with someone else used to sharing heavy loads.

The phone rang in Starkey's office. 'Good morning, you're through to Janine, Dr Starkey's secretary.'

'Janine. It's Brenda, Brenda Brown, I saw Dr Starkey yesterday. I want to apologise for rushing out so rudely after you'd been so kind. I'm really sorry.'

'Not a problem, Brenda. It's not always easy in there.'

From that remark, Brenda felt that perhaps Janine had been in the chair herself. 'Can I come back and see Dr Starkey again. Please? I've calmed down. I don't know what came over me, hormones probably,' she said, giggling like an embarrassed schoolgirl. 'I'll be alright, promise.' Brenda was starting to sound pathetic, desperate, slightly scatty even.

'Dr Starkey would be delighted. He hoped you'd be back and thought you'd made excellent progress, for a first visit. He has a lunchtime appointment free today, one o'clock. Shall I book you in?'

'Please, Janine. See you then.'

Brenda turned up at one with a box of chocolate ginger for Janine. *Everyone likes chocolate ginger.*

Oddly, she couldn't wait to get back in *that* chair, must be a mother's womb thing, a subject she expected shrinks to talk about, read it somewhere.

Starkey smiled and came straight to the point. They both knew why she was there. 'Are you ready to talk about Pap?' he asked.

When he'd mentioned Pap on Brenda's first visit and she'd burst out of his office, he may have thought she'd just lost her dad and his death was too raw to speak of. But Starkey had worked it out and decided it was rather more complicated than a simple bereavement.

'Pap is not my dad, if that's what you're thinking. Got over Father's death years ago, we weren't that close. This is someone else, someone who hurt me, someone I don't like…You're not recording this are you, Dr Starkey?'

'Of course not, I'm not even taking notes, I want you to feel completely free to talk, off the record. That's what you want isn't it? I know this is tough, Brenda.'

'Thank you,' Brenda sighed. She hardly noticed the flesh tunnel this time, only the feeling of peace when she sat in *that* chair and he started to hypnotise her.

She slipped under his spell with hardly any effort on his part. This usually happened when the patient was ready to be totally honest. Brenda trusted him and knew that whatever she said now would never leave his clinic.

He used his bog standard professional dialogue to start, a kind of warm up for the big event: *Are you comfortable? Don't forget, you can stop the therapy at any time. Don't hold your breath, get that nice easy rhythm we talked about last time—let go.* What surprised him most was how quickly everything came out, like an avalanche or spray from a jet hose. The force of her staccato confession, because that's what it sounded like, took his breath away. She never mentioned her husband. A string of names peppered Brenda's story, but the one that came up most often was Pap. And with it Starkey's realisation that she was the person holding Melvyn Greenstone, the guy who'd been all over the news and internet for weeks. He was pleased with a connection he'd already considered; surely Pap and Melvyn Greenstone were the same man!

'Do you have a plan for Pap, Brenda? Would you like to talk about why you're holding him and what you intend to do with him before you fly off to Australia?' Starkey pitched this gently as if trying to talk her out of leaping off a tall building.

'Not sure now. The police and media have been getting close. I'm under suspicion, I know it. Not long 'till I leave though. They won't catch me before I go, will they?'

Starkey said nothing. He wouldn't know how to answer that question.

'Will you leave Pap in the basement?'

'Well I'm not likely to let him out, am I? He'll kill me.'

Starkey was worried now. He couldn't possibly leave Greenstone to die. 'So what's the plan?' he ventured.

'I'm handing the key to someone. They'll know exactly what to do. The end game won't be pleasant. Not after what he's done to all those women: messed up their lives…and mine,' she added.

'Can you tell me who that someone might be?'

Brenda sat up with a start, completely alert, before slumping back in her favourite chair.

Starkey wasn't surprised at the sudden end to the session. From his experience, as mesmeriser extraordinaire, he knew that patients would not reveal things that deep down they didn't want to. Hypnotism, in the world of the psychoanalyst, was like that, it would not, could not work against the patient's will, nor should it.

'How did I do?' asked Brenda, rubbing her eyes as if she'd slept for hours. It was, in fact, just over ten minutes. She took the glass of water from the table at her side and waited for Starkey to reply before sipping it.

'Very well, Brenda. Do you feel better for getting things off your chest?'

She did indeed, a problem shared and all that stuff.

'You told me all about Pap,' said Starkey, fingering his flesh tunnel.

'You won't tell anyone, will you?' She took a long drink from the glass of water, wishing it was gin.

There was no doubt in Brenda's mind that Starkey had done her a power of good. She wondered quite how he'd managed to make such a difference to her burden. He hadn't done much; spent a few minutes helping her relax, asked a few questions, but nothing like the interrogation she'd expected. She couldn't be sure of exactly what she'd been prompted to say under hypnosis, but that didn't matter. The purpose of this visit was to let rip and not hold anything back. The feeling was that of stripping naked in the sun and running into a warm sea. Something she'd never actually done, on account of her upbringing.

Starkey, however, was not surprised at how well Brenda had performed. It often happened in his practice. 'Letting it all hang out' couldn't help but solve problems for a whole bunch of people.

When he'd reassured Brenda with the words, *Nothing will go outside this office,* perhaps he should have said, *Nothing will go outside this building*, because cases were discussed in practice meetings. One was due at the end of the day. Psychiatrists and psychoanalysts swap ideas and perform psychological post mortems on difficult cases and tricky patients. The patients' names are kept anonymous, of course, but no doubt the practitioners present may well recognise certain characters, especially if they appear to be the subjects of current press coverage.

Two more experts from another practice joined the case discussion group, but the floor was opened by Smut and Starkey. Mr. Smut, the psychiatrist, had not taken to Starkey's ear tunnel. Told him so as soon as he'd had it done, that it looked totally unprofessional, juvenile even, and added that in his opinion it made Starkey less credible as a therapist. Starkey wasn't worried by Smut's analysis but it had put a little distance between them. They were less chummy, less likely to consult each other when they had a problem. But this Brenda Brown case was such a coup for Starkey, he wanted Smut's take on it, if only to brag about the infamy declared in his clinic.

It came around to Starkey's turn, to talk about an interesting patient or problem he wanted to share. Smut looked stonily at his 'punk' psychoanalyst, but warmed to him once Starkey started talking about his latest case, picking up immediately on the story connected with the huge media coverage of the prisoner, Melvyn Greenstone. He settled back in his chair, quite taken with his colleague's account.

'So what do think her real problem is, from a psychoanalytical point of view?' asked Smut.

'Although Miss X talks about all the women Mr. Y has betrayed. I can't mention his name but we all know who *he* is...'

'Melvyn Greenstone,' interrupted Smut, grinning.

Starkey didn't answer. Smut was testing his partner's professionalism; never reveal a patient's name. Then Starkey told Smut about Brenda's visits in more detail. ''What do you think?' he asked, at the end of his disclosure.

Smut almost forgot the flesh tunnel. It was like having the old Starkey back.

'I think she's a woman seriously scorned. This is not just about Greenstone's women and wives. I think Miss X feels unloved, not sexually fulfilled. Suitors not exactly queuing round the block. She has been married, of course, but it doesn't sound like her husband was that interested either, from what you've told me. She's been celibate, probably since he died. This is about Miss X thinking a man was seriously interested in her, expecting love maybe, but betrayed just when her dreams were taking flight. She wanted revenge. She wanted to punish the man, and the only way she could be in control of his suffering was by kidnapping him, and depriving him of things he enjoyed, get him to think outside his underpants.'

Starkey had a similar take, but kidnapping, going to the lengths Brenda had, seemed totally over the top. Maybe they were wrong. Or maybe, despite many years in the business, they still had no idea what depth of feelings such a situation could incite in a woman. Brenda was not mad, he was sure of that, yet her actions were bordering insanity.

'What should we do?' asked Smut. 'If she's leaving, we can't let Greenstone rot in a cellar, can we?'

'What then?' asked Starkey, aware there was only one possible decent way out. One choice, or they might have a death on their hands.

'You could drop an anonymous letter into the police station,' suggested Smut.

'Saying what?'

'You don't have to say much, a few words: *Check Miss X's cellar,*' no need to elaborate,' said Smut, pleased it wasn't his problem.

They'd save Greenstone, but if word got out that he'd betrayed patient confidentiality, would anyone ever trust Dr Tristan Starkey again? So Starkey wasn't sure about the note. It would need to be posted, not hand delivered; couldn't risk going in and being recognised or arrested—as an accomplice even—a nightmare scenario for all concerned.

They were still struggling with the enormity of what Miss X was doing. It really didn't add up, an overreaction to her situation was putting it mildly. There must be more, something else, something they'd all missed; the police, the press, everyone.

Starkey, despite—according to Smut—being reduced in standing by his flesh tunnel, took control with his latest theory. 'There is one thing that would change everything. And I think I know what it is, though how we're going to prove it in the short time we have, I really don't know.'

Smut, an arrogant individual at the best of times, was itching to know what he *might have missed*. 'I'm listening. Spit it out, Tristan.'

Starkey sipped very slowly from his glass of water, noticing the impatience in Smut's expression. This reaction in his colleague gave Starkey the feeling of being in charge. He could see Smut getting irritated by the whole thing, maybe a little envious of Starkey's coup.

'Miss X must have known Melvyn Greenstone before all this,' declared Starkey.

'Wouldn't that be an obvious line of enquiry for the police?' said Smut dismissively. 'They'd have found that out fairly quickly and checked all the women in Greenstone's past, surely.'

'But they must have missed one, because her one-woman campaign could not possibly have been triggered by the reasons she's given us. Just work it out. A little kiss by someone she possibly fancied, until he got a bit rough and put his hand up her jumper would not, on its own, make even the most unstable person kidnap a man and keep him in a basement for weeks. Think of the time it must have taken to organise? The risks? And, providing she hasn't killed him already, what on earth could she possibly get out of it?'

'Any past association, if there was one, must have been way back. No one's come up with the evidence so far, because if you listen to the news or read the papers, they only ever show Greenstone in his cell, or some photographs of him abroad on business, never anything about his past relationships.' Starkey steepled his fingers and fell silent. His colleagues adopted similarly thoughtful postures.

There was knock at the door. Janine came in with coffee. She smiled and gave Starkey the morning copy of his favourite tabloid. On the front page was a picture of Greenstone at the seminar and right next to him, staring straight into the camera, was Brenda Brown.

There must have been twenty people in that photograph. Starkey decided not to point Miss X out to Smut, who was scrutinising the picture and reading the article below. They were appealing for anyone in the photo to come forward and talk about their relationship with Greenstone. The article didn't mention Brenda but as far as Starkey knew, Miss X was Brenda Brown, Greenstone's captor.

'I also believe that Miss X has a history of anxiety and depression, maybe even suicidal ideation. Difficult to prove as she's come to me privately and didn't want me to contact her GP,' said Starkey.

'Of course she's anxious and depressed,' huffed Smut. 'Why else would she come? So would we be, in her situation, but suicidal ideation? What on earth did Miss X say that gave you that impression?'

'It's not so much what she said but what she didn't say, what she left out. And I was talking about a history of anxiety and depression, not her present episode.'

'So..? Without her actually saying she felt suicidal, how can you be sure?'

'Not absolutely certain, but my years of experience in the field draws me to that conclusion.'

Smut had to admit that Starkey was very successful in practice. He could never quite grasp the idea that talking, alone, could possibly make people better. Smut's view was that depressed people suffered chemical changes in the brain and the only obvious way out was to prescribe chemicals that would put things right.

'Well. Even with all that information, there's not a lot we can do,' said Smut, taking the high ground. 'You say she's off to Australia soon, Tristan? I still think we should get that note into the police station and make sure Melvyn Greenstone isn't left to die. Get Janine to type it up and I'll pop it in the post now. It'll be at the station by morning.'

Starkey didn't want Smut popping anything in the post. If anyone was going to write the note, Starkey would type it himself. He didn't want Janine asking too many awkward questions about the man in the basement, and didn't want Smut to get any more involved in the case than he already was. After all, Brenda Brown was Tristan Starkey's patient!

Chapter 64

She'd read or heard somewhere, that when someone is at your front door, choosing between bell or knocker, it depends on the type of visitor and how urgently they need to grab your attention. A neighbour might give a polite single press on the bell; a postman, a little more of a sustained ring so you don't miss it, and him not wanting to hang around with your parcel. People selling stuff tend to knock. Jehovah's Witnesses and political campaigners—both convinced they have been sent by God with an urgent message—tend to give sharp raps of the knocker.

The vigorous knocking Brenda was hearing now, combined with the continuous ringing of the bell until it started to fizzle and fade electrically, was obviously of some urgency. The kind of visitor who might be accompanied by armed police and a warrant to search the house. Handcuffs would be available and a woman police officer present to ensure there were no sexist issues involved in the arrest. Brenda's car was in the drive, so whoever it was would know she was home, nothing to do but answer the door. If this was the end, so be it.

She opened the door quickly, hoping a confident manner might be in her favour. The woman standing before her was not a police officer, or a Jehovah's Witness. It was someone she wouldn't have guessed at seeing again in a million years. With her hair swept tight back in an unruly bun, a long green coat that looked as if it had been made out of an army blanket and not a scrap of makeup, stood Olive, Brenda's mother.

'Mother?'

'Ten out of ten, Brenda. I can see you still have part of your brain intact.'

'Where's Arthur?'

'Dead.'

'What of? 'Spect he electrocuted himself fiddling with that old Black and Decker, or got himself buried under a collapsing wall somewhere,' said Olive, suggesting causes without waiting for Brenda to respond.

'Heart attack,' said Brenda sadly. 'I'll put the kettle on.'

'Won't be stopping, Brenda, a cup of tea would be good, but don't bother to make up a bed.'

As soon as she saw her mother at the front door she recalled, with utter clarity, why they hadn't been in contact for all those years. Olive was a controlling spiteful woman who maintained that the plainer you looked the less likely you were to be bothered by the sex maniacs who she believed had virtually taken over every UK town and city.

'I've seen the news about Melvyn Greenstone, our nemesis. It's you, isn't it? You've got him down in Arthur's cellar. I want to see him. Now.'

'What makes you think it's me?'

'Saw the news, read the papers, didn't I? Heard the police were looking around the area where Greenstone was last seen; The Avenue and Blackstone Road, and bingo, thought of you, remembered you living in the locality. I called in years ago, when Arthur was alive. No one in, or at least no one answering the door. We're damaged women, Brenda. I'm not surprised how far you've gone with Greenstone. You must have been smouldering for years, something had to give.'

Olive was right. Like a long lit fuse spluttering slowly toward a stick of dynamite. 'Please leave, there's nothing more to talk about. He's my problem now. We've been over and over our past, what you've been through, what happened to me. I'm sorry about Dad, angry at him too, it needn't have ended like that. We could have worked through it together.'

Olive looked down at nothing in particular and let out a huge sigh, one of defeat and resignation.

'I'm off to Australia soon and it's all taken care of. Pap will get his dues. No need for you to be involved,' said Brenda.

'Pap?'

'It's a nickname,' said Brenda, not about to go into detail.

'I don't intend to get involved, Brenda. I'm not here to interfere with your misspent life. But I do want to have my say, then I'll be gone and you'll never see me again. I'm going to check the basement for myself.'

They never got on, but the words 'never see me again' tugged at Brenda's heart.

'I don't want you to go down there.'

'Why, is he dead?'

'Course he's not dead. However badly you think of me, I'm not a killer.'

Olive pondered this a little too long for Brenda's liking, as if weighing up whether her daughter was actually capable of murdering someone.

'Then if he's not dead, I want to see him. Half an hour and I'll be gone.'

'I don't have to give you the key, Mum. Leave it, it's over, there's nothing else to do or say.'

'Give me that bloody key or I'll go straight round to your favourite journalist, Kev Strong, and talk to him instead.'

Brenda's complexion went from argumentative red to puce. 'You know S-t-r-r-Strong?' she stammered.

'Let's say our relationship is recent and cosy. He doesn't know who I am, not yet. I told you I'd been following the story and I took the trouble to find out who the local reporter was. I quite like

Kev, he'd sell his soul for a scoop. He's invited me out for coffee, after I've finished my business.'

'So how'd you get to talk to him without setting off alarm bells?'

'Told him I knew you way back, we don't look like mother and daughter so that didn't trigger any suspicion. I said if he gave me a bit of info about what was going on, I'd give him a story really worth printing at the end of it.'

'The end of what?'

'The end of my stay here. Co-operate and I may not have that coffee with Kev. Depends on how this little scenario pans out.'

'I'm your daughter, we've been through a lot. Considering my wishes is not going to work then?'

'No point trying to bond now, Brenda. We've tried before, it never worked, did it? I'll follow you down.'

Brenda unlocked the basement door. Olive heard two healthy clicks as Brenda pulled the retaining bolts back. No creak, it was well oiled and well used. Olive was more nervous than she'd ever admit. It had been some time.

'Give me thirty seconds, Mother. Please.'

Olive grunted impatiently. Brenda took that to be a 'yes'.

Pap looked lazily up from his bed. Had she come with his food? He didn't bother to get up.

'I've got a visitor for you, Pap.'

She'd never seen him move so quickly. He hadn't seen another soul in weeks. He suspected she must have been tumbled somehow, someone was coming to get him out, he was sure of it. Or was this the end game Brenda kept rattling on about, some hit man coming down the stairs with a baseball bat, or an irate husband linked to one of his women about to give him hell?

He looked toward the staircase and heard the clumping of sensible shoes, a steady step, more womanly than manly, but only just. The hem of a long green coat appeared followed by a worn handbag and the rest of Olive with her pale tight face, devoid of any makeup or sympathy. She squinted at the wreck in the cell, her eyes adjusting to the poor light from the single bulb. Brenda turned the dimmer up a notch.

'That's not Greenstone,' said Olive, moving dangerously close to the bars.

'I wouldn't get too close if I were you,' said Brenda, 'He'd do anything to get out of there.'

'Who the fuck is this?' asked Pap, suddenly relieved to see a little old lady looking at him sternly, as if he'd just failed his 'O' Levels.

'Guess,' said Olive, as she began to realise this was after all, the notorious bastard, Melvyn Greenstone.

'Mary Poppins?' asked Pap, chuckling with the confidence of a man who'd concluded she was no threat. 'What did you do, Brenda, pay some homeless person on the street to give me a fright? Or is she an undercover cop? Oh I get it, the handbag prop. It's Miss fucking Marples.' He laughed again, both hands on his stomach, shaking with exaggerated mirth. His relief had made him flippant. 'I've never seen her before, so what are you up to?'

'Look closer, Pap.'

He screwed up his eyes, feigning fresh scrutiny of the woman in the green coat. 'Nope. Never seen her before, ever, cross my heart and hope to die.' He was certain.

'It's been a while,' said Olive.

'Give me a clue then? What's your name?'

'Olive.'

He shook his head. 'Can't help you there, don't know any Olives.'

'Olive Burton.'

Pap's memory experienced a sudden eddy of flashbacks. Then he passed out and hit the concrete floor like a sack of potatoes.

Brenda wanted him alert. She didn't want Mother hanging around, questioning her while Pap decided when to open his eyes. He might choose to lie around for a bit, and listen in to her and Mother while they discussed the situation. So she gave the back of Pap's head a quick three-second blast from the Karcher, which had been kept in the corner—*good to go,* as they say. Olive looked shocked but Brenda guessed it was more to do with her daughter's ingenuity than the ferocity with which she delivered Pap's wake up call.

Pap stirred, looked at Olive, then Brenda and backed up against the furthest wall of his cell. He was shaking, he started to cry like a baby, suddenly realising the shit he thought he was in was about to become a whole lot deeper.

'No point crying now, it's all a bit too late. A million years too late if you remember. That's when you wrecked our lives, Greenstone. Stop blabbing and I'll tell you how you're going to pay for it.' From her worn bag, Olive took out a plastic folder containing sheets of typed paper. 'You need to sign these—both copies.'

'What this?' he said, wiping his eyes with his sleeve.

'Can't you read, Pap? You used to be able to, back in the old days.'

Brenda looked on, completely taken aback by her mother's actions.

Pap read the document, then read it again. If he was pale before, he was ashen now. He looked at Olive then at Brenda and back again. He rubbed his palms on the soiled boiler suit, as if trying to wipe something unpleasant off his hands. There was a mini-nuclear reaction going on inside his body, a rising mushroom cloud promising devastation. But Pap was no stranger to tricky situations. Being cooped up for weeks had taken the edge of his snappy response to adversity, but he still had some battery life.

'It's not legal, Olive, not worth the paper it's written on. If you want this watertight you'll need a solicitor then you'll have to go through the courts to enforce it. And I'll fight you all the way,' said Pap, pleased for the protection afforded by the bars of his cell.

Olive's thin lips turned up at the ends, hardly moving her pale cheeks, the barest semblance of a smile. 'I have better assurance than that, Pap,' said Olive, rather taking to Greenstone's nickname. 'I have the press on my side. They'd have real fun if this was let out. Heard of Kev Strong? He's hot on your case, hungry for more dirt.'

'How would I have heard of him? Don't know any reporters.'

'Well let me tell you a little about Kev. He's close to solving the mystery of where you are. According to all the stuff I've been reading and watching there's quite a bit of public support for you. It's only there because people don't yet know the truth. Conspiracy theories abound. Some poor idiots even think terrorists are involved. Now here's the rub, Pap. Sign this and settle your dues and you may still keep a bit of that support, not exactly a hero, but at least a victim who really looks the part. I'd never have recognised you myself, until Brenda told me who she had hidden in her cellar.'

'That's a lie, Mother,' interrupted Brenda, 'and you know it, I never told you he was here, you just turned up out of the blue. No wonder Pap didn't recognise you, I hardly recognised you myself.'

'How come no one is recognising anyone?' growled Olive. 'No matter, I'd have bet my pension he was here and you let me down to see him without too much persuasion.'

Brenda was furious. 'What's the paperwork about?'

'It's between me and Pap. No need to get involved—unless he refuses to sign, then the whole world will know.'

Pap was holding the papers. 'I need a pen.'

Olive took a black biro out of her bag and handed it to Pap. The pen was the first potentially dangerous weapon he'd got hold of since he'd been there, but useless now. He put the papers on the floor and signed both copies.

Chapter 65

Barker, Smithy and Kev Strong had re-bonded, after a fashion. Strong, who Smithy and Barker now considered a loose cannon, had been charged with attempted burglary, then released on some technicality. The intrepid trio had shared what information they had, the most recent being that Greenstone's boss had confirmed that his erstwhile imprisoned employee had indeed done deals in Lahore. Strong was now trying to get an interview with the lady from Pakistan. And then he'd report back, hopefully with enough hard evidence to authorise a raid on Brenda's property.

Monday morning, Raihana left her flat alone. Kev Strong dropped into an easy pace alongside her. She recognised him.

'I'm Kev Strong, by the way, *Daily Moon*,' said the reporter, offering his hand which Raihana ignored. 'We've nearly got Greenstone now,' he said. 'The police are closing in. Do you want to comment, as someone who knows someone who knows him?'

'I'm not stupid, I know you've been following us, we spotted you. You're wasting your time if you think Brenda knows where Greenstone is. But I'll make a bargain with you,' she said, keeping her cool. She knew how important the next couple of days were, if she could only play him along for a bit.

'Not sure I can do that. The case is nearly closed, I don't want to deprive the public of its right to a free press.'

Raihana was not taken in by the reporter's apparent attack of ethics. 'Please yourself. Do you want something to add to your scoop or not? I need a guarantee though, that you won't mention names, I don't want my parents dragged into this.'

Strong offered Raihana a cigarette. She waved it away but he lit one for himself, while he thought the situation through. 'How do I know it'll be any good?'

'You'll find out soon enough, if you agree. And if you don't, you'll get nothing. If you go ahead and print anything at all, without running it by me first, you'll be in big trouble.'

'How come?'

'Because I have something on you too. Something other tabloids might be interested in. On film.'

Strong laughed, 'Can't have.'

'Don't forget, I'm Brenda's friend. Her neighbour called and said you'd been arrested for breaking and entering Brenda's property. Why would you do that to a woman living on her own? If she'd been at home you'd have frightened the life out of her. Your failed burglary attempt is all on video. The neighbour gave us a private view straight from his mobile; you're quite recognisable, despite the disguise.'

Kev reminded himself that reporters don't blush and just about managed to abort the scarlet wave creeping up his neck.

'I'll be honest with you, Miss...What shall I call you?'

'Raihana, is fine.' She didn't even want to hint at the family name, Khan.

'Well, Raihana, we... no, I, thought that Brenda had something to do with Greenstone's disappearance. Thought you were in on it together at some point. I'm an investigative journalist, I have to follow all leads. Not always nice, but that's how we catch the baddies. We make mistakes and I'm sorry if this was one of them.' He wasn't going to reaffirm his suspicions, certainly not to her friend, that Brenda was still very much in his sights.

'Then have we got a deal?'

'I've no idea what you're going to tell me. If it's not to do with Greenstone I'm not interested, but if it is, then yes, I'll leave names out.'

'Of course it's about Greenstone. What else?'

'Okay, tell me what you have.'

She opened her coat to reveal a swollen belly. 'This is his child!'

Strong was speechless. Controlling his jaw drop reflex, he quickly undid his reporter's bag and took out his notepad.

'I came here to find Melvyn Greenstone and make him pay. My parents think he'll never be found and in any case, they don't want me anywhere near him. They want me back home in Lahore.'

Kev scribbled a hurried note. A photo was crucial for his article: everyone loved a visual and he was certain he'd got her on side. How hard could it be? He took a few long drags of his cigarette before crushing it into the pavement with the flat of his shoe. 'Any chance of a photo, just a distance shot? You can cover your face, we'll keep you anonymous?'

'How many women do you see around here wearing these clothes? I'd be recognised in no time.'

'I have to ask, I'm a reporter. The article will mention you're from the East, can't avoid a bit of publicity if you want the truth out there. Of course there are others in Surrey dressed like you but no one's going to hunt you down, are they?'

'Probably not, but you did!' she reasoned.

'Approached, not hunted, Raihana. Anyway, we're here now and this is an important interview, for you and for me. Shall we carry on?'

She nodded.

'And how do you know Brenda Brown?'

'She helped me find a place when I came to the UK. We became friends, she's been good.'

'Did you know that Brenda had met Greenstone?'

'Yes of course I knew. That's the only real reason you're interested in me, isn't it? She met him at a party or business seminar, ages ago.'

Kev thought this response a bit too neat. 'Do you know where he is now?'

Raihana laughed. 'How would I know that?'

Kev had to play it a little more cautiously. 'So how did you meet Greenstone?'

'He was on a business trip to Pakistan, buying up products for resale in the UK.'

'And what, he just put you in the family way?'

Raihana didn't like how cheap that sounded. But to the eyes of the world that's how it would seem. 'In the East, Mr. Strong, things are changing, the world is changing. We are learning to trust other nations, foreigners, we do business with them. The West seems sophisticated and attractive. I was taken in by Mr. Greenstone, had this stupid romantic idea he was in love with me. What that relationship did and how it affected my family life will stay with me forever. He will eventually pay for his mistake, when they find him of course.'

'So can I pitch this story of you as a young innocent woman from the East being exploited and badly treated by the Man in the Basement, forsaken by her family and left alone to search for him; the treacherous womaniser and bigamist who ruins women's lives on a global scale?'

'Sounds about right. By the way, in case you think I'm hiding Melvyn Greenstone, Mr. Strong, I most definitely am not, but I'd like to know who is. I've come all this way to find him and I want Greenstone to pay for his mistakes.'

'A photo would help…You can check it out first, you'll be in control.' He'd get his pic, whatever it took.

Raihana, placated by his explanation, covered her face and stood across the street. He took a number of distance shots, his sophisticated camera clicking away as she walked toward him. Raihana asked him to stop, then removed the covering from her face.

Kev Strong checked the images.

'Show me,' she said.

Strong tilted the camera screen toward her and swiped through the dozen or so pics he'd taken. Raihana nodded at each one. She was unrecognisable in every shot.

Raihana filled in the rest of her story, though heavily edited, about her business dealings with Melvyn Greenstone. He turned a page and took more notes, glancing up to see if she was kidding when she mentioned Greenstone's magnetic attraction. She was quite a beauty, Greenstone was a tubby-ish chancer. Strong realised that Raihana was not going to let anything slip about Brenda. But he had a damn good story.

'I saw you with two older people, are they your parents?'

'Yes, they want to take me home.'

'Are you going?'

'Yes, but not quite yet.'

Strong gave all this info to Barker and Smithy. 'Well, well, well,' said Barker. 'The way this is going, it wouldn't surprise me to learn that Greenstone would rather stay where he is.'

'I'm going to search all the basement properties in The Avenue. If we target the lot, Brenda Brown can't complain she's been singled out.' Barker looked up the relevant documentation with regard to a search and angled his computer screen toward Smithy, to show a warrant is only needed if the owner refuses to allow entry:

Q: When can the police legally search my premises?

A: If you give police the permission to search your premises, then this can happen at any time. Section 8 to 18 of PACE, 1984, gives the police statutory protection to enter and search your premises for evidence. These powers can be put into practice with or without a search warrant.

'Get on to it, Smithy, will you? Put all calls straight through to me, saves delay. We've still no proof, but Brenda's name keeps popping up all over the place. The wives have calmed down, the ex-girlfriends are now silent and the girl from Lahore is not a suspect.'

'Should we question Raihana's parents?' suggested Strong, choosing to disregard his recent conversation with Raihana. Anything goes when there's a story to be had, he reckoned. 'They must be pretty pissed off about their daughter and Greenstone. Perhaps they're in it somehow.'

'Doubt it, they've only been here a couple of days.'

'Perhaps they're in for the kill. Not kill as in death, I don't mean. I Googled family relationships in Pakistan, they can do nasty things to each other when daughters stray from the fold. Extramarital affairs are not tolerated, even amongst their own people, never mind taking up with a spiv from England.'

'Well let's sort the Brenda Brown thing out first, before questioning Miss Khan's parents. If we've made a mistake, she can be on her way,' said Barker. 'And if she refuses to let us in, we'll have her anyway.'

'I've got a feeling that something significant is going to happen. And very soon,' said Strong, 'Raihana is going back to Lahore with her parents she says, but not quite yet. What's she waiting for? Brenda is about to fly off to Australia and as far as we can tell, no one knows exactly why she's going, something vague about a long lost uncle. *To start a new life*, doesn't explain much, but the words conjure up a certain amount of suspicion. The wives and girlfriends are keeping pretty quiet. Lull before the storm,' said Kev, forgetting where he was, about to light another cigarette, only to have it pulled straight out of his mouth by Barker.

'Let's take a look at the facts, reasons to give us a case for entering Brenda Brown's house. She knew Greenstone, probably better than she's led us to believe. He was dropped off by taxi in the area of The Avenue and Blackstone Road on the night he disappeared. A girl from Pakistan, pregnant by Greenstone, makes close friends with Mrs. Brown, who finds a place for her to stay. The friend's parents arrive, to take her home presumably, around the time Brown is getting ready to leave for Australia—with Greenstone still missing. The wives, as far as we know, are in the clear. There's no evidence that he's met up with any of his old flames. Brown lied about her basement. We can only think of one obvious reason she'd want to do that. Obvious now at least, she's hiding something, whether it's Greenstone or not, we're about to find out.'

Chapter 66

The North Terminal at Gatwick was buzzing. Saturday night, and half the world seemed to be on their way out of the country. Brenda checked in at the Emirates desk with a certain amount of anxiety. She wondered if next week's Virgin flight would show up through some Internet link, flashing on *check in* screens across the globe: a passenger on one flight booked in for another; some sort of terrorist alert system.

Brenda christened the Emirates check-in girl, the 'bag lady'. Bag Lady smiled but Brenda's ticket made the machine flash alarmingly. She was asked to wait. Bag Boss was called for. People took Brenda's place in the queue. The machine repeatedly refused to accept the ticket. Bag Boss held the ticket up to the light, muttered something under his breath, then made a phone call. He nodded at whatever was being said at the other end. Brenda was anxious; someone might have alerted the police, or found out about her booking with Virgin. He kept nodding and whispered something to Bag Lady.

Brenda was unable to contain herself. 'Is there a problem?'

'Sorry to have to ask you this, Mrs. Brown...'

Brenda was sweating, her hands clammy, beads of perspiration trying to assemble in the deep lines on her forehead.

'...but did you print your boarding pass off in draft quality?'

'What?'

She kept calm but was inwardly tearing her hair out, thinking she was about to be arrested and all they were worried about was the economy of her bloody printer cartridge!

'Perhaps you'd reset it by mistake. Draft quality doesn't leave the bar code solid enough to be validated, the detail shows up too pale to be recognised by our scanner. I've checked the details on your ticket manually, it's valid, I'm pleased to say. We'll issue you with a boarding pass but it's worth remembering about the print issue in future,' he said, giving Brenda a sympathetic smile. 'Thank you for choosing Emirates, Ms. Brown,' he added, leaving her wondering if he was being sarcastic. It clearly stated Mrs. on her passport.

She remembered now, setting draft quality. All those extra letters! Pap had made her a lot of work.

Brenda almost fainted with relief. She placed her case on the conveyor, an identification tag was stuck on, and Brenda's bag travelled smoothly along toward the Emirates Airbus 380. First stop, Dubai.

Always a nice feeling, when your bag trundles off to the plane and you can walk freely around the shops and restaurants with your passport and boarding pass nicely tucked away. Nothing to stop her leaving now.

Brenda chose Jamie's for her bite to eat, ordering a bacon sandwich and coffee. It was noisy and crowded. Now and then a police officer walked by, but rarely looked into the cafe.

The bacon sandwich reminded her of Pap aborting his hunger strike. She wondered what he was doing right now. First thought; *Brenda hasn't brought me any soup*. Second thought; *Brenda's not here today*. It would be deathly quiet. Third thought; *Brenda has gone, after all, but forgotten to let me out. Cow.*

Brenda's phone rang. 'Hi, Brenda, it's Raihana. Everything alright? Checked in yet?'

'Everything's fine, all okay your end? Got the keys to let the new people into number twelve for me?'

'Yes, I took the other set to Raymondo yesterday, as a backup. He was a little surprised that you hadn't dropped them in yourself.'

'I couldn't possibly have told him about the earlier flight. He might have spread the word then we'd be snookered. He'll get over it. Mum and Dad okay?'

'They will be, once we leave England. I'll tie things up for you first then we'll be gone. I'll be travelling back with them after all. Some of the Shalmi Market crowd will shun us. To them, wayward daughters should be severely punished. But I belong in Lahore. I can tell already that Dad will learn to love the baby. He's drinking the water without sniffing it and talking about taking me home. I'm certain it will be a boy. Just what Dad needs, to help with the business.'

Brenda didn't understand the significance of water sniffing but guessed from Raihana's tone that it was a positive sign. 'How close are the police?'

'Very close. My friend Kev Strong,' she giggled, '...says they're poised to search your house. They still seem to think you're flying out next week; they've got your Virgin flight number, departure time and everything. I didn't inform them otherwise.'

'Good girl, Raihana, it's been fun. Well most of it has, a few dodgy moments, but it will all be worth it. I hope we'll meet again. I'll visit. Can't be that far to Lahore from Australia.'

'About six thousand miles, I think,' said Raihana, sniffing gently before blowing her nose, disguising her sadness.

Brenda was going to miss Raihana, even thought they might both have ended up in Australia together at one point. But Brenda could see the love in her parents' eyes, when they were together. Despite Khan looking as if he might wring his daughter's neck on occasion, it was because he was scared of losing her. Men always get angry when they're scared, that's why they're frightening most of the time. That was Brenda's theory anyway.

Brenda checked her watch and wondered what Pap would be doing now—well not exactly doing, he wouldn't be doing anything, not yet. But what would he be thinking? Probably still wondering where the hell his soup was. He'd be getting hungry now, ten hours without anything to eat. He wouldn't have long to wait, there was a new carer on the way, though maybe not with the same menu in mind.

Then she thought how close she'd got to being caught. If she hadn't left the other flight booking in place, God knows what would have happened. She thought of Barker, Smithy and Strong having extra cups of tea before searching Brenda's house: *plenty of time, lads, we've got another week yet.*

Ha, bloody ha, thought Brenda. *I've won.*

Chapter 67

Being deprived of normal everyday sights, smells and sounds had bestowed certain qualities on Pap. His senses had been sharpened. His ear could detect sounds he would not have previously heard and he could see and mentally magnify every defect in the walls, floor and ceiling. He hadn't seen his own face, there was no mirror, but he often lay there studying his arms and fingernails as if he'd observed them for the first time. It was peculiar. His nervous system had become ultra-sensitive. He sensed when a rain cloud was approaching, just by the change of air quality entering the small vent which had guaranteed enough oxygen for his survival. Dust motes circulated on warmer, drier days. He watched them in fascination.

He ran scenarios of his life through his mental movie screen and tried to change the script, edit out the bad bits, a virtual post mortem before sewing the whole sorry parcel up as if it were a gutted cadaver.

He could hear something now. He'd got used to Brenda and her strong perfume. He could detect her mood from the way she opened the cellar door and negotiated the stairs down to his cell; could tell when she was in shoes or slippers, whether she had food, by the smell.

He'd noticed a big difference when Olive had taken the stairs; a different sound, different atmosphere about the place, even before she'd appeared. The clatter at the basement door now was different again, it wasn't either of them. Someone seemed to be having trouble opening the door, a clumsy kind of noise like a key rattling around in an awkward lock... Then click, click, followed by a palpable hesitation, maybe someone who didn't know he was here. A surge of optimism overcame him. This must be it. Someone was going to let him out!

The door finally opened and a smell of musky perfume drifted towards Pap. Not Brenda's fragrance, but he'd smelt it before somewhere. He gripped the bars and tried to prepare himself. It was definitely a woman; flat shoes, a pair of baggy cotton trousers, a shift covering most of the upper half of the body, and carrying a bulging shoulder bag. A beautiful but unsmiling face appeared as the woman checked it was safe to continue down the stairs. Perhaps she thought he'd got out and was preparing an attack! Pap froze, when he saw who it was. He hardly dared look.

Raihana couldn't believe this was Melvyn Greenstone. She'd seen the YouTube video but he'd deteriorated since then. His hair was matted and wiry, his cheeks more hollow, his eyes sunken and dark, flushed with small red veins. He was stooped, using the bars as if to hold himself up. His beard had completely changed his face. If Brenda hadn't told her what she'd actually done, Raihana wouldn't have believed it. She'd have gone back upstairs and shouted, 'False alarm. It's not Greenstone,' and called an ambulance. She took a deep breath. There was a plan to follow. She couldn't let Brenda down, not after all she'd been through.

Raihana, shaking like a leaf, broke the silence, her voice betraying anxiety. 'I've come to let you out, Pap.'

He was in shock. *The girl from Lahore,* how the hell did she find him? And she was calling him Pap. He hated that, but he was staring at her now; a rabbit caught in the headlights.

Raihana moved the shoulder bag and lifted her cotton shift to display her swollen belly. A boy surely! 'This is yours, Pap, your son. There was a time when I'd hoped to say 'our son' with pride.

But you've wrecked my life. Have you any idea what it's like for women in Lahore to have a baby outside marriage? It's bad enough with someone from my own land and culture, even then we can be thrown out, stoned or beaten, or hidden away with our little bastards. Some women in this condition have been killed for bringing disgrace on their families. Honour killing, heard of that, Pap?'

He winced, squirmed at the confrontation, didn't know what to do or say.

'...But a European! Can you imagine?' asked Raihana. 'I thought you loved me. I really did. But it was the same act you used on all the others. I've had a lucky escape, which is more than I can say for you, Pap. My mother and father are here and we have to make arrangements for the baby. You need to pay your share.'

'Of course I will,' said Pap, in a reassuring tone. 'Once I'm free, we can talk it through. I'll sign all the paperwork, anything to make amends. I'm sorry, I can't remember your name. I've been down here so long, my brains gone to mush, I need help, can hardly remember my own.' He smiled weakly. 'I'm so sorry.'

'You will be, Pap, you never came back to Lahore. We got engaged! That's a step away from marriage in most people's eyes. And you were excited about doing more business together. All those plans we made.'

He didn't have an answer for that. Not right now. 'Where's Brenda?'

'She's gone, Pap, flown off to sunnier climes. A new life. You'll never see her again.'

This was at least one bit of relief, but he couldn't understand why she'd go to all that trouble, keep him alive for weeks, then bugger off without being around to let him out and witness his inevitable humiliation.

Sure, he'd been a naughty boy, but she'd certainly done her best in the revenge department, she'd texted everyone, dumped his wife, thrown his job in and done everything possible to mess up his life.

But once he was out and everyone knew it was Brenda spreading all this rubbish, he could put the record straight, get his old job back. Simon would understand, he'd make him another fortune.

The bigamy issue might be tricky. But the two wives didn't really know each other. The worst that could happen is that they'd want no more to do with Melvyn Greenstone. He could live with that. They'd want money, but his son should come first. He'd promised Raihana, given his word on that. But they couldn't have what he hadn't got, could they?

Raihana approached the cell door. 'Step back, Pap. And by the way, don't try to hurt me or do anything silly. Mum and Dad are waiting. Any funny business and I'll scream. And I can say, with absolute certainty, that if they hear me cry out, you're a dead man.'

There was something metal sticking out of the lock. Raihana gave it a quick pull. It didn't give easily. She watched Pap standing against the back wall looking even more shamefaced.

The straightened piece of Raihana's broken engagement ring came away in her hand. She looked puzzled at the cheap silver fragment then recognised what it was. Despite the situation, her eyes started to fill. Not only had Pap ditched her, he'd used their engagement ring to try and break out of his cell.

Pap couldn't look at her. She threw the remains of her ring at him. It bounced lightly off his chest and hardly made a sound, like the proverbial pin dropping, as it hit the concrete floor.

She took the key from her pocket and turned it carefully in the lock. The last thing she wanted was for it to get stuck or snap off. There was a reassuring click. She tugged at the cell door.

Pap held his breath. He was about to be free. As with all prisoners released back into society, there was a certain amount of trepidation. He shuffled toward the door, like Papillon after he'd been starved, tortured, and kept in solitary confinement. His throwaway boiler suit was stained with sweat and sticking to his body. He ran back to the toilet and threw up, wiped his face with his damp sleeve and apologized once more.

Chapter 68

Brenda was waiting for the gate number to come up on the digital screen. She checked her watch. Raihana should be letting Pap out about now. She was tempted to text her, see how she was holding up, but that might not be a good idea. She'd wait until the plan was due to be finalised, about an hour or so at a guess. But Brenda would probably have boarded by then and mobiles couldn't be used during take-off.

There seemed to be an awful lot of police around; she'd forgotten the world had changed, it had been some time since she'd flown out of Gatwick. There'd been much in the news about increased terrorist alerts at stations, airports and ferry terminals, CCTV and security guards keeping an eye out for suspicious packages and people. She was a suspicious person herself, but not a danger to the public, yet somehow she felt especially vulnerable. Maybe the police had got to her house before Raihana, run off photos of her while she was sitting in Gatwick waiting for her gate call, and were now circulating them to every transport hub in the country. Her mind ran riot.

A security guard came over. 'Is that your bag, madam?'

'Yes it is,' said Brenda, a flush pinking her cheeks.

'Please keep it next to you. Security's hot these days. Don't want it confiscated, do we?' he smiled.

Brenda had heard the PA announcing on a regular basis— *Please do not leave your baggage unattended, or it may be destroyed*—but stupidly, when she'd checked her mobile, she'd left her bag and stepped away from it, long enough to cause concern, it now seemed. She was mightily relieved, a silly mistake but no more than that.

There were no text messages.

Brenda was anxious now. No messages and no gate number coming up. They should be boarding. No one had announced a flight delay. Several scenarios ran through her mind. She gave herself a good talking to. She'd asked Raihana to text her if necessary. But if the plan was going well, not to bother until Pap had been released—and to let Brenda know she was safe.

A bearded young bloke with a rucksack and laptop, plonked himself next to her.

'Going anywhere nice?' he asked.

'Melbourne.'

'Me too,' he chirped, 'Backpacking right across Australia if I can.'

The further away the better, she thought. Not being unkind, but she wasn't exactly feeling sociable.

'How about you?'

'Holiday,' she said, hoping it wouldn't lead to awkward questions. 'Shouldn't the gate number be up now? We should be boarding, shouldn't we?'

He looked at his watch. 'Bugger, we should.' They both looked at the digital information board. Only the flight number and their first stop destination *Dubai* appeared.

'Keep an eye on my stuff, I'll check at the information desk,' he said, leaving Brenda with a stuffed rucksack. It could have contained a bomb for all she knew, that's how terrorists carried them, wasn't it?

The minute he left, the *flight delayed* sign came up and Rucksack Man came back, looking annoyed. 'The plane's gonna be late, something technical, that's all they'd tell me. They'll give us an update when they have news.'

'That's a nuisance,' said Brenda, in a matter–of-fact voice, as if delaying her escape was no more than a minor irritation.

'Wanna go for a coffee?' he asked.

'Better not. They may fix whatever's wrong quickly and the gate might be right down the other end of the walkway. Some of them are fifteen minutes away.'

'I'll get you one to go, what d'you fancy? I'm having a cortado, if they do them. I travel a lot, cortados are big in Spain and Latin America. I love 'em,' he said.

Memories of Coffee 4 Us with Raihana flooded back, when they'd planned Pap's demise. How things had moved on since then.

'That's very kind of you. I'll have the same, if they do them, or Americano with milk if they don't.'

He strolled off, taking his rucksack with him this time.

She didn't want to get stuck with this guy. Suppose he had a seat next to hers?

He came back with an Americano and had bought her a doughnut too. They sat quietly for a moment. He switched on his laptop and searched for the world news channel. Brenda glanced sideways, hoping Pap wasn't strutting his stuff in front of the cameras. No doubt her photo would be superimposed somewhere on the screen. Her imagination ran wild: *Brenda Brown wanted for kidnapping. Anyone who knows her whereabouts should phone this number. She may be desperate. Do not tackle her on your own.*

She smiled at her idiotic fantasy. There were more important news items. But she had to admit her surprise at how much publicity she'd got for Pap. Apparently the media loved this stuff. And let's face it, when was the last time anyone heard of a woman imprisoning a man?

Chapter 69

The door, unopened for weeks, needed an extra pull. Ever the gentleman, Pap tossed his head slightly, indicating he could help.

'Stay where you are, Pap. I don't want you near me, I can manage.' Raihana pushed the lever down hard and yanked, and the door swung back, the heavy bars nearly knocking her off her feet.

Pap froze, petrified, panic-stricken. He began to move cautiously from the back of his cell, hesitating at the threshold as if crossing it might unleash some unknown disaster.

'Who's up there?' he asked, walking slowly toward the bottom of the staircase.

'My parents, they're not happy.'

His bowels felt suddenly loose, he broke out in a sweat. 'I'll make sure the baby's looked after. You won't have to chase me for money.' In his weakened emotional state, Pap felt a surge of love for the pretty little thing carrying his child. He'd thought himself incapable of fatherhood. Hadn't managed it with Angie but after a couple of quickies with Raihana... So his low sperm count couldn't have been that low after all. His baby. His son? He'd probably never see him. No doubt Raihana would give birth in Lahore with her parents clucking around. Melvyn Greenstone would be forgotten.

He gripped the bannister, took the first step and felt his knees hurt. His thigh muscles were already starting to cramp, shooting pains ending up knife-like as far as his groin. Stopping for a moment, he looked back pathetically at Raihana.

She was trembling, wondering if he was going to make it...'No good looking at me like that. I won't be helping you. Don't want to touch you and I'm staying well back. Can't risk you falling on me and hurting the baby.'

He took the next few steps slowly, groaning as he went, like a man who'd just had a hip replaced. 'I think the door's slammed shut,' he shouted back to Raihana. He wanted her to walk out of the cellar first, terrified of coming face to face with her parents in this state. Well in any state really, but especially in this state.

'It's not locked. Turn the handle and you'll be in the kitchen. There's a glass of water on the worktop.'

He turned the handle cautiously and opened the door. The sunlight flooding the white-walled kitchen hurt his eyes and he rubbed them like a sleepy child waking from a dream. Was he leaving a nightmare or about to enter one? There didn't seem to be anyone else in the room, or the house. He was puzzled. He'd expected two grumpy Pakistanis waiting to give him hell.

He grabbed the glass of water from the worktop and downed it in one, spilling much of it on his sweaty one-piece. He saw himself in the kitchen mirror; shaggy haired, bearded, red-eyed, pathetic. The face staring back was not Melvyn Greenstone—he really did look like Steve McQueen in *Papillon*, just before he escaped on that dodgy raft.

This was a big moment for Raihana, for all sorts of reasons, but mainly closure for her and for Brenda. She told Pap to walk to the front door.

'What, like this?'

'Yes, like that, Pap. It's just along the hall, my parents can't wait to meet you again, you made such an impression on them in Lahore. Don't you remember?'

'Can I shower before I go out there?'

'No. We need to get the formalities over with first. Anyway, Brenda wouldn't want you clogging up her nice clean bathroom before the new owners arrive.'

Chapter 70

Brenda's mobile pulsated in her bag. She took it out and looked around; no one was close enough to see the text from Raihana.

'*He's out!*'

This was what Brenda had been waiting for, but it was supposed to happen when she was on the plane, flying over the south-east and out toward Dubai. The gate number hadn't come up, the police still had time to stop her leaving. Rucksack Man had gone for a pee but she felt sure he'd be checking the news again shortly. She needed the loo fast so didn't wait for him to return. The PA echoed its message around the airport. *Passengers for Emirates flight to Dubai please go to gate...* She finished as quickly as she could, grabbed her shoulder bag and ran toward the nearest digital display; her gate was at least ten minutes' walk away. There were police hanging around. They seemed to be eyeing everyone heading toward the Emirate flight gate. Her flight! They'd stopped Rucksack Man up front and were asking him questions. She kept her head down and hurried past to join the queue already starting to board. Why had he been stopped? They'd have checked all his bags before he'd got this far, wouldn't they? Perhaps he was telling them about her, a woman he'd recognised from a newsflash, someone he'd been sitting next to and bought coffee for?

Only a few more to board, she was at the tail end. Rucksack Man came into view running toward her.

'What happened?' she asked.

'Dropped my wallet in the Gents, needed to make sure I was the owner before handing it over. Phew!'

Lots of people were trying to locate their seats. She watched Rucksack Man put his bag in the overhead locker and sit two rows back. They belted up and Brenda mentally ran through the arrangements she'd made.

*

Raymond hadn't been too surprised when Brenda turned up a week early to say goodbye. She'd already primed him for it: *So much to do,* and she'd wanted time to say a proper goodbye before she left.

'We're really gonna miss you, Brenda. Any further instructions for your buyers?'

'Don't think so. You have a set of keys and Raihana will drop the other set in after she's given the house the onceover. I've left an envelope on the kitchen worktop with all the boring stuff: when bins are due to be put out, neighbours' names and phone numbers, how to contact handyman, plumber etc. They left me a cheque for the odd bits of furniture they wanted. The rest is being moved and dumped ASAP. *Big White Van Man: no job too small,* is going to take care of it.'

She didn't mention the two illegal immigrants who'd been paid a tidy sum to smuggle Pap's cell door out in the mattress it came in; too much information.

Instead of celebrating in the office, Raymondo had been kind enough to take the staff across to the pub to bid Brenda a fond farewell. She could have done without it.

The pub had been fairly packed. She thought she'd spotted Kev Strong slip into the public bar but couldn't be sure.

Raymondo had taken the orders and returned with a tray of drinks and some nibbles.

'Here's to you, Brenda, and all that sunshine.' They'd raised glasses and cheered. 'If you ever come back, there's always a job for you,' said Raymondo.

Brenda had been touched by the sentiment, it felt genuine and prompted her to say too much. 'If you're ever in Melbourne, please drop in, you've got my email address. I'll send pics when I get there...' *Stop now*, her brain had told her.

'They never solved that Greenstone thing, did they?' asked Raymondo, of no one in particular. They'd all looked at Brenda, knowing the police had been sniffing around because of the photo.

'They probably will,' said Brenda, gulping her half of shandy a bit too quickly.

'It all seems to have quietened down. Do you think he might be dead?'

'Doubt it,' said Brenda. 'Not still asking questions, are they?'

'All quiet on the western front,' said Raymondo.

They'd all hugged and wished Brenda good luck.

She'd looked through the crowd into the public bar. It was Kev Strong! He'd raised his glass for no obvious reason. Brenda had swallowed hard.

At Coffee 4 Us, Raihana and Brenda had sat opposite each other in the Little Conservatory, both sniffing back tears they'd refused to let fall. 'It's nearly over,' said Brenda, passing Raihana the spare keys to the house and Pap's cell.

'When you've let him out, leave the cell key in the door and drop the others in to Raymondo.'

'What about the cell bars?'

'Some guys are coming to remove them before the new owners arrive. They have a key and I've asked them to pop it through the letterbox when they've finished. There's nothing of value left to nick. The new owners won't escape the publicity but then they shouldn't have been so mean about the price in the first place. By the time they move in, the house will be as good as when they first saw it. I've cleaned it from top to bottom.'

'Mum and Dad okay?' asked Brenda, 'Have you told them yet?'

'This morning. They were shocked to learn where Melvyn was. Viewed you in a different light, Brenda, thought you were a gentle soul. Dad nearly burst a blood vessel. I thought he was going to hit me, he wanted to go straight down and face Pap. Then I told them about the plan...'

'And?' queried Brenda, feeling a bit sad that Raihana's parents had been involved.

'They liked it, especially the bit about Pap paying for the baby.'

Chapter 71

Barker, Smithy and Kev Strong had put their heads together about how best to raid Brenda Brown's cellar. Not a raid as such, but a search without a warrant had all the excitement of one. According to their notes, Brenda was due to leave next week, nineteenth of May from Gatwick. So they had a time frame. They needed to get on with it, so the next morning was picked for Brenda's 'day of judgement'. They decided to call in at Butts first, see how they'd tied things up with Brenda, administration wise: paid her up to date, sorted National Insurance details, provided references and stuff.

'Check it out please, Smithy,' said Barker as he drained the last of his coffee. 'And while you're at it, see if there's any hint of Brenda not being the full ticket.'

Meanwhile he phoned the Virgin helpline, to make sure Brenda was still on the list for the nineteenth. She was.

Smithy parked in the town car park and walked to Butts, in plain clothes. The place was empty of clients but all the staff were either on the phone or using their computers. Smithy wondered if people actually needed estate agents these days, it all seems to be done online with slide shows of houses and even video tours of the bigger properties. You could imagine punters signing up to Houses 4 Us or some such company and a button being pressed—*Buy Now with one click*—like having an Amazon Prime account.

'Good morning, officer, how can I help?' asked Raymond, recognising Smithy immediately.

'Just a routine visit, sir. Seen Brenda Brown at all?'

'Matter of fact we have, we had a little celebration to see her off.'

'I thought she wasn't going 'til next week.'

'She's not, but had lots to do, so we said goodbye while she had the time to have a drink with us all. Is there something wrong?'

Smithy felt uneasy about Brenda tying things up so early. But they'd checked the flight and she was still booked in. Nevertheless, he couldn't help thinking…

'We haven't found Greenstone yet. Wondered if there's anyone else in that seminar picture who we should be interviewing?' Smithy hoped that Raymond wouldn't see through this weak attempt to keep him in conversation. 'Anyone dodgy, d'you think?'

'It's a bit late to ask that. I thought you'd have interviewed the others already,' snapped Raymond.

'We didn't think Greenstone really knew anyone else in that photo. But we're clutching at straws now.'

Raymond was suspicious. He couldn't quite work out why Smithy was here at all. They had the seminar photo and a list of everyone in it, so what was the problem?

Smithy was satisfied that Raymond was innocent of any collaboration. Brenda was some cool cookie. If she had Greenstone locked away, then she was a very clever woman. The big question was; what on earth would drive her to do such a crazy thing? She could end up with a heavy sentence, for kidnapping!

'Anything to report, Smithy?' said Barker when the young officer got back to the station. He could smell the remains of Kev Strong's tobacco even though the reporter had left.

'Nothing much. Brenda Brown had called in to say goodbye earlier than expected. On the face of it, there didn't seem to be anything in that. But it doesn't feel quite right.'

'Well she's flying out next week and we're raiding tomorrow, so whatever she's up to, we'll find out pretty soon.'

'What time tomorrow, guv?'

'Eight am, before she gets a chance to go shopping. Kev Strong will be there for the press.'

'This is global news stuff. Shouldn't we alert all the media, make it big? We'll get medals, we'll be famous!'

'Only if Greenstone's there, if he's not, we'll look a right pair of pricks. By the way, Smithy, seeking fame should not be on our agenda, we're the silent seekers of justice, not bloody Rambo. Don't want our mugs all over the papers either, otherwise every criminal in the area will have us on their list. Besides, I promised Strong a scoop.'

'Bound to be TV and radio crews getting wind of it, they usually do…' said Smithy.

'That's an unknown, Smithy. We may get lucky,'

Barker's phone rang, and the receptionist said, 'Call for you, sir. Sounds urgent, it's about Brenda Brown.'

'Barker here, who am I speaking to?'

'Tristan Starkey, I'm a psychotherapist. Sorry to bother you but I've been rather worried about a situation…'

There was a long silence, Barker thought he'd been cut off. 'Are you still there?'

'…Obviously I try to ensure patient confidentiality but I fear a man's life may be at risk. I've not made this decision lightly, you understand.'

'Are you talking about Melvyn Greenstone?'

'Yes.'

'And your patient?' Barker knew exactly who it was, but didn't want Starkey to stop what he might be about to reveal. 'We'd like to see you straight away.'

'I'll come to the station. Ten minutes,' said Starkey.

'Put the coffee on, Smithy. A guy called Starkey is on his way. He's a shrink and it looks like Brenda Brown was his patient.

Greenstone's life may be in danger.'

'So she's bonkers after all,' said Smithy. 'Thought she might be.'

'Not everyone who has mental health problems is bonkers, Smithy. And please don't use the term in front of Starkey.'

Smithy mentally toyed with the words, *Starkey, staring bonkers.*

Starkey entered the station and was directed through to Barker's office. Smithy was halfway through his second coffee. He spotted the flesh tunnel and couldn't help but smile. He shook Starkey's hand, still smiling as if pleased to meet him. Barker kept a straight face.

Barker and Smithy's phones vibrated at the same time. Picking up their mobiles in sync, they stared at each other across what seemed like a void.

Text from Brenda Brown.

Chapter 72

It was exactly ten am when Raihana heard the police siren. Pap was still standing in the kitchen looking dazed as the sun streamed through Brenda's kitchen window. It lit him up like a stage spotlight, picking out the stains and creases in his orange jump suit.

'Time to move, Pap, time to face the world. Walk to the front door,' said Raihana, breathing heavily. Pap tried to stand tall, head up, to face the Khans but his legs felt powerless at first. Then he began to move with short uncertain steps; stiff from lack of exercise plus a creeping terror emanating from somewhere way down in the pit of his stomach.

'I'm behind you, Pap, open the door, it's not locked. No need now, is there?'

Pap couldn't explain why he chose to open the door slowly rather than getting it over and done with, but it was all the better for Kev Strong's camera; a series of shots that would serve his story well. There were arc lights and Pap could see the outline of a TV crew with an overhead woolly microphone picking up the hubbub and an interviewer stepping forward with a hand mic for some up close questioning.

Raihana reached into her shoulder bag and removed a significant number of envelopes. She offered one to Smithy, as his boss began taking control.

'Step back!' shouted Barker. He aimed his command at everyone gathered, as he dashed toward Pap. Brenda must have texted the world and his bloody wife about his pending release. Despite Barker and Smithy waving their credentials, no one took much notice of them.

The Khans stood staring in astonishment. They'd seen Pap on the YouTube video, but they were shocked. Tristan Starkey hovered in the background fiddling with his flesh tunnel, uncertain as to what role he might be playing in this drama. Several women, some smiling, others in a state of shock, surged forward as Pap froze on the steps of number twelve. They were the ghosts of Pap's past, some from not that far back.

The Free Melvyn Greenstone crowd were smaller in number than when they'd first formed. Gloria was standing in front of them but left the banner-holding to others more sympathetic to the cause. She glanced across at Angie and, while not exactly ready to throw their arms around each other, they exchanged a look that only two women betrayed by the same man could understand. The cameras whirred. Reporters shouted at Pap who'd been swiftly escorted by Barker and Smithy to the centre of Brenda's front lawn. They weren't sure what to do first: call an ambulance, give Strong the interview they'd promised, or arrest Pap for bigamy. Brenda was gone. All they'd had was a text from her saying, '*I'm on the plane and you can collect Greenstone at ten am. You know where he is...*'

The Avenue was blocked in both directions—most people thought they were witnessing the making of a film or TV programme. There seemed to be little control and the crowd was becoming unmanageable. Barker rang for backup and an ambulance.

Raihana had filmed Pap's exit from the house on her iPhone. The video, shot from behind as she followed him through the front door, added drama as he faced the waiting crowd. She panned the scene before stopping the sixty-second clip and pressing send.

Brenda smiled when she saw Pap sneaking out of the front door of her house, as if he'd just burgled the place and was checking the street. She couldn't remember exactly how many texts she'd sent from his contact list and realised quite a few of those on his list must have been in the scene, but she couldn't begin to put faces to them. Some spectators would have simply walked in off the busy street. Starkey was there! No matter. She was on the plane with her mobile in flight mode and Raihana keeping her up to speed on everything. All was well.

Raihana walked quickly through the crowd handing out envelopes from her shoulder bag like a canvasser touting for business. There were no names on them. Nearly everyone stuffed them in pockets or handbags, thinking she was advertising a trade or promoting a product of some sort.

It really was worth Brenda booking that earlier Emirates flight, otherwise they'd have caught her and the trip to Australia would have been nothing but a dream. They'd been cleverer than she'd expected but there was still one final piece of the jigsaw. Her missives to Barker, Smithy, Kevin Strong, Raihana and the world at large, would be something of a revelation. It would be a surprise to Pap too. It was fairly obvious he still had no idea exactly why he'd been given such a hard time and so much publicity.

Pap was panic-stricken. He took a deep breath and, with the stage fright suffered by even the most experienced actors, decided on acting out his role as Papillon to Steve McQueen standard. He gave a half but determined grin, a man who'd been through hell, but not broken. He didn't raise his head too much, didn't want to look arrogant. He rubbed each wrist as if he'd just had manacles removed.

Kev composed a dramatic shot. Cameras were rolling. Attempting a brief announcement, Barker took the floor, waving his arms at the advancing media. He wasn't being heard and had to clear his throat to recalibrate his virus-stricken voice box.

'Ladies, gentlemen. I am happy to say that at ten am this morning, following a text from the owner of this property, the search for Melvyn Greenstone is over. An ambulance is on its way and I ask for your patience. As you can see, Mr. Greenstone is in no fit state to be interviewed. I will issue a statement once he has been debriefed.'

The crowd became defiant.

A woman ran toward Pap and hit him with her outstretched palm. Only Pap knew her identity. Angie moved next, she pushed Barker aside and, holding Pap's shoulders, stared him straight in the eye. Pap twitched, uncertain of her intention. She cursed loudly and spat in his face. He twitched again. She let him go, walked back toward Gloria and kissed her gently on the cheek, a silent collaboration.

Starkey was thinking of Brenda. She'd been clever. He would never see her again but his professional curiosity needed to witness first hand, the source of her anger; not to judge Pap, but to observe a womanising bigamist brought to heel in as dramatic a scene possible. He'd like to write a paper on it.

Backup arrived to control the growing crowd as people got out of their cars and pedestrians diverted their step to see what was going on. An ambulance, siren still blaring, spewed out its crew with their bags of equipment. They slid a gurney from the back of the vehicle as police and medics tried to clear a way toward Pap. Starkey, as an observer, also headed toward Pap, intrigued at this puzzling character finally appearing in the flesh.

Pap wiped Angie's spit from his face as Barker stepped forward with a pair of handcuffs. Pap held his up hands defensively. 'You won't need those, officer, I'll go peacefully, I'm a sick man,' he said, watching the approaching ambulance crew pushing the gurney toward him. 'I know you are going to arrest me...'

A gasp came from the crowd, to a man and woman; they weren't expecting that!

Kev Strong elbowed his way through and stood next to Barker and Smithy, to make the best possible use of his new camera. Photographers and film crews, some with stepladders, shot scenes over the top of the crowd.

The Free Melvyn Greenstone ensemble tried to raise their banner high enough to be seen on film, but it was pulled down and stamped on by a few angry women. Unladylike punches were exchanged, the backup of extra officers intervened and, due to his prominent ear tunnel and proximity to the action, Starkey'd had his collar felt. He'd been viewed by a strict sergeant (ready for retirement) as an ageing punk rocker, a potential troublemaker running amok. However, he was released, once they'd searched him and verified his credentials.

Raymond, who'd had a similar text about Pap's release, looked on agog, unable to associate any of this with Brenda Brown, his good natured, hardworking letting agent.

Simon, Pap's boss from Ethical Global Logistics also turned up. He was shocked beyond belief. He wanted to throw his arms around the errant Melvyn Greenstone, get him bathed and shaved, buy some new suits to fit his leaner image and get him back out there earning another million for the company. He'd been missed, takings were down. The main earner had been out of the game for too long. And the publicity, good or bad, could only bring the name Ethical Global Logistics to a whole new swathe of business magazines and websites across the world.

Olive, guessing she'd never see Brenda again, couldn't resist one last look at the bastard Melvyn Greenstone; to revel in his downfall, to see him arrested, reviled and ruined. How dare he traipse around the world treating women like tarts.

Chapter 73

As the farce proceeded, Brenda enjoyed Raihana's clips sent with amazing regularity from her iPhone. She particularly liked the bit where the Free Melvyn Greenstone banner had been trampled into the ground and punches exchanged. Professional protestors were there for the publicity, adding fuel to the confrontation between Melvyn and his ex-lovers. Brenda was surprised to see her mother at the scene; thought she'd left for good but could understand the bittersweet moment, as much revenge as one could expect from such a sober human being.

Australia-*aah*. She couldn't wait to get there now but the flight to Dubai was not without its pleasures. She put her headphones on and watched the world news. Pap's release was the second item, with live coverage. Police, ambulance and film crews fought for priority. Pap was holding up his hand as if to speak…

Annoyingly, the clip was cut short. It happens, from time to time on long-haul journeys, when the aircraft entertainment screen on the back of the seat, replaces whatever you're watching with the plane's progress. The flight path showed an aircraft, out of proportion—the size of Dubai it seemed—superimposed on a map of the route. And the following details: *Time to landing: 6 hours. Air speed: 450 knots. Height: 30,000 feet.*

Barker and Smithy stepped forward to read Pap his rights and charge him with bigamy. Pap held his hands aloft for theatrical effect, taking advantage of the moment before entering the ambulance.

'I'd like to speak, before I'm taken away. While you're all here to listen...'

Kev Strong got closer with his voice recorder. Others jostled for position. Cameras whirred and people stopped shouting their memorable sound bites for the media.

'Brenda Brown has kept me against my will in the most appalling conditions. As you can see, I am not the man I was...'

A shrill voice piped up, 'Thank God for that.' Cheers were heard from some of the women. Not celebratory, due to his release, more of an unsympathetic nature.

An arm rose above the crowd and a takeaway coffee winged its way toward Pap leaving a heavy dark stain around his crotch.

He watched as the remaining Free Melvyn Greenstone contingent swapped notes with the women from his past. Margo who had, so far, remained loyal throughout, rolled up her FREE MELVYN GREENSTONE: RESPECT HUMAN RIGHTS banner. The overwhelming evidence before her was proof that she was just a passing fancy in his life.

Unfortunately for Pap he was living in the age of social media. iPhones and Androids came out, iPads and digital cameras were capturing every moment. A series of rapid clicks, like crickets in the early evening, signalled that many scenes of Pap's release had been recorded. Some had switched to video, panning the crowd, picking up angry and bemused faces and attaching them to messages before Tweeting or putting them on Facebook or attaching shots to emails. For the titillation of those he was about to post to, a creative photographer took a shot of the dark stain around Pap's crotch. Already, five minutes into his freedom, Pap's image had gone to thousands of people, who'd passed them on to thousands of others. No time lapse, it happened in seconds, minutes at the most.

A sudden migration occurred; a groundswell of feeling against the prisoner was building. Pap got their drift and, what with the impending charges and questioning, felt the time right to feign collapse. He did this with dramatic effect. A gasp went up from the crowd. The ambulance crew pushed past those who'd been expecting him to elaborate on his opening statement and slid Pap onto the gurney and smoothly into the back of the ambulance.

The Khans, taken completely by surprise at the chaos, stepped back, lest they got caught up in some racist incident: Pakistanis attacking a freshly released prisoner might look like a new tactic dreamt up by radicals to incite unrest in Surrey.

No doubt Pap had stopped trying to work out why Brenda had put him through all this. He'd branded her a spiteful woman who needed to lighten up. His memory being what it was, only Olive and Raihana confronting him in person had finally encouraged the penny to drop.

The ride in the ambulance didn't take long. The media followed and the same vultures turned up to see what else they could glean from his sorry condition. He kept his eyes screwed closed while he was wheeled into casualty, reminding him, momentarily, of Gloria, when they'd had sex with the lights on.

Closed eyes did not stop reporters firing questions at him:

'Have you been treated badly?'

'Terribly; too painful to recall at the moment.'

'What were you given to eat and drink?'

'Broccoli soup and water.'

'Did you have a television?'

'No.'

'Were you tortured?'

'Water-boarded, more or less, and threatened with some sort of injection.'

'Have you been sexually abused?'

'She made me take all my clothes off.'

'Did you try to escape?'

'Tried, but she caught me and gave me hell.'

'How did you spend your time?'

'Wondering why I was there and how I could escape. I thought a lot about death.'

'Did you know the news of your disappearance had gone global?'

'Yes, Brenda Brown showed me her video going on the Internet and Facebook and stuff—and the news.'

'Did you know your boss had put up a reward for any information leading to your captor or captors?'

'No, that is so kind. We have a good relationship.'

'Will you recover from the trauma of it all?'

'I don't think I ever will. Even if she pays me compensation, it won't take away the suffering; a piece of my life has gone forever.'

If he'd not feigned collapse he could have answered all these questions even more convincingly to gain maximum support. Perhaps he'd been a little hasty collapsing so soon after his release. But it was giving him time to think. There'd be lots more questions, some he hadn't even considered and he wanted the best possible chance to put his case and give Brenda Brown the punishment she deserved.

The hospital staff wired him up, checked his pulse, his heart, his lungs. Gave him an ECG, tested his blood sugar levels (borderline diabetic), then his reflexes. Taking no chances, due to the fresh stains on the front of his trousers, they provided an incontinence pad. They shone a torch in his eyes and watched his pupils respond to light. Someone asked him a series of questions designed for those who may have suffered brain damage: where was he born? Who was the present prime minister? It seemed endless...*Never could remember who the bloody prime minister was anyway*. They checked his body for bruises or signs of physical abuse. There were none, just weight loss and a body odour typical of someone who hadn't washed for weeks. No lice in his hair or beard, despite both areas being a perfect environment.

Pap decided to show further signs of life. Slowly, at a pace commensurate with his fragile state, he allowed himself to be sat up and supported with pillows. Staff nurse decided he could be moved from casualty and into a private room. Barker and Smithy stood outside, waiting to question him. Gloria and Angie, both claiming family representation, stood next to them. No longer fuming, they'd decided, wordlessly, that they were now both on the same side and that entering the private room together would be just the ticket for their wayward husband.

Pap, who'd spotted the foursome through the obscure glass partition, thought it too soon to collapse for a second time, but was sorely tempted. He closed his eyes. A nurse asked if he needed anything before the consultant came round to question him further about his ordeal. Staff nurse, smiling, asked if he'd like his wives to visit once the doctor had finished. Pap felt a sudden need to visit the toilet and was grateful when the nurse turned up with a bed pan and drew the curtains over the glass partition of his room. He'd take his time.

'Mr. Greenstone? The police need to interview you while things are still fresh in your mind.'

Pap opened one eye. Time to face whatever was coming. The top doc had done his bit and declared Pap in reasonable health, considering. They wanted to keep him under observation for a couple of days then he'd be free to go. But not *free*.

Barker and Smithy introduced themselves for the second time. They each pulled up a chair to Pap's bedside, took out their notebooks, and started a gentle preamble to mollify the sickly looking patient. 'You have been through quite an ordeal, Mr. Greenstone but we need to get the facts so that we can bring proper charges against the person who kept you captive. You can stop us at any time if you feel unwell. There'll be a nurse standing right outside,' said Barker, omitting to tell Greenstone that a nurse would be keeping an eye on him twenty-four-seven: they feared he might take his own life. No telling what someone might do in his situation.

'Are you feeling okay, Mr. Greenstone?'

'Yes thank you,' croaked Pap.

'There are certain accusations being made against you. But let's start with your story, Mr. Greenstone. Tell us in your own words. What happened to you on...'

Barker checked his notes and confirmed the date.

There was no way round the fact that he was drunk when that bitch locked him in the cellar. 'I'd been drinking. I met a girl.'

'Someone you knew?' asked Smithy.

'No. I was drunk and she came on to me in the bar. I'm a bloke and like all of us, I'm a sucker for a pretty face. I like women.'

Everyone knows that, thought Barker and Smithy, smiling in unison.

'We got into a cab...we stopped in a dark street...she took me down some stairs. I thought it was her place...didn't really question where it was. Thought I was getting a reward for the good time I'd given her...cost me a few quid she did. Next thing I knew I was behind bars in a filthy cell.' Pap sniffed, the whole thing was so uncivilised.

'Then Brenda Brown came down and said she was going to keep me there. Must have been her idea, using a friend to get me pissed and trick me.'

'Kidnapping is a very serious crime, do you know why you were taken down there?'

'Not really. She said I'd made a beeline for her at a seminar, made advances and touched her up or something. But we were all drunk, ask anyone who was there. That's what goes on at these gigs. Can't imagine how that would give her reason to keep me imprisoned for all those weeks.'

'Apparently you're quite the ladies' man,' said Smithy.

'We all like the ladies, don't we, officer? And they like us. Human nature.'

'What about your two wives?' asked Barker. He noted a little colour appear on Pap's cheeks.

'I thought I'd divorced Angie, I really did. We split up ages ago.'

'She said you left. A divorce wasn't discussed, never on the table.'

'Ah. Memory isn't so good right now. Being imprisoned does things to your mind.'

'From all accounts your memory has never been good.'

Pap looked down at his shape under the sheets and was pleased to note he'd lost that bit of the belly he'd been developing. 'What exactly are you expecting me to say about all this? I've been kidnapped, tortured and starved by a mentally deranged woman and all you can talk about is my past. What about her, what about Brenda Brown? I hope you stopped her getting on that plane and clapped her in a cell of her own.'

'We tried. We'd had her under surveillance, questioned her neighbours and her boss but the links were tenuous. We were planning to search the place, once we had good reason, but we really didn't have enough evidence to prove that you were there— until we got her text...' Barker blushed at his incompetence. *Too much information*, he thought. He was supposed to be conducting the interview, not the prisoner!

'What text?' asked Pap.

'May I remind you, Mr. Greenstone, that we're doing the questioning,' piped in Smithy.

'Anyway, Mrs. Brown is no longer with us.'

'Suicide was it?' asked Pap, hopefully.

'Not dead. She's on a plane,' said Smithy. 'Let's get back to you...'

'There's a lot of public support for Mrs. Brown's actions, now that facts are emerging.'

Pap said nothing.

'The Free Melvyn Greenstone cohort seems to have lost interest in you, since your dramatic release. We're used to this stuff, these banner wavers are often professional protestors who turn up at the drop of a hat just to get on the telly or the Internet.

None of them knew you. We asked around, interviewed the main players. I think one of your wives and a girlfriend may have been sympathetic initially, but not now it seems. There's a television in your room, you can catch up with the latest,' said Barker, unsure just how much use this interview was going to be.

'From our point of view there'll be the bigamy charge. Quite a stiff sentence, I'm afraid,' said Barker.

Pap said nothing.

'A poor memory will not get you out of that,' said Smithy, helpfully.

'So Brenda Brown will get away with it then?'

'Let's wait and see what our pals in Australia say. We've alerted them to Mrs. Brown's arrival and asked them to check out the person she is supposed to be visiting,' said Barker, without adding that the police in Australia thought the whole thing very funny. He doubted they'd take it seriously or be much help: *a Sheila kidnapping a healthy male—and then letting him go with no damage done, you couldn't make it up, could you?*

Pap let his eyes half close. A young nurse entered holding a tray with his lunch; soup. How could they? He grabbed the stainless steel dish at his bedside and threw up, much to the disgust of Barker and Smithy who just missed a splattering.

'You'll have to leave now, gentlemen,' said the sister, who'd heard the commotion. 'You can interview Mr. Greenstone further when he's had a rest,' she said, adopting the air of a seasoned matriarch. Both men felt it.

Pap looked pale. The nurse wiped his mouth, rested his head back on the pillow, took his temperature, checked his pulse and went off to fetch some soap and water.

'We can continue this at the station, Mr. Greenstone. You'll be out in a couple of days. We'll have an officer check in regularly. We don't want you having problems with that memory of yours— and forgetting you have an appointment with us.'

Pap, eyes fully closed, trying to shut out the world, was not having a great deal of success. His memory, which up until now had erred on the side of self-preservation, had begun to play up. He was remembering things buried long since and spent a lot of energy trying to keep them there; like molehills, appearing haphazardly in a manicured lawn, forcing his past escapades to surface. It was not a nice experience.

There were no distractions: no booze, no fags, no flying off to cut a deal and—no women. He doubted his ability to ever form another relationship and even began to doubt whether he would experience an erection again. It had been nearly six weeks and his favourite toy had lain dormant for all that time, apart from the brief moment when, half asleep, he'd been stirred by Brenda's perfume. Unable at the time to pin the smell to his gaoler, it had been a mild aphrodisiac with a short shelf life.

And all those women, standing outside Brenda's when he was released! Some were only vaguely familiar, from way back. But he was ashamed to admit, although a few may have been introduced to him as friends of the women he'd had affairs with, they could, equally, have been the ones he'd had sex with! Life could be so confusing.

Sister, starched and freshly bunned, returned. 'I wanted them to leave,' she barked at Pap, who was still wrestling with his memories and the memories were winning. 'I want you...' she hesitated but there was no other way to put this. '...I want you to have a little time...with your wives, Mr. Greenstone.'

Pap felt as if he'd been shot. He gripped the sides of the bed. Startled by Sister's booming entrance, he could hardly go back to his eyes closed reverie now. Shit.

Gloria and Angie entered the room. They didn't attempt to touch him, which seemed ominous to Pap. They pulled up two chairs, scraping the concrete floor, making him want to hold his front teeth.

Angie put her hand on Gloria's knee. Gloria covered Angie's hand with her own.

Pap said nothing.

'We've come to screw up your life, Pap, just like you screwed up ours.'

'Sorry,' said Pap, the only suitable response he could think of. He couldn't imagine a worse scenario: two wives who'd no idea the other existed, just sitting there with him confined to a hospital bed and nowhere to run, nowhere to hide and no chance of trawling his not insignificant library of *Save Melvyn's Arse* lines.

'We don't need to remind you of what a cheating lying bastard you are. Even with your rhinoceros hide you must be fully aware of that now.'

'I don't feel well,' said Pap.

'You gotta feel worse before you feel better,' said Angie.

'No pain, no gain,' added Gloria.

'Quick, pass me that bowl,' said Pap. He tried to retch but nothing came up. Angie and Gloria smiled.

'Nice try, Melvyn.'

'I really do feel sick. I think I've got a bug.'

Gloria and Angie sighed as one. 'We'd like to have been a fly on the wall when you were in that cell,' said Gloria. 'What is it they're calling you now? *Pap? We like the name. I guess you know what it means. If not, I'm sure the hospital keeps a dictionary.'

'You must've driven Brenda Brown crazy,' said Angie.

'What do you want?'

'Closure, justice, our dues, we won't get our lives back but we have agreed, Angie and I,' said Gloria, squeezing Angie's hand, 'on what we want: the marital homes, the ones Angie and I are now living in, plus half your assets signed over to us. We understand there will be other claims against you...If they are to do with the women you've messed with, you'd better make sure they get their fair share.'

'I'll need to live,' said Pap. He was tempted to give a short speech on human rights, but didn't feel this was the moment.

'You don't deserve to, but we heard from Simon that you'll get your job back. Imagine that, Pap, someone still wanting you after all you've done,' said Angie.

'I'm a good worker, that's why...'

'You're a fast one, we'll grant you that.'

'Anyway, that's the deal,' said Gloria. Angie nodded agreement. 'You'll be charged with bigamy, no doubt, but we've both accepted that neither of us wants to claim you. Let us know where you'll be staying because solicitors need to know where to send paperwork. You'll still be working for Simon, but we don't want you to spend all your money, well ours really, hiring a private detective to root you out.'

Pap grunted.

'Don't try and hide away, because your face will be everywhere, showing you before and after your recent adventure. When you're all cleaned up and ready to go, the media will make sure they get current pictures and interviews.'

Pap said little, apart from, 'I didn't mean to hurt anyone,' which seemed ridiculous, given his current situation.

Gloria and Angie both felt he actually believed what he'd just said. But then wasn't that the way he'd always lived his life? *He didn't mean to hurt people by being a bigamist, or a serial womaniser, or a liar or a cheat. He thinks he's so-oo innocent.*

'Goodbye, Pap. We'll be in touch.' They scraped the metal chairs back across the floor.

Pap gripped his front teeth.

Pap—Chambers Dictionary: *mediocre, stultifying or worthless entertainment.*

Collins Thesaurus: *rubbish, trash, trivia, drivel.*

Chapter 74

Brenda didn't see much of Dubai. She hadn't intended to, and had managed to lose Rucksack Man. In the few hours she'd had before transferring to the Melbourne flight, she'd stayed around the terminal shopping area, read a book and watched the world news. She was delighted to see Pap being given a further spot on it, but he didn't get to say much before he was whisked off in the ambulance. She'd spotted Raihana and her parents watching Pap giving a fair impression of a wounded war veteran as he was transported away.

About now, Brenda's revealing letters were probably being delivered to all concerned. More of a short story than a letter: her thoughts, reasons and feelings about The Prisoner of Brenda. She was still thinking what a good film it would make.

There'd be another spate of press and media interest. She might get sought out in Melbourne. Obviously the police would be alerted and want to interview her. But the press coverage and the weight of her argument would surely win them over in the end. The worst that could happen might be a bit of community service to make it look as if the Australian police had actually done something to appease the UK legal system.

But once the preliminaries were over, she intended to lose weight, travel a lot and go blonde again. She'd bide her time, find out exactly what was happening to Pap, how it would turn out for

Gloria, Angie and Margo, whether Raihana had got his guarantee that her baby would be cared for financially. And whether Pap might be targeted for recompense by any of the other women who'd turned up to watch his release. Raihana was on the case and would report back, right up until she went back to Lahore with Ma and Pa Khan.

Brenda was grateful to Starkey, for seeing her through the worst part of her experience. She'd felt compelled to invite him to witness Pap's release, but never really thought he'd be there. He really had done more than she'd expected, saved her from a mental breakdown. Mind doctors were not something she'd ever admit to using, but following the abortion in her teens and the strain of juggling the last tricky stages of Pap's incarceration, they'd turned up trumps.

Brenda's gate number was called. She walked the striking concourse of Dubai terminal wondering what might happen to Pap and his *followers* by the time she landed at Melbourne airport.

Chapter 75

Brenda's uncle, her mother's only brother, had had enough of the UK with its deteriorating lifestyle and miserable climate. He'd fallen out with everyone, apart from Brenda who he'd loved since she was born; his little soul mate (sole mate, Fred's wife called her, after deciding to leave him, following years of near total silence).

An eccentric who had a knack for playing the stock market and investing in the right company at the right time, Fred now owned property dotted about Australia and the only one he could think of to take over the reins when he'd gone, was Brenda. He was convinced that, as well as being his favourite person, her work as an estate agent qualified her nicely for keeping an eye on his small property empire. Even so, he had a property manager and investment team, so it wouldn't be too onerous a task and she'd have plenty of Brenda time.

He'd written to Brenda about his prostate cancer, said he was having chemo, couldn't manage his life so well, and asked her if she'd like to take over his business. He'd worked out that with husband Arthur gone and no kids, she'd be ready for a new challenge. And she was. Fred was excited, but not long for this world; about three months they'd given him.

'Don't tell anyone about the business, Brenda, just say you're on a visit to help me through my illness. If your mother hears about the legacy...who knows what spiteful thing she'll get up to. You may be my favourite but you're certainly not hers.'

Chapter 76

A good night's sleep can do wonders. Pap had slept like a baby. Two young nurses had been checking him all night, one on suicide watch. Come the morning they asked if he could get out of bed and stand. He made a meal of it, couldn't help playing the sympathy card and, half stooping, he tottered to the en-suite. This was the first time in weeks he'd seen himself in a full length mirror. He was shocked, frightened that he'd aged disproportionately and doubtful as to whether he'd ever get back to his old self. The only positive sign was the weight loss; he was struck by his slimmer figure.

But his face looked jowly, pasty from lack of daylight. His eyes were red-rimmed and his hair, like steel wool with a matching beard which seemed to emanate from his ears like a hairy waterfall, to end at his Adam's apple in a ragged eddy of tight curls. But he didn't feel half bad, considering.

He was able to shower, which was hot and plentiful. He thought of the Karcher and shuddered. A male nurse was assigned to cut his hair and shave him. The blunt scissors snatched at Pap's tough beard and it took all of half an hour to get his face ready for a razor. The nurse apologised for the few nicks he'd inflicted, explaining how sensitive skin becomes when it's not been exposed to shaving for several weeks. Pap already knew that.

He felt light-headed from his morning groom, the air and

revitalized circulation had an astringent effect, leaving him icy fresh. He stood more erect as he examined the results in the mirror, ignoring the scraps of toilet tissue covering his razor wounds. The 'years' accumulated during his incarceration were already beginning to drop away. He managed a half smile.

That morning, apart from medical staff and the hospital padre, he had his first sympathetic visitors. His boss Simon came, bearing a box of chocolates. Much to Pap's surprise, he was accompanied by Margo, Simon's secretary, Pap's current lover. She carried a small bunch of flowers and although angry with Pap for the way he'd treated her, was not totally lacking in sympathy for his predicament. She gave him a peck on the cheek but didn't smile, and stood back while Simon did the talking.

'Well this is a fine old mess you've got yourself into, Melvyn,' he said, in an appalling accent, reminiscent of an old Laurel and Hardy film. Simon was half grinning and patting Pap on the shoulder as if it were all a bit of a bloke joke. 'Your old job is waiting as soon as you feel up to it,' said Simon, almost rubbing his hands, anticipating his profits on the rise again. 'Lots going on, Melvyn, we need you out there, flying the flag.' He hoped Melvyn hadn't lost his touch. 'You'll be up and about soon, we'll have lunch. You can choose somewhere to celebrate, wherever you like. Anything we can do in the meantime?'

Pap could think of many things but none that his boss would be capable of helping with. He looked at Margo and resisted the urge to smile. The last time he saw Simon's secretary, she was getting dressed in a hotel bedroom, but he guessed that wasn't on her mind right now. She lowered her eyes. They'd be working together again...

Mid-morning, the nurse brought Pap a coffee and a stack of letters and cards. 'You're very popular, Mr. Greenstone, there's this lot and a whole load of people outside waiting to see you. TV, press and everything. Don't worry, a police officer is standing guard at the entrance. No one will get past him.'

He didn't know what to open first. He ripped the envelopes with more vigour than he'd shown so far. Requests for interviews, good luck cards (mainly from his male friends), a few from various reporters looking for a scoop: the inside story. There was an amusing request from an exclusive men's association, a group of guys calling themselves The Endaway Club, wanting him to speak at their monthly meeting and consider becoming their president. The request was on official looking paper but the logo had a peculiarly phallic quality about it...

There were some business cards from radio and TV companies and a ghost writer asking if he could 'have the honour of writing Pap's story'. Pap was pretty puffed up about it all, but it was too early to start making important decisions. After all, it was only his first day out of captivity!

Pap was tired now, too much exposure much too soon. The nursing staff felt it a good idea to keep the newspapers out of the way, for now. The press were at odds as to which was the best story.

The most popular tabloid went for the throat:

CAPTIVE BIGAMIST RELEASED FROM BASEMENT CELL

> *Melvyn Greenstone, the man held captive in a basement cell by Brenda Brown for six weeks, is to be charged with bigamy.*

(Below the caption was a picture of Pap in his cell, one inset picture of him standing next to his first wife Angie, and another with Gloria on their wedding day. Pap would have had no idea how the last two photos had been obtained.)

> *Two women claim to be married to Greenstone but only one officially, as he never sought divorce proceedings*

from the first. The sentence for bigamy in the UK can be anything up to seven years. So Melvyn Greenstone may be out of the frying pan and into the fire...

Broadsheet, somewhere on an inside page:

MELVYN GREENSTONE FREED

Following six weeks of being kept prisoner in a basement cell, Melvyn Greenstone has been released without harm.

Greenstone was described as, 'a shadow of his former self', when he was led away by ambulance crew, from his underground prison.

No details have yet been released as to why the kidnapping took place. There were no demands of any kind. The police admitted they had never experienced a case like it. Typically, a financial demand is usually made before the prisoner is released.

Chapter 77

The envelope from Brenda, containing part letter, part memoir, and given out by Raihana, was addressed: *To all who may be interested.*

By now you will have witnessed the release of Melvyn Greenstone and probably be asking about my reasons for keeping him in captivity for so long. Some of you may question my sanity, a question I asked myself at times. Was I mad? I certainly had to seek help, before I could wrap it all up: wondering if I'd tied up all the loose ends or left it too late to leave the country. Fortunately, everything turned out better than expected.

I have to admit to one little trick I played, just to keep the mystery going, had to use it from the start, otherwise someone may have realised that Greenstone was not where he was supposed to be. I got hold of his mobiles. Yes, he had a couple, one for his lady loves: past, present and probably future too, and the other for his day to day life: work contacts, business associates etc. plus his latest wife's number (second wife Gloria, you may already know he had a first, hidden away in another part of the country— despicable—he never divorced, you know). So all those messages sent while he was in my basement were actually from me. Clever eh? He will have fun sorting that out. Who are you gonna believe? Am I telling the truth?

No doubt Greenstone, known as Pap throughout his incarceration (ask him why) will have his own story. I'll warn you now, most of it will be lies. Pap tells porkies on a mammoth scale. This will be proven over the coming weeks as his story unfolds. Evidence of his bigamous marriages and abandoned girlfriends will come straight from the mouths of the women he's cheated, especially those who witnessed his dramatic release from captivity. It will make interesting copy. Already I can imagine a whole new batch of YouTube clips of his release going viral. He'll be Tweeted, Facebooked, Instagrammed, Googled and newsworthy for some time yet. He may even wish he was back in his comfy cell with his ex-girlfriend gaoler; yes me, me, me, the one he got pregnant, the one he couldn't remember because he'd dumped me and left the country, a very, very long time ago.

Then I was petite, blonde, seventeen, naive, didn't need a bra until the hormones went into overdrive. But hey, look at me now! I thought Pap was the greatest bloke around, but then so did he, it seemed.

My father on the other hand, never thought Pap was the greatest, didn't take to him right from the start (then what do parents know?). Dad paid for my abortion before dying of a massive heart attack: a broken heart, my mother said, his 'little girl' disgraced by Greenstone's miserable indulgences.

Mother never forgave me, but then, I never was her little girl. To my mother, Olive Burton, I was a mature woman with a number of brain cells missing. In her opinion, any girl, of any age being fooled by the likes of Melvyn Greenstone, didn't deserve one iota of sympathy. As far as she was concerned, I'd broken Father's heart, caused his death, and deprived Mother of a future with the only man she'd ever loved. As if I'd murdered him!

Likewise, I could never forgive Melvyn Greenstone. I gave up searching for him after an agonising year wondering whether he'd died or simply rejected me.   Whatever the reason, he was gone and if still alive then it was pretty obvious he no longer wanted me.

But the past always has a way of surprising the present. And so it happened, Greenstone turned up in my life again, some thirty years later.

The first shock was the incident at the seminar. Initially I didn't even recognize Greenstone, until he got close (that man always gets too close). Next day, in spitting blood anger, I Googled Ethical Global Logistics, the name on Greenstone's tag at the seminar, and looked up their contact details. I plucked up courage, pretended I was someone else, tried to get them to put me through to his desk. I couldn't stop shaking. He was away—always away— weeks at a time.

I knew I'd catch him off guard at some point, but when? And what would I actually do? What could I do?

As time went by and contact seemed almost impossible, I calmed down, shifted the mind set from angry to cunning. Then Raihana, my friend from Lahore, appeared on the scene. We made a spooky connection and a plan started to develop, something more than a confrontation in the street or in Greenstone's office. A bigger plan, something life changing, something with a bit more revenge: a punishment to fit the crime.

One Wednesday morning. I was on my way to work, having dropped my car in for its yearly service. I was standing at a bus stop, one I only happened to use when my car was in the garage for servicing, not that far from the office block of Ethical Global Logistics.

Something made me walk toward the company building, on the opposite side of the road. And there he was! My eyesight was not great at this distance but Greenstone surely; smartly dressed, standing at the entrance talking to an attractive woman who was having a cigarette, in the doorway. The way he pushed his hair back as he spoke; the way he touched the woman's arm, pressing home what he'd just said; the way he smiled at her, as if he either knew this woman more intimately than it first appeared or was in the process of chatting her up; he'd invaded her 'personal space', so too close for it to be anything else.

It was an approach, a Greenstone ritual I'd experienced myself, a very long time ago. I wanted to make absolutely sure it was him. I positioned myself just across the street, amongst a crowd of early commuters and shoppers. It was him! Then rage came in spades. I experienced chest pains and dizziness. A headache started at the back of my neck before creeping across my forehead and behind the eye sockets which seemed to be burning like hot coals. I supported myself against a shop front, trying to control the symptoms. I took some deep breaths. Greenstone entered the building but left the woman outside to finish her fag.

I popped into the newsagent, bought a cheap Welcome Home card, and wrote—Melvyn Greenstone, Ethical Global Logistics— on the envelope, and 'gotcha', in large print on the inside. I put the card in the envelope and delivered it, by hand, to Ethical Global Logistics.

'Sorry to trouble you,' I said to the receptionist, 'but I wonder if you could pass this on to Mr. Greenstone, I believe he works here.'

The receptionist gave me the once over, then winked and gave a knowing smile. 'Yes he does, everyone knows Melvyn,' she said, 'I'll make sure he gets it...Nice perfume by the way.' I wanted to smack her face.

Sure, it was possible the receptionist might describe who'd left the envelope, but the description of me now would be nothing like the Brenda he'd dumped all those years ago. So Melvyn Greenstone was back from his travels, and not a million miles from where I lived, just half an hour away. I had plans—it was payback time; time to tell his story to the world and save others from a similar fate which, to a young woman in love, really can be worse than death.

So this is it. This is the reason I kidnapped him and stuck him in the basement. He never did remember who I was, until my mother Olive turned up and reminded him. Fair enough I suppose,

I'd matured from a flat-chested seventeen-year old-blonde, to a buxom, dark haired fifty-year-old.

Anyway, remembering every woman he'd exploited was not a priority in Pap's life. But he'll remember them now. They're standing outside my house making eye contact. Two wives who didn't know each other existed, a young pregnant woman from Lahore whose name he'd completely forgotten, her angry parents. My pissed-off mother might be there too but I wouldn't be surprised if she wasn't. She'd already visited Pap in his cell and done the necessary. You're all probably wondering what the 'necessary' might be. Well ask Olive Burton and she might give you an interview, for a small remuneration of course, before she disappears out of our lives.

My story would make a good film: The Prisoner of Brenda. Who would play Pap? Someone who could carry off 'unhinged': Ray Winstone, John Malkovich or Tim Roth maybe. And for my part? Penelope Cruz? Might be too petite though. Kate Winslett then, still a bit thin but curves in the same places, though I'd have to admit, Kate will need to dress down a tad and dye her hair for the part. Stephen King could direct.

But I digress. Pap might come through this a better person, though given his reluctance to put his life in order so far that may be overly optimistic. The women from his past, most of them wishing they'd never met him will, perhaps, have closure.

The law may have to do something about me; suspended sentence hopefully, a bit of community service maybe. I realise that kidnapping should not be taken lightly, but my guess is, that the reasons for my action will be found perfectly understandable. I made no financial demands and no injuries were inflicted. The women of the world will be on my side. That's for damn sure...

Chapter 78: Epilogue

Brenda Brown: Uncle Fred didn't last long. A month after she arrived in Melbourne and drove out to learn the ropes of the business, he had a stroke. Not too much of a surprise, he'd been overindulging for years and had a history of high blood pressure and a particular liking for strong beer and salty food.

Brenda took to the business like a duck to water. She liked the heat and the wide open spaces of Australia. But Uncle Fred had exaggerated her importance to his projects. On reflection she guessed he just wanted her to be there when he died, she wasn't really needed. The staff running everything had been with Uncle Fred for yonks, they were excellent, reliable. It was no problem to Skype, phone or email them, and she could pay occasional visits from wherever she was in the world. Money and time were not a problem now.

Pap wasn't completely out of her mind. The Australian police had contacted her after emails and calls from DS Barker. They'd seen the media coverage and the YouTube clips, but the Australian team, led by a woman officer, found the whole situation highly amusing, replaying the videos whenever they needed cheering up, especially when more horrific crimes presented themselves. Even so, they couldn't let Brenda completely off the hook. She ended up with a suspended sentence.

She'd had offers to appear on television, take part in a documentary, a possibility of that film she'd thought about. But for the moment, Brenda decided to chill out a bit, and make sure the business was running as it should.

She'd never forgotten Pap at *the* seminar, a truly unexpected shock. Under the influence of alcohol, some deep seated déjà vu emotion had responded to his advance. It was a moment she'd regretted immediately…but once the whole of her history with him had been revealed, Brenda's revenge had been sweet.

Melvyn Greenstone (Pap): The bigamy issue was taken care of nicely by Gloria and Angie. Pap was in custody and maybe, because of it, uncharacteristically celibate. Anyhow, his problem had become less of an 'intensity' issue and veered more toward impotency in nature. He'd consulted experts for advice but found it all too much like the programme he'd been given when he'd last sought help.

He did everything he could, to cash in on the publicity surrounding his prison sentence. Even managed to set up a YouTube channel on which he posted the original video of himself in the basement, followed by a host of interviews with various interested parties. No film offers yet, but he was certain there would be. During his confinement Pap received a significant amount of correspondence, including; a couple of death threats, some hate mail, and number of marriage proposals from women in countries he'd never visited.

He never quite got over Brenda being his teenage lover. Or the fact she'd been pregnant. Were it not for Olive turning up to enlighten him, he might still be wondering what his imprisonment had all been about.

Once Melvyn was out of prison and had finished his spell of community service, Simon gave him his job back. He continued to make the company a lot of money. Despite all his efforts to the contrary, most of it went to compensate wives, some to Raihana and the remainder to keep him out of the way by financing the rental of a small flat in the city.

Arthur Brown—Brenda's husband: Remains a fond memory in Brenda's mind though she thanked her lucky stars that when she needed work done at her new place in Australia, Arthur wasn't around to offer his services.

Raihana Khan—Brenda's friend: The stress of the past couple of months were blamed for her losing the baby. It *was* a boy! Raihana took charge of the business which prospered even more when Khan decided to retire. She kept in touch with Brenda who was planning to visit Lahore that very spring.

Raymond (Raymondo)—Brenda's boss: Business as usual. The infamy surrounding his best salesgirl Brenda Brown had done him no harm, though at one point, when the stress had got too much, he was tempted to light up a fag or try vaping but his sinuses said no.

Simon—Melvyn's boss: Immediately put Melvyn back to work after his release. There was a lot of mileage in that employee of his and already his takings were up.

Gloria—Pap's second wife: Decided on a divorce and with the share of Pap's estate, intended to start over.

Angie—Pap's first wife: Ditto...

Barker and Smithy—detective and constable: They'd worked hard on the case. They were praised by colleagues for their combined efforts and duly acknowledged in reports, and in the press. They remained a formidable team in the force but neither were promoted, due to the fact they hadn't actually found Melvyn Greenstone and brought Brenda Brown to justice.

However, they did arrest Greenstone for bigamy under the Offences Against the Person Act, but he'd had a clever barrister, Olga Slowinski, a tough Eastern European determined to win at all costs.

A woman defence lawyer didn't seem the best choice for the bigamist in the dock but he need not have worried. Bigamy cases are relatively rare in the UK and Olga argued that Melvyn Greenstone had led a complex life and was involved in a complex and unique set of circumstances. Greenstone, keen to help Olga's winning record, argued that imprisonment would prevent him earning enough to pay for his misdemeanours, including the essential support of a child due to be born in Lahore (there was a gasp from the court at this juncture—even Olga blanched at having to deliver this news). The fact that Raihana lost the baby, was not known until after sentence had been passed.

Angie and Gloria, wanting nothing more to do with Greenstone, helped simplify the court's decision and ruling. He was held for a short while in prison before ending up with a Community Order: a substantial period of unpaid work, and the wearing of an electronic tag while he was doing it.

Kev Strong—*Daily Moon* reporter: Kev became a source of amusement to his colleagues. His reputation as an undercover reporter, being caught and charged with attempted burglary, was further damaged when Brenda's neighbour sold the iPhone clip of him trying to break into Brenda's house. It went viral on YouTube. Some viewers questioned whether the clip was a cleverly choreographed set up as they doubted a hard bitten undercover reporter could be that stupid.

The Khans—Raihana's parents: Never quite got over their daughter's disgrace but managed to keep news of Raihana's pregnancy secret. Khan was sad he'd lost a grandson but pleased his daughter had another chance to regain her respect in Lahore. No one ever needed to know! Mother Khan was torn between sorrow and relief. On the positive side, she had escaped the further mortification, of Pap ending up as her potential son-in-law.

Olive Burton—Brenda's Mother: Olive had got Pap to sign a confession; a document admitting he was the father of her daughter's aborted baby and that he was liable for a bill of £10,000 plus expenses to be paid back into the Burton account. This was the money Brenda's father had paid for the abortion, aftercare and counselling required by Brenda, the year following her disgrace. Goes without saying, Brenda was never forgiven for her disputable contribution to her father's death.

Tristan Starkey—psychoanalyst: Wrote his paper *The Prisoner* which was published in *The Global Journal of Progressive Psychotherapy*. It was an important study on his favourite psychotherapy topic; a woman scorned. He lectured on this all over the world, citing his strangest case and congratulated himself on being the most important factor in seeing Brenda through her crisis, enabling other women to find their potential, when partners strayed from their commitments.

Margo—Simon's secretary, Pap's lover: It all died down and Pap came back to work looking contrite and fitter after his forced health regime and his subsequent detention at Her Majesty's Pleasure.

Margo thought she might ask him out to dinner...

Also by Geoff Green

PAYING FOR THE PAST
My true life crime story

Everyone knows the extent of their crime…but only one man knows where they are. September 1975. Jim Miller and John Bellord, two wealthy men of impeccable character, fly to France and disappear without a trace. A blackmailed bishop, forgery, faked suicides, a multimillion pound fraud and many lives ruined as police, Interpol, the media and a psychic investigator join in a fruitless search for the two outlaws. Only Geoff Green knows where they are. He plans and executes their escape and finally gives them up following their hideaway year on remote Priest Island surviving a sub-zero winter. This is his account of what they did, how they did it, and why he confessed all. It is not only a crime adventure, but a personal story of total trust in a mesmerising mentor and his philosophy of life.

THE SAND HIDE
Alcoholism, abuse, betrayal and escape to the desert

Robert Dexter makes a lot of money before turning to alcoholism and abuse. When he draws blood and puts his wife Laura in hospital, things have to change. Robert wants to win her back, but in a moment of madness he commits the ultimate betrayal. Nothing would stop Laura leaving now. And where she was going, he'd never find her...

COLD FRIENDS

Someone is about to reveal your past

Ben Taylor wants a quiet life. But when civil servant creep, Frank Carson, threatens his job, and daughter Beth seems intent on wrecking her future, he thinks it's as bad as it gets. Until he spots his old friend, Craig Thomas, looking like a ghost on Victoria Station, and knows he should have walked on. Past secrets threaten their comfortable suburban lives: from the moment they shake hands and exchange cards, Ben's life takes a downward spiral.

Acknowledgements

So many thanks to my wife Carol—reader, critic and most patient friend—for her unending support.

Many thanks to my book production team, whom I have never met but through the miracle of the internet and social media, produce the best possible results from my manuscripts: Julia Gibbs, Proof Reader, Cathy Helms, Cover Designer at Avalon Graphics, and Allen, of eB Format, for his expert formatting of both paperback and Kindle versions of my books.

Made in the USA
Columbia, SC
30 May 2017